W9-CUH-514

LADY VANISHES

Also by Carol Lea Benjamin from Walker & Company

This Dog for Hire
The Dog Who Knew Too Much
A Hell of a Dog

LADY VANISHES

A RACHEL ALEXANDER AND DASH MYSTERY

Carol Lea Benjamin

WALKER & COMPANY
New York

First published in the United States of America in 1999 by
Walker Publishing Company, Inc.

Published simultaneously in Canada by Fitzhenry and Whiteside,
Markham, Ontario L3R 4T8

Library of Congress Cataloging-in-Publication Data
Benjamin, Carol Lea.
Lady vanishes: a Rachel Alexander and Dash mystery/Carol Lea
Benjamin.
p. cm.
ISBN 0-8027-3335-2
I. Title.
PS3552.E54455L34 1999
813′.54—dc21   99-25682
CIP

Series design by Mauna Eichner

Printed in the United States of America
2 4 6 8 10 9 7 5 3 1

For Zachary Elijah

Joubert,

one with everything

The beginning and the end reach out hands to each other.

CHINESE PROVERB

ACKNOWLEDGMENTS

The author wishes to thank:

Detectives Daniel O'Connell and Bill Golodner of the Sixth Precinct, Greenwich Village;

Temple Grandin, whose remarkable book *Thinking in Pictures* added greatly to what I had learned doing pet-facilitated therapy with institutionalized autistic people;

Gail Hochman;

Michael Seidman, George Gibson, Chris Carey, Cassie Dendurent, and Krystyna Skalski at Walker & Company;

Julian Allen, who will be sorely missed;

Beth Adelman and Stephen Solomita, friends indeed;

and Serge.

With special thanks to my darling husband, Stephen Lennard, hugs for Stephen and Victoria Joubert, an *oh, no* for Zack, and pats to Dexter and Flash, incomparable wags.

LADY VANISHES

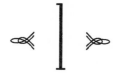

WE FOLLOWED DASH

urry," Chip said, "we can make the light."

He grabbed my hand and began to run across Hudson Street, the Don't Walk sign flashing. Dashiell broke into a run too, hitting the end of his leash as if he were in a weight-pulling contest.

We stopped in front of the Cowgirl Hall of Fame to catch our breaths, and I gave Dash the eye to stop him from lifting his leg against the flimsy faux Western fence that separated the out-door diners from the rest of the sidewalk. Had he marked one of the wagon wheels, the patron dining at the adjacent table would have gotten what's called a golden shower, not everyone's cup of tea, even here in Greenwich Village, the neighborhood that invented *de gustibus non disputatem est*.

I didn't ask Chip why we had to risk getting mowed down in the prime of life. It's not as if Waterloo took reservations. But New Yorkers don't argue about their relationship with time. It's always of the essence. You never kill it. More often than not, it kills you. Worst of all, if you're caught in the act of not rushing, people will think you're from Kansas.

We headed uptown a block, turning left on Charles Street, passing the little farmhouse that had been moved down here intact from the Upper East Side. On the other side of Greenwich Street, we passed a co-op that used to be a couple of warehouses, then a rental building called the Gendarme because that's where the cops were before they moved to Tenth Street. Waterloo was on the corner of Charles and Washington. It used to be a garage. Like it or not, things change.

It was midnight, and the place was in full swing. We were greeted cheerfully and shown to the only empty table, one near the pull-down frosted glass wall, which was raised high enough for us to see passersby only from the waist down, but allowed a full view of any dog who passed. Dashiell positioned himself to enjoy the show while Chip ordered a bottle of Vouvray.

"You look especially beautiful tonight," he said after the waiter left to get our wine.

A thick-set little man with ruddy skin delivered our bread, crusty rolls that, as soon as we began to tear them apart, would cover everything with fine white flour.

Chip was grinning. He reached across the table and took my hand.

"What's so funny?"

"Nothing," he said. "It's just that I love you very much."

A waiter with a ponytail came with our wine.

My cell phone rang.

Listening to the caller, I watched the waiter pull an opener from the back of his belt and begin to uncork the wine.

I said, "Uh-huh" and "I do," then "I'll be there," before hanging up and slipping the phone back into my jacket pocket.

Then I picked up my glass of wine and held it, thinking about what I'd just heard.

"Work?"

I nodded.

His eyes darkened with concern.

"You'll be careful?"

"I promise." I took a sip of wine. "When do you have to leave for the airport?"

"Seven."

"We shouldn't have left Betty home alone."

"She'll be fine."

I tapped my nails on the thick white paper that covered the table.

"I'm not all that hungry," I said. "Are you?"

Chip grinned. "I'll be back before you know it."

"Still."

He took a sip of wine.

I slipped off my sandal and slid my bare toes up under the bottom of his pants leg.

He raised a hand to get the waiter's attention.

"Check, please," he said.

The waiter nodded.

Chip paid in cash, leaving a generous tip. Hand in hand, we followed Dash into the dark, quiet night, walking home without saying another word.

Afterward I got up, slipped on his shirt, stepped over Betty, who, typical shepherd, was sleeping in the doorway, and tiptoed through the dark cottage, Dashiell padding along behind me. Once outside, I sat on the steps, looking up at the night sky, the air I inhaled coming from the heavens, the air I exhaled returning to the stars, feeling completely alive and one with everything.

She'd said her name was Venus White and that she was the manager of Harbor View, on West Street between Twelfth and Jane, a small, privately owned residential treatment center for throwaways, high-maintenance people who needed more care than their families were willing or able to provide. Those who even had families.

She was whispering.

"Can you hear me?" she'd asked.

There was a pause then.

"Right," she said. Loud. "Remember that pin of mine you *love*, the Art Smith with the tiger's eye? Well, there's an exhibition of his work over at the gallery across the street from Florent, on Gansevoort Street. Do you know it? I'm going tomorrow, about noon," she'd said, for whomever she thought was listening. "Can you meet me? We can look at it together."

She whispered again. "Noon, tomorrow, the Gansevoort Gallery."

Why was someone at Harbor View calling a detective? If she were calling for pet therapy, she wouldn't have been whispering. She simply would have asked. And she wouldn't have called so late at night.

I looked down at Dashiell. Lying near the bottom step, he was asleep again, his big head leaning against the side of my foot, the way he'd always slept leaning on Emily, an autistic eleven-year-old we'd worked with at a small Brooklyn shelter. I would sit next to her and hand her crayons, and she would copy pictures out of old magazines, Dashiell snoring under the table, using her foot as a pillow. Without his presence she wouldn't have sat there, wouldn't have drawn those pictures and colored them in so carefully, wouldn't have let me sit so close or touch her once in a while.

I remembered the last visit we'd made, right before her parents had moved her to an institution upstate: how she'd stood in the window of the little front room where I hung my coat, watching me leave with Dashiell, how she'd put her hand up on the cold windowpane, as if to wave good-bye, as if she understood that she was never going to see us again, how when I'd lifted my hand to wave back to her, the tears rolling down my cheeks, her face had remained expressionless and her hand had stayed where it was, an aura of moisture surrounding it, the tips of her fingers white against the glass.

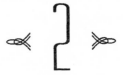

WHAT DID SHE WANT? I WONDERED

At noon, I pointed my finger at the bell for the Gansevoort Gallery, and Dashiell did a paws-up, one big foot smacking the bell dead center. A moment later we were buzzed in.

It was easy to spot Venus. She was the only one there. She was leaning over a round, glass-topped display table, dreadlocks covering her face like a beaded curtain. I picked up the price list and moseyed toward the back of the gallery.

Venus glanced up as I approached.

I began to look at the jewelry too, graceful silver pieces, mobiles and stabiles to be worn instead of exhibited on pedestals. Venus walked around the table and began to look at the pieces near me.

"What are they asking for that one?" She pointed to an elaborate necklace, a rigid, graceful arc of silver that would circle the neck, a green stone surrounded by delicate silver leaves dangling down from the center.

When I opened the book, she took a step closer, as if to read the price over my shoulder.

"Thirty-five hundred," she said. "I wonder what my pin is worth."

The pin was on her lapel, a free-form bow with a tiger's eye on one side and a matching hole cut out on the other, the white linen of her jacket showing through.

"It's lovely," I told her, turning back to the display of necklaces, watching her out of the corner of my eye.

"I couldn't speak last night," she said softly, even though there was no one near us, the manager off in the other room. "I was calling from work. It's been chaotic, and I've been staying over, to keep an eye on things, be there if I'm needed. You never know who might be outside your door, listening."

I looked through the Plexiglas shield at pins and earrings, each sitting on a round red circle attached to a tall pole, like the leaves of a surrealistic tree.

"One of the owners died two days ago," she said, her voice a monotone, as if she were reading from the newspaper. "He was on his way home. He'd barely stepped out of the door when he was hit by a bicycle, riding on the sidewalk. It plowed right into him and killed him."

"One of those freak accidents you hear about," I said, remembering the coverage on the news Saturday night, thinking, good lord, what next, a hit-and-run on the sidewalk. And on Sunday morning, when Dashiell brought in the *Times*, there was a small article in the Metro section, saying the police didn't know who it was, riding where people walk, going so fast he couldn't stop, hitting this old man on his way home from work.

"Only this isn't something that happened to a stranger," Venus said. "This is the man I've worked for for fourteen years. And try as we may, keeping up as usual, the grief, the loss, it's getting to the kids."

"His children?" I asked.

"No. He never had children of his own. I mean the people we take care of at Harbor View, the kids. Well, none of them are really kids. The youngest, Charlotte, turned twenty in April. On the ninth. The oldest, the Weissman twins, are ninety-two. Dora's eleven minutes older than Cora and never lets her forget who came first."

What did she want? I wondered. Was I supposed to go undercover as a bike messenger, ride around in spandex shorts, a canvas bag full of padded envelopes on my back, listen to rumors, hunt this guy down? I was the wrong sex, the wrong color, the wrongest possible person for the job. If that's what she had in mind.

Or was she thinking the accident had been caused by some little Asian guy, delivering someone's egg foo yung? Rain or shine, day and night, the streets were full of diminutive men on bicycles delivering for the Chinese restaurants, keeping the folks in the Village from starving to death. Maybe Charlie Chan could do the job, but not Rachel Kaminsky Alexander.

Or was it someone out exercising, looking for a place to get by the never-ending reconstruction of the Westside Highway so he could ride along the Hudson, catch a breeze or two? This I could do, but toward what end? I'd never find out, no way. There'd be no connection, no bridge from the doer to the done.

"We always call them that," Venus said, "the kids, because, well, they can't take care of themselves, can't live on their own. Some of them you can talk to, though at times it makes you feel like *you* need residential care. Some of them talk back, say a few words when they feel like it. Some don't talk at all."

Venus shook her head, the clumps of hair twirling one way, then the other, finally landing on her shoulders.

"Jackson's been with us nine years. All he does is paint. We don't even know his name."

"But—"

"We call him Jackson because of the way he paints. Well, *paints*. He dribbles it, you know, like Jackson Pollock. Only not quite that good." Venus smiled for the first time. "Don't get me started on my kids," she said. "I love them to pieces, and I'll bore the hell out of you."

Her eyes teared up, and she wiped them with the heels of her hands, then flapped a hand at me and let it land, finally, on her chest. She closed her eyes for a moment before continuing.

"Here's the irony of the situation. I was going to call you anyway. After Lady disappeared, the whole joint was a disaster, no one eating, no one sleeping, it was something awful. Lady was our resident therapy dog." Venus looked down at Dashiell, then back up at me. "Eli Kagan, he's the other owner, our shrink, he saw this show on PBS about pet-facilitated therapy and felt that instead of having a volunteer come in once a week, we should have a full-time dog of our own. If it helped, he said, how could we limit it to an hour or two a week?

"I began the search for the right dog, and within two weeks I found her, a female puli." Venus lifted up a handful of her hair and smiled. "The kids love to touch my hair. It fascinates them. I thought a puli would be a good choice for them. She was one year old and had actually done a little visiting, at a local nursing home. She was perfect for us. She loved everyone and was patient, more than most humans. Of course, her owner loved her, she wasn't looking to give her up. But she had eleven of them and lived in a three-dog town. Her neighbors had gone to the zoning board more than once. Even if she let them out three at a time, figuring a puli is a puli is a puli, the neighbors weren't fooled. It's not that they knew one from another. It's that one day the snoop next door saw two dogs in the window when three were in the yard."

Venus checked her watch.

"So we lucked out, because she said if she couldn't keep her, she couldn't think of a more appropriate place for her, and the next day Ragmop's Lady Day came to live at Harbor View."

"That's some name for a Hungarian dog."

"Tell me about it," Venus said. "Rachel, I know you've done pet therapy with Dashiell, so I don't have to tell you what happened. It was fantastic."

I nodded.

"It was one of those small miracles you pray for in a place like this. That was a year ago. Then two weeks ago, Lady vanished. I left one day after work, she was there. I came in the morning, she was gone."

"Had someone left the door open?"

"At Harbor View? No way. The door is always locked. That's rule number one. The kids can't go out without an escort. Not only would they get scared, confused, and lost, even right out in front of the building, but we're right on West Street. The Westside Highway is steps away from our front door. Even with the construction, there are still six lanes of moving traffic."

"And no one saw anything?"

"You got it. No one saw anything. No one knows anything. It's not like there's anyone around *to* see anything. We don't have neighbors anymore. The place to the north of us burned to the ground. Last winter. You heard about it?"

I nodded.

"We're lucky we didn't go up along with it. The other side, there's a bar. But it closed one night and never opened again the next." She shrugged. "Maybe tax problems, too much cash going into the pocket, not enough going to Uncle Sam."

"That happens," I said.

"So we're alone on the block. And our residents, they're with us because most of the essentials of reality don't factor into their lives. You don't ask these people who, what, where, why, and when. Information? Forget about it. We don't have one iota of information in the whole damn building. What we do have is frantic human beings, people who need everything to stay exactly the same, and now things are different and it's no damn good."

"You looked around the neighborhood, of course?"

"We looked. We called the shelters. We put up signs."

"Any response to those?" I asked, remembering seeing one, wincing at the thought of yet another lost pet.

"Yeah, two calls. One lady had a brown dog she'd found two months earlier. The other was from a man I wouldn't mind strangling. Hard voice. Sounded like a lawyer. He offered us his own dog, in case Lady didn't turn up. Said he didn't want her anymore, she was way more work than he expected. That's it so far, so we still don't have a clue as to what happened to our Lady Day.

"Finally, in desperation, I called the Village Nursing Home, hoping they could recommend one of their volunteers who might come in with a dog until we found Lady. Or replaced her. That's where I got your name and number."

"So all this secrecy has to do with asking me to come with Dashiell and—"

"No. That's just how I got your name. And in that conversation, Muriel, at Village Nursing, mentioned that you didn't keep a regular schedule. She said it didn't matter there, no one knew the time of day anyway. She asked if it mattered to us, if we needed someone who could commit to the same time every day. She said you and Dashiell were especially gifted with her residents, but that you kept weird hours, that sometimes you'd visit after breakfast, sometimes at bedtime, sometimes not for weeks at a time, that you did what you could, and would that work for us? Then she told me why, that you were a private investigator."

Venus turned to face me now, her eyebrows raised, as if she wasn't sure it were true and I was supposed to tell her it was or it wasn't.

"And that's what you need, a private investigator? To find out who mowed down—"

"Harry Dietrich," she said. "Yes, that's what I need."

I waited for more.

"I'm not buying that it was a random accident, Rachel. I just don't believe it. Maybe I don't want to believe it, I don't know."

"Terrible things happen for no discernible reason. Look at the population you take care of at Harbor View."

"I know," she said. "Still."

"And are you hiring me on behalf of Harbor View?" I asked.

"No," she said. "That's why we're talking here, not there. I'm hiring you on behalf of myself."

Once again, I waited for more. It seemed to me that there was no end of more I hadn't been told. I didn't need a tarot deck or a crystal ball. It's just how human beings are, always keeping the most difficult stuff for last. Or not telling it at all.

"What I want you to do is this. I want you to come in with Dashiell and work with the kids, but you'll be working undercover. I want you to find out who killed Harry. And I need you to do it as fast as possible."

What had the cops found out? I wondered. But I figured I'd get that answer straight from the horse's mouth.

"Do you know what kind of bike rider hit him, Venus?"

She shook her head.

"I know I'm not giving you much right now. But something's wrong. I just feel it, and I'm scared."

"Of what?" I asked, thinking I should have said, Of whom? But it wouldn't have made any difference. She wasn't going to answer me either way. I could see it in her eyes. The conversation was over.

"I have to get back now," she said. "I'm already late. Come later this afternoon, two-thirty, can you do that? I go to the gym every day after work, Serge's on Bank and West, just a couple of blocks from Harbor View. I'll arrange a pass for you. It's a good place for us to talk. We can meet there every day and fill each other in. Five-thirty. On the treadmills."

"Then there's more you want to tell me?"

"Lots more," she said. "But it'll have to wait. I'm never late, and I don't want to draw attention to myself right now."

"Venus, if I'm looking for a bicycle messenger or a delivery man, then why—"

"I don't know *what* you're looking for," she whispered. "But whatever it is, we only have until Friday for you to find it."

"Why?" I asked. "What happens on Friday?"

"I'm late," she said, turning to leave, but not before I saw the fear creep into her dark eyes.

Then she was gone, and I was standing there alone, holding the price list, wondering what was going to happen on Friday. Would her coach turn back into a pumpkin, her fine white horses into mice?

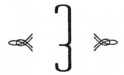

SOME PEOPLE HAVE ALL THE NERVE

A s I approached Harbor View, I was assaulted by the deafening sound of jackhammers. They had already come so close to the building line, chopping away half the sidewalk out in front, the institution looked as if it might fall over forward onto the half-constructed roadway.

Harbor View was neither grand in scale like some of the commercial buildings facing the river at the northwestern edge of the Village, meatpacking plants that had been converted into high-priced housing, nor small and funky like the bar that had been its neighbor to the south, a squat little hovel painted aqua so that on the occasion when it wasn't your first stop, you still couldn't miss it, not even if you'd been drinking for a million years.

In its previous life, Harbor View had been a hotel for seamen, a place where they could keep a watchful eye on the river while waiting to sail again. I didn't need the *AIA Guide to New York City* or *Greenwich Village, How It Got That Way* to tell me that. It was written in stone, right over the front door. Harbor View, it said. And under that, Seaman's Rest. Harry hadn't changed the name.

It was a neat little building, four stories, about fifty or sixty feet wide, red brick with that stone trim over the door and the windows. There was a narrow alley on either side, leading, I supposed, to a rear yard. Half the rooms would face the back, a quiet oasis in a noisy city. The others looked out over the river, the very view that made the price of housing along West Street so high.

I stopped in front to let Dashiell drink from the squirt bottle I carried for both of us. There was a young man standing in the skinny window to the right of the doorway, a sidelight with a rectangle of stained glass at the top, blue for the sea, yellow for the sun. He seemed to be looking at us, but I doubted he was. More than likely his view was inward, to some dark place only he was privy to.

I rang the bell. A moment later, Venus opened the door.

"Ready to begin?" she asked.

I nodded, too hot to speak, glancing at the man in the window, my eyes drawn to his hands because of the bandages, his fingers sticking out beyond the waterproof tape tap-tap-tapping against each other as if they were piano keys. Venus touched him lightly on his shoulder, then headed for her office, to the right of the front door. Dashiell and I followed behind her.

"You're going to have to work one-on-one to begin with. We don't know exactly how the kids will react to Dashiell. Some of them won't *see* him. Maybe not for the first few visits. Charlotte, when she gets overstimulated, scared, whatever, she acts out, beats herself on the chest, moans, rocks. Just let her be. She'll stop on her own.

"If it goes on for more than a few minutes, you can take her to the squeeze machine. It's on the second floor. You can't miss it, the door is always open. Are you familiar with them?"

"Is it something like the thing they use on farm animals, to keep them calm during veterinary procedures?"

Venus nodded. "Works here, too. Most of the autistic kids know when they need it and control the machine themselves. They determine how much pressure and for how long."

"It's like a mechanical hug?"

She nodded. "They can't take—"

"I know that part," I told her. "Only I found it wasn't true across the board. One of the kids I worked with, a *real* kid, she was eleven, we got to where I could hug her."

Venus looked as if she wanted to say something but was holding back.

"I know they're not all the same," I said.

"Just go slowly," she said. "Don't expect too much."

"Okay."

"And if you have any doubts about how to proceed, or if you should proceed at all, don't be shy about asking. You'll never bother me with a question, Rachel. It's what I'm here for. For them. And for anyone working with them."

"Good. Thanks."

"You're not working alone—on *any* of this."

I nodded, holding her eyes for a moment. They were nearly black, her gaze steady and serious, as if she'd seen a lot, maybe more than was good for her.

"So," she said, "if Charlotte reacts well to Dashiell, you can take her out for a walk, let her hold his leash. She'll love that. It'll help her to trust you, too, the three of you going out together.

"Jackson will probably ignore you and keep on painting. But he'll know Dash is there.

"Some of them speak, once they trust you. Some of them don't. And there'll be these moments, times when the person you're with will seem lucid and you'll find yourself wondering if, hoping . . ." Venus sighed. "Well, that's what keeps us going, those moments. And knowing we're doing the right thing.

"David, the man in the lobby, we'll save him for later. Don't want to scare you off, have you deal with David your very first day." She rolled her eyes. "Just remember, you never want to take *him* out, because, well, you just don't."

"He's right by the door. He never—?"

Venus shook her head. "That's his post," she said. "He's there most of the day, just looking out. He never tries to leave."

"Was he there Saturday?" I asked. "When—"

"He was," she said. "But he doesn't communicate, and it's doubtful he sees what's right in front of him. So whether he was there or not, it doesn't make a bit of difference."

"Nothing changed with him since the accident? He didn't seem frightened, agitated, he didn't stop eating?"

Venus got that look again—should she trust me or not? Go slowly, she'd told me. She was taking her own advice, something few people do.

"Despite Dr. Kagan's warning and my pleading, one of the detectives tried to question him. At first, nothing happened. Nothing is our middle name. But the detective didn't get it. He kept right on asking questions. Eventually, David began to keen, really loud."

"To block out the detective's voice," I said.

Venus nodded.

"Did that stop it?"

"No—the detective only got more aggressive. And so did David. He broke the window with his hands. He needed eleven stitches in one hand, seventeen in the other. *That* stopped it."

"And now?"

"He's on extra meds, and before bedtime, Molly rolls him in gym mats. That calms him more than the squeeze machine."

"Molly?"

"Our den mother. She helps with bedtime, baths, meals, whatever's needed."

"So aside from increased tension, no other changes with David?"

"Not that we can tell. He doesn't speak about what he saw, if he saw anything, if that's what you were hoping. I'm sure it's what the detective was hoping for. But as we told him, David doesn't speak, *period*. Aside from some occasional *agitation*"— Venus said each syllable separately—"nothing's changed with him in the five years he's been here. And before he came to us, he was in another institution. And nothing changed there either. Still, I love that kid, but I'd be hard-pressed to tell you why. It's more or less like loving a statue. The most difficult ones, the ones you worry about most, sometimes those are the ones that grab you hardest. Do you know what I mean? Taking care of them, you just get attached, even when they don't seem to know you from a hole in the wall."

"And why shouldn't David go out?" I asked, thinking it was something I ought to know. "Doesn't he want to?"

Venus didn't answer me right away.

"Is it too much stimulation for him? Too much change? Too much noise?"

Venus straightened the books on her desk—a dictionary, some medical reference books, the PDR—standing between two bronze bookends, African heads atop long necks, one male, the other female.

"He's gotten violent a couple of times. Dr. Kagan took a risk accepting him here. But he always says, If not here, then where?

"We can do it here. We have such a small population, only sixteen right now. Somewhere else, it would be like jail for him." She shook her head. "Anyway, it's only happened twice. But we can't predict it. So you don't want to take him out in public."

"Oh," I said.

"He's been pretty stable on medication for several months, he's sleeping through the night, he's eating better, but I'd rather err on the side of caution. He would love some time with Dashiell, though."

"You mean he'll interact with him?"

"I didn't say that, did I? I'll be with you the first time. You'll see for yourself what happens. And listen to me, Rachel, if he makes you uncomfortable, if anyone does, if you have any problem at all, tell me about it, talk to me. You're not obliged to work with everyone. We'll play it by ear, see what happens. Okay? Also, I don't want you staying more than an hour and a half, tops. You're going to get really stressed, and so will Dashiell. We took Lady for a run across the highway by the waterfront early in the morning so she could start her day clean, you know what I mean? Dashiell will need something like that, too, a way to blow off all that tension he'll be absorbing. The same goes for you."

"I'll go to the gym," I told her. "That should help."

Venus nodded.

"I wouldn't trade this job for anyone's," she said very quietly, "but that doesn't mean it's easy, working here. It can get to you something awful if you don't take care of yourself, 'cause but for the grace of God—"

I put my hand on her hand to stop her. "This isn't my first time working with a difficult population. But I hear you. And I appreciate what you're saying."

"I'll have you start with Charlotte, our youngest. Charlotte didn't say much of anything until Lady came. She just used to ask for her parents, that's all."

"Do they visit?"

"You see a line at our door, Rachel?"

I looked down at Dashiell.

"Yeah, they visit. A couple of times a year. It tears them to shreds to see their daughter like that, all their dreams come to nothing, then they go home and try to live their lives for another five, six months before coming back. She's their only child." Venus shook her head. "Life's not easy. But we have a dog visiting, and that's going to make today a lot sweeter, isn't it?" she asked Dashiell, leaning down and scratching his big head. "He's registered, right?"

I nodded. He was wearing his tag.

"Funny noises, weird movements, they won't bother him?"

"Are you kidding? He lives in the Village."

"So he's cool?"

"Cool's his middle name."

"Good." She handed me a wad of paper towels. "He might get drooled on. You'll want these."

I folded the towels a couple of times and stuffed them into the back pocket of my jeans.

"Charlotte's on the top floor, the southwest corner, best room in the house. Knock and then open. Almost no one responds to a knock, but Dr. Kagan feels it's an important sign of respect to let them know someone is coming into the room."

Fine. I knew what to do with the kids, but what about what I was hired to do?

"Venus, about Friday—"

The phone rang, and she reached for it.

"Yes, of course. Why don't you tell me what the problem is." She slid over a form and picked up a pen.

No use hanging around. I could see this was going to be a long one.

I took the stairs. I'd gotten in the habit of walking instead of using the elevator on a recent job. Dashiell ran ahead, waiting for me at each landing. When we got to five, he began to spin around with excitement. He always knew when he was wearing his therapy dog hat, and the chance to work filled him with ecstasy.

I knocked twice on Charlotte's door, waited, then walked in.

She was sitting on the end of the bed, a soft doll on her lap, buttoning and unbuttoning its blue gingham dress. As soon as she smelled Dashiell, she dropped the doll. Arms moving stiffly up and down, Charlotte resembled an arthritic bird trying to fly. Dashiell went slowly toward her, his tail waving from side to side, and put his head in her lap. At this, instead of touching him, Charlotte began to wail, hugging herself and swaying from side to side.

I waited to see what would happen, already starting to feel the confinement of the place, bars on the windows, things bolted down. Even though I'd only been at Harbor View for fifteen or twenty minutes, I always reacted the same way when I first came into an institution like this one, as if the walls were closing in on me.

Charlotte was quieting down, so fortunately there was something I could do about my claustrophobia, something that could help all three of us.

I began to talk softly, using her name, telling her mine, mentioning that Dashiell needed a little walk, asking her if she'd like to be the one who walked him.

Charlotte went straight to the dresser across from the foot of the bed, stepping over her doll on the way, then opening the bottom drawer and taking out a pair of red woolen gloves.

"It's pretty hot outside," I told her.

Even knowing better, I waited for a response.

"Hey," I finally said, "take them along, see if you need them or not. It's always best to be prepared."

She was rooting in the drawer again. This time she came up with fur earmuffs. She smelled them before putting them on.

She was almost pretty, her short hair, the color of buckwheat honey, framing her face and curling against her cheeks, her skin fair; and despite the stiffness of her movements, she didn't seem clumsy. There was something graceful about her, in the careful way she moved about, never looking directly at anything, still knowing what was around her.

Charlotte took Dash's leash from around my neck and hung it around her own neck, heading for the door. Before heading down the stairs, she slipped on the red gloves, making sure each finger went in the right place; then, holding the banister, she began to descend the stairs, Dashiell rushing ahead, then running back up to butt her with his big nose before running down to the next landing, turning, and coming back again.

"Lady's back," I heard with still a half a flight to go to get to the lobby.

"I knew she was. I told you—"

"First. Lady's—"

"Back. She's back."

It could only be Dora and Cora, the Weissman twins. When we arrived on the main floor, they looked up at me, confused.

"Who's—" Dora began. She rolled her wheelchair closer.

"She?" Cora finished. Her chair stayed put, but she leaned forward and eyed me suspiciously.

"Rachel. And Dash."

"Why is she—" Cora said to her sister.

"Talking to us? We don't—"

"Know her," Cora finished. She shrugged her shoulders, rolled her eyes, and dismissed me with a flap of her liver-spotted hand.

"Know who?" Dora asked.

Cora looked at me, then back at her sister. "She's taken every dime I have. Some daughter—"

"She is," Dora said, nodding in agreement, Charlotte waiting at the door, Dashiell at her side.

"Hang around, ladies, I'll see you when Charlotte and I get back."

I poked my head into Venus's office to tell her I was taking Charlotte out.

"Does she have her earmuffs?"

"She does."

"Sound sensitivity," she mouthed, making me feel pretty stupid for not looking beyond the surface. She probably wore the gloves so she wouldn't have to touch unfamiliar things.

At the door, Charlotte took the leash from around her neck and hooked it to the D ring on Dashiell's collar. Things like that were what kept me up at night when I'd worked with Emily, knowing that there was more inside than we could get to and not knowing how that could be changed, or if it could.

"Ready?" I reached for the doorknob.

"Where is she taking—"

"Lady?" Dora shouted.

"Some people have—"

"All the nerve. What is she doing—"

"Here anyway?" Cora asked no one in particular.

Leaving the Weissman twins for later, I opened the door, and we walked out into a wall of heat and noise. As fast as I could, I headed for Jane Street, hoping to get Charlotte away from the din, though she seemed oblivious to it. Perhaps she felt protected by the earmuffs, or was so happy to be out with Dashiell that nothing else registered. Suddenly she began to sing. Holding tight to the loop of the leash with one gloved hand, the other hand firmly in mine, a behavior I was sure she had been taught, she began singing, "Old McDonald had a farm, eeyieeyioooo," again and again. Twice I sang the rest of the song, but she never changed her routine, as if that line were the only one she could remember.

I didn't mind Charlotte's repetitious, tuneless singing. I rather liked it because I knew it meant she was happy, but the noise of construction was getting to me, and I was concerned for Dashiell's sound sensitivity as well. He wasn't wearing earmuffs. When we got to Washington Street, it only got worse. A new building was going up on the corner, and the first of the evening's delivery trucks was leaving the meat district, which ran from Fourteenth Street to about where we were standing, waiting for a chance to cross what the locals called "accelerator alley," drivers in too much of a rush to consider the needs of pedestrians.

We headed for Hudson Street, leaving the noise behind us. Dashiell walked slowly, pacing himself to Charlotte, looking up at her with his goofy grin, already best of friends. I wondered if Charlotte, too, thought Lady was back, the way the twins did. Some puli he was, rolling from side to side as he ambled along as if he had nothing better to do, his short white coat revealing every rock-hard muscle, an anatomy lesson in motion.

On the way back, my hand sweating from Charlotte's woolen glove, we came around the other way, on Twelfth, crossing the cobblestone street and approaching Harbor View from the south, as I had earlier.

There was music playing in the dining room. We turned right, toward Venus's office. I could hear her through the closed door.

"Can't you postpone beyond Friday?" A pause. Then "Me, too. Damn scared."

When it grew quiet, I knocked.

"How did it go?"

"Fine. It got her singing."

But Venus didn't respond. "The service is going to be on Wednesday morning," she said, speaking about Dietrich's funeral in a way that Charlotte wouldn't understand. "Are you free, Rachel? I'd like you to come with me."

"I can do that," I said, wondering what she was going to tell me later at the gym, wishing I knew what was going on here.

"Let's go into the dining room for a few minutes. Samuel's doing a movement class. It's one of Charlotte's favorite activities."

I raised my eyebrows.

"Samuel Kagan," she whispered. "One of Eli's sons."

Venus locked her office, took Charlotte's hand, and headed to the opposite side of the lobby. I unhooked Dashiell's leash, and we followed along behind them, stopping for a minute to look at the two closed doors next to Venus's office, primitive drawings taped to the middle one, nothing at all on the other.

The doors to the dining room were open. Venus let go of Charlotte, who went to join the class, a bizarre tableau of movement and stillness in the center of the large room, the tables and chairs all pushed against the walls. The man in the middle of the room could only have been Jackson. His clothes splattered with paint, he stood with his arms aloft as if he were a tree, his green hands the leaves reaching toward the sun. Very dramatic. Around him, the Weissman twins moved their hands in time to the music coming from a portable CD player that sat on one of the tables. And in various states of confusion and disarray, the oddest group of human beings I'd ever seen swayed and moved, some holding hands, some holding stuffed animals, or blankets, one holding a shoe, and now Charlotte, in her shorts and T-shirt, wearing red woolen gloves and white fur earmuffs, twirling around Jackson and singing "Old McDonald Had a Farm" at the top of her lungs.

But which one was Samuel? I was about to turn and ask Venus when I got my question answered. He was at the far end of the dining room, near the kitchen door, a short guy with a fringe of brown hair sticking out around a major bald spot. He had been gesticulating in such an exaggerated way that I thought he was one of the residents, but when he spotted Venus, he pointed to himself and then toward the kitchen, asking her to watch the class for a minute. When Venus nodded, he disappeared.

One by one, the kids spotted Dashiell. Some froze, faces expressionless, mouths hanging open, eyes blank. As if sleepwalking, they headed for him. Dashiell's tail began to stir the air. He sneezed and cocked his head to one side.

There was an older woman with an aluminum foil crown on her head and a wand in one hand; a Down's syndrome man, short and wide, his eyes fixed on Dashiell but his feet taking him nowhere, so stunned, it seemed, by Dashiell's presence that he couldn't move; a youngish woman the color of molasses, her black hair in a long braid that lay on the line of her spine, a teddy bear in her hand, holding it out, her treasure, for Dashiell to take.

"Lady," one of them said, a man of about thirty.

Or maybe he was fifty. Here, the old people looked young, the young ones looked old.

He dropped the shoe he'd been carrying and reached out for Dashiell.

Cora began to cry, having forgotten, I guess, that she'd seen him just half an hour ago. "She's—"

"Back," Dora said. And she began to cry as well.

They all gathered around him, fluttering, moaning, babbling, he the eye of a daisy, the residents the petals surrounding him.

When I heard something behind me, I turned. It was David.

He was standing in the doorway, looking up at the ceiling, his forefingers and thumbs drumming away, exhaling audibly, as if he were trying to speak.

I wondered if he'd been in the lobby all along, if when I'd come back with Charlotte, I hadn't seen him—so still and quiet, he'd all but disappeared.

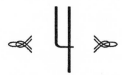

YOU WANT TO EXPLAIN THAT?

L eaving Harbor View, I crossed the highway and took Dashiell to the long, skinny park that ran along the river, a wide roadway, part of it marked off for bicycles and skaters, the rest for walkers, a line of benches facing the Hudson.

This used to be dog heaven, the only place in the neighborhood where a dog could be off leash and really run. Then the city designated the area a park and began to ticket off-leash dogs. Unhooking Dashiell's leash meant risking a hundred-dollar fine, but after an hour and a half at Harbor View, it would have to be considered a necessary business expense.

We headed for the Christopher Street pier, where he could run and I could keep an eye out for the green trucks the rangers used to patrol the city's newest park. At five-fifteen, I headed for Serge's gym to meet Venus.

We crossed back to West Street at Eleventh, where there was a traffic light, though if you wanted to make it safely across, you had to run. Heading north a block to Serge's gym, I noticed again how broken up the sidewalk was, big fissures in the concrete because of the reconstruction of the roadway. In some places, cracks had been filled in with gravel, making walking there even more treacherous because the danger was now more difficult to spot and would be slippery whenever it rained. Why would anyone ride a bike here if they didn't have to?

I began to wonder where the rider had been going when he plowed into Harry Dietrich. If someone was riding for pleasure, he would never ride on a broken sidewalk when there was a smooth bicycle path just across the road, a safe place to cross three short blocks away.

Was he a messenger, I wondered? But then, I thought, to whom would the messenger be delivering? Unless Harbor View was getting something, there was no one else on the block. In fact, most of the buildings on West Street had their entrances on the side streets, Bank, Twelfth, or Jane, not on West itself.

As for the Chinese food delivery theory, again, to whom would the food be going? Riding along on West Street would be the long way around for a delivery.

A lot of the delivery guys would cadge a nap at Westbeth. I'd seen them many times, sleeping on one of the wide, low walls that divided the courtyard, finding a spot in the shade of one of the trees. I'd throw the ball for Dashiell, watching him race by the sleeping delivery men, one of them waking up once, seeing a pit bull heading his way, ending his break one, two, three.

But they napped after a delivery, not before. I never saw one letting the food sit and get cold while he slept. And there were no Chinese restaurants along West Street. So leaving the courtyard, they'd head back along Bank Street, toward Washington or Hudson, where the restaurants were.

Venus was waiting in the lobby, dreadlocks pulled back with an elastic band, wearing shorts and a workout bra, her midriff bare, big multicolored cross trainers on her feet. She was ready to work out, except for the necklace, a pavé diamond heart on a long gold chain. What an odd thing to wear to the gym. To each her own, I thought as she showed me where to sign in and waited while I tied Dash's leash to the red metal bench near the front door. Then together we headed for the treadmills.

There was an arch in the wall to the right of the entrance so that, walking on the treadmill, I could see Dashiell and he could see me. What I saw after turning on the power and setting the speed was Serge bringing a green plastic basin of water for Dashiell, and though he'd just had a drink from the squirt bottle, I could hear him lapping over the sound of the music.

Venus and I began to walk on the moving belts, side by side, no one saying anything at first. There was a short, muscular man on a Stairmaster, also on the front wall, windows facing west, the traffic in front of us, the river beyond.

"Which way was that bicycle going?" I asked, breaking the silence.

"North," she said. "It hit him on the right side of his chest. So he saw it coming."

"But didn't have time to get out of the way."

"Maybe he didn't realize—"

I nodded.

"He could have thought it was going to turn at the last minute."

I nodded again.

Venus turned away for a moment, then began to fiddle with her treadmill, increasing the speed.

"Nothing much there," I said, "to the north. Could be this incident was more on the intentional side than the accidental."

"That's what I've been thinking, too," she said.

She took a sip from her water bottle.

I took a sip from mine.

I was on the corner treadmill, a window in front of me, one to my left. Looking south through the honeycomb iron grating protecting the window, I saw a delivery guy on foot, looking around, confused, checking the address on the fat manila envelope he was carrying, no one else on the street to help him out.

"What else makes you think it wasn't an accident?"

Venus didn't answer me, and I wondered if she'd heard me or if she was listening to the music Serge had on, a Billie Holiday song, the volume not set so high you'd lose your hearing, maybe thinking about the other Lady Day, the puli, wondering where she was. If she was.

I turned to look at her. She seemed to be concentrating, gathering up what she needed to say. Then she said it.

"What would you do if your life was in danger?"

"I'd go to the cops."

"What if you couldn't?" Turning toward me now, staring.

For a moment, I was the one gathering thoughts.

"You want to explain that?"

Venus nodded. She did.

"I was very lonely," Venus said, "working hard at Harbor View, taking care of people, no one in my life to take care of me, take me out to a fine restaurant, tell me how pretty I was, hold my hand, call me darling, say I smell good, listen to my day, make me feel valuable. Oh, I felt valuable at work, of course. Don't need anyone to tell me how good a job I do at Harbor View. But personally, it was bad. You know what I mean?"

"I do."

"I thought you would. No one volunteers in institutions who doesn't know what it's like to feel left out of things."

We each took a drink from our water bottles. I looked over at Dashiell, asleep on the cool marble floor.

"I have a computer at home. I do a lot of research on-line, see what I can find to help the kids. Sometimes I do the autistic chat groups. I'm not family, but I *feel* like family. I need the support, for sure, but it also helps me to hear the questions, the answers, the concerns of the parents. Sometimes someone stumbles onto something wonderful—that music can help a kid to learn, that some of the kids smile once in a while, that a kid began to talk when she was soaking in the bathtub, maybe the warm water relaxed her, but whatever it was, it was better than it had been before, an improvement. Or this other kid, a pacer, a bath at night helped him sleep better. Vitamins. Herbs. Acupuncture. Flower drops. Breathing exercises. Homeopathy. Massage. People will try anything to help their kids. Me, too. Cautiously, but me, too.

"Someone started a different chat group a while ago, nine, ten months back. It's part of the autism web page, but it's social. This one's about us, the caregivers, not the kids. A lot of families, they have a kid this difficult, they split up. They can't take it, maybe each one thinking it's the other one's lousy genes caused the kid to be so fucked up. So there's a lot of people with a difficult kid, a kid needing supervision, patience, lots and lots of care, and now they're alone, and sometimes they want to talk about something other than the kid, but to someone who'll understand what their life is like.

"So now people get to talk about how much they love Indian food or going to a concert or playing tennis, everyone saying what they like to do. But we all know we can't do it, we can't go out for Indian food, go to a concert, play tennis, we have to stay with the kid because no one else will, not for love or money.

"Of course, that's not my problem, right? I can go home and forget all about it.

"Fat chance of that. Just like them, even though I'm not

with it twenty-four hours a day, I'm stressed out. I'm drained. I don't have the energy to go out and find myself a sweetheart. And even when I'm not dealing with these kids, I've lost my ability to make small talk, doesn't seem to matter that they're not mine, they inform my life as if they were.

"Not mine. Of course they're mine. Who else is there to worry about them but me?" Venus was talking to herself, telling me her story at the same time, both of us looking beyond the traffic at the river, the light dancing on the water, a boat passing now on its way to the ocean.

"How do you get close to someone who doesn't understand the peculiar strain of what you do all day, of what you're devoted to? And Rachel, someone doesn't know these kids, they could never understand.

"But just when I'm convinced this is it, for ever and ever, I meet a man."

"On line?" I asked.

Venus nodded. "On this chat group."

The traffic light on Eleventh Street was red, the cars looking like the runners in the New York City Marathon, lined up, tense, waiting for the shot, see who's the fastest one.

"It was like a miracle," she said.

Meeting someone on-line, I thought, what does that even *mean?* On-line, it could seem like one thing, be something else entirely.

"After a while, we're not in the chat room anymore, it's just the two of us, staying up late writing long, long letters every single night, no exceptions, letting it all hang out, hopes and dreams and fears, nothing we couldn't say.

"All of a sudden, everything's different. Someone's listening to me, and me to him, listening to my problems, saying I'm kind, and funny, taking my advice, giving me some too. And, you know something, Rachel, I'm not so lonely anymore. I got 1346@Compuserve.com to talk to."

"No names?"

"No *real* names. Just made-up names we use on-line. That's how it worked in the chat group, and we stuck to it. I never asked for more. Neither did he. We both had so much more than we'd had before. Why rush? Why be greedy when you already feel rich?"

"Weren't you concerned?" I asked. "Meeting on the net, you wouldn't know anything for sure. You wouldn't know who he really was."

"Who he was? Of course I knew that. I knew he was kind, intelligent, sad, but funny too. I knew he was warm. I knew he cared about me and that I cared about him. What else did I have to know?"

Lots, I thought. But I didn't say so.

"I know what you're saying, Rachel—that he could be a kid, fooling around, or a con artist, about to lay a big story on me and ask for money, or an old lady in a wheelchair, passing the time away on her computer; that nothing I knew was real, that I could get myself one big hurt doing this. But in a short time, I knew that there was nothing I could find out about this man that would change what I felt for him. Not one thing.

"And shortly after I knew I felt that way, that's when he told me he was married."

Fortune, a Jewish proverb says, is a wheel that turns with great speed.

But Venus didn't look upset. She unscrewed the top of her water bottle and took a long drink. Then she hit the cool-down button on her treadmill.

"I have a meeting." Very businesslike now.

She stopped the belt and shut off the power.

"I have to get back. I'll see you tomorrow, at two-thirty, then again here at five-thirty, and I'll go on with this."

"Venus—" I said.

But before I got the chance to ask anything else, she was off the treadmill and on her way to the ladies' locker room, leaving me alone, the belt of my treadmill moving rapidly along, me getting nowhere, fast.

5

I LEFT MY NUMBER, JUST IN CASE

didn't go directly home from Serge's. First I crossed back over the highway, walked uptown to the Gansevoort Street dog run, a private, locked run for members only, and looked through the chain link fence at the dogs playing ball to see if there were any pulis there. If I wanted to hide a purebred dog, I'd hide it in plain sight, especially a breed like the puli—cords hanging over their faces, most of them black, except to their owners, they all look pretty much alike.

But there were no pulis there, only the more popular breeds—two Goldens, a chocolate lab, even more popular now that President Clinton had one, a Dalmatian, two mixed breeds, and a border collie, crouching, her eye on the ball she was waiting for her owner to throw, as intense as if she were herding sheep.

I waited for the toss.

"Get it, Mavis," the woman said, the dog halfway there before the words were out.

We crossed the highway at Gansevoort Street, heading for

Beasty Feast on Hudson. If someone were bringing a puli in, or having food delivered for one, they would know it. That is, if Lady were still in the Village and if her new owner spared no expense, feeding her premium dog food in lieu of a supermarket brand.

The woman who ran the store began to shake her head.

"No one came in with a puli in the last few weeks."

The delivery man shook his head, too.

"No deliveries for pulis." He scratched the tip of his nose with one finger. "There's a new Tibetan terrier on Jane Street. Cute as a button. And Jack Russells, you're looking for a Jack Russell, I can give you twenty addresses."

I left my card, just in case.

I tried their other stores, too—the one on Washington Street near Charles and the one all the way over on Bleecker, near Sixth Avenue.

If I was going to meet Venus at the gym every day, I needed new shoes. The ones I was wearing let me feel every crack in the sidewalk. I walked around the corner to Sixth Avenue and dropped an obscene amount of money on a pair of cross trainers that made me feel as if I were walking on marshmallows.

The salesman, a skinny old guy, his mustache wiggling as he slowly enunciated each word, cradled one of my pathetic-looking old sneakers in one hand.

"There are only so many miles in a pair of shoes," he said, turning my shoe over, shaking his head. "Do you want me to toss these?"

"No. I'll give them one last walk," I told him. "For closure."

On the way home I stopped at Beverly Hill's Laundromutt to see if anyone had a puli bathed recently. No one had.

At Pet's Kitchen, Dashiell put his paws up on the counter, and Sammy inserted a doggie bagel into his mouth. We both listened as Dashiell crunched, a viscerally pleasing sound, as basic as it gets.

I asked my question. Sammy shook his head. No new customer with a puli. But he promised to call, just in case.

When we got home, Dashiell hit the water bowl in the garden big time, then crashed at the base of the oak tree, too tired to make it into the house. I went inside, dropped the shoe box on the table, and snagged the cordless phone and the directory, calling the rest of the grooming shops, same question: Someone new come in with a puli to be bathed?

"Saw the sign," one guy said. "Didn't see the dog."

"Too bad."

"Good luck, lady," he said. "Tough thing, losing a dog like that, never knowing what happened to her."

I left my number, just in case.

I sat on the steps, the phone in my hand, thinking about the bunchers—people who steal pet dogs to sell them to laboratories to be experimented on—but I thought they mostly worked the 'burbs, taking dogs off porches and out of yards, dogs left outside when the owner wasn't home, trusting dogs, lonely dogs, easy as pie to steal.

Lady wouldn't have been out alone.

And the door at Harbor View closed and locked automatically. You couldn't leave it open if you tried, not unless you put something in front of it to hold it open. Surely someone would have noticed, had that been the case.

I looked up the animal shelters and called those, too. Sometimes even when you report a dog lost, the report gets lost, falls through the cracks, and when the dog comes in, no one puts two and two together, gets it back where it belongs. But no, no pulis had come in. And when I asked if there'd been an unusual number of thefts reported, I was told no, there weren't, not this summer.

"Thefts in the city usually take place in Central Park, or Riverside," a man with a gravelly voice told me. "Owners have the dogs off leash and get involved in a conversation, they turn around, seems like a minute later, the dog is gone. Last time we got a lot of those calls," he said, "was last fall, Riverside Park, mostly way uptown, near the university. Nothing recently."

Dashiell had rolled over onto his side and fallen asleep, his head resting on one of the exposed roots of the tree. I sat there, the directory on my lap, just thinking. Then I got up, switched directories, got the residential one. When you don't know which pieces of information are significant, you need to gather them all; as my erstwhile employer Frank Petrie used to say, you never know.

I looked up Harry Dietrich to see where he might have been headed the last time he left Harbor View. The Upper East Side. Park Avenue. Where else would a rich man live?

Had he been heading north, toward the subway? Had he heard the wheels of the bicycle bumping over the broken sidewalk? Had he turned around, curious?

After a moment, I looked up Eli Kagan, because knowing more is always better than knowing less, and besides, I was too hot to climb a flight of stairs and take a shower. No Eli Kagan in Manhattan. Either not listed, or in another borough. I'd find out tomorrow.

Sitting there, not wanting to move, I looked under *W* next. There was a Venus White right in the neighborhood, at the Archives, the pricey rental building that formerly housed the Federal Archives, with a gym, a supermarket, a dry cleaner, and a catering place on the ground floor. The building was bounded by Christopher, Greenwich, Barrow, and Washington Streets— an easy walk to work, nice, open views, maybe even a river view, just like at work.

I wouldn't have thought a nonprofit institution would pay its manager enough to live at the Archives, but she did have that lovely pin she was wearing at the gallery, and the clothes she wore didn't look as if they came from Kmart.

Thinking about Venus's story, I pictured her at the gym, remembering the necklace she wore while she was working out. It must have been under her shirt at work, because I hadn't seen it there; but at the gym, there'd be nothing to hide it under, not an ounce on her body she needed to cover up with a big shirt or loose pants, everything out there, looking terrific. Including that necklace.

It looked like the heart Cartier advertised every few weeks in the *Times*—the ad saying, Start something, or, Because she has your heart, something like that, the heart and chain sold separately, the whole shebang costing slightly more than my yearly nut for renting the little back cottage on Tenth Street I've lived in for four and a half years.

It sure didn't look like the kind of jewelry a woman would buy herself.

If Venus had been so lonely, where had it come from—the married man she met on-line?

And why was I hearing about him anyway? What did he have to do with a missing dog, a dead old guy, a bunch of witnesses who don't speak and couldn't tell you the time of day if they did, and this gorgeous, mysterious black woman who hires me because she thinks her life's in danger, then won't tell me why?

⫷ 6 ⫸

I KNOW A LOT OF STUFF, HE SAID

After showering, I gave Dashiell his dinner, then went back upstairs to my office and sat at my desk, now covered with the equipment my brother-in-law kept sending me so that "we could be a family again," not understanding that a fax machine, a laptop, and a printer are not the route to this girl's heart.

Why was I still so angry? Lillian wasn't. She was acting as if they were kids again, as if they had just fallen in love, as if they didn't have two pimply, whiny, selfish teenagers, as if Ted hadn't cheated on her with one of his models.

I opened the laptop and turned it on, thinking about the case while it booted up, beeping and whistling to let me know how hard it was working on my behalf. Then I waited again while it dialed my internet provider, gurgling and flashing some more, making sure it had my attention.

When the home page was there, wiggling annoyingly, promising free upgrades and all kinds of other things I didn't want, I typed in "puli rescue" and hit the search button, waiting while the computer found what I was looking for.

I left a message on the lost-and-found bulletin board of the closest group, hoping for some exposure, that someone checking my post might know where Lady was. Of course, there was no sense describing her, a thirty- to thirty-five-pound springy little black dog, cheerful, noisy, smart, easy to train, with dreadlocks. That wouldn't exactly cut her out of the pack. But since she'd been a trained visiting dog even before she'd arrived at Harbor View, she probably knew some unusual commands. Those were the things I included—that she might do back-up and walk-up, commands sometimes used to position a dog close to a wheelchair. She might do paws-up on the knees of someone who wanted to pet her, and she wouldn't get spooked by canes, walkers, or any other institutional equipment. She hadn't been tattooed or microchipped. But she did answer to her name. Big deal. Lady is by far the most common name for a female dog, Ginger or Muffin only a distant second.

I also read the lists posted at the puli rescue groups, paying careful attention to the dates. But none of the found dogs could be Lady. Of the three on the lists found after Lady had gone missing, two were males, and the bitch was old, ten or eleven, hard of hearing, her teeth worn down to little nubs.

Downstairs, in the pile of newspapers on the far side of the couch, I found the two recent articles about Harry Dietrich, the small piece that ran in the Metro section the day after he was killed and a larger one, an obit, that I hadn't paid any attention to the first time around.

When the phone rang, I was studying the photo that ran with the obit, Harry Dietrich's grim, scrunched-up old face.

"It's even hotter here than New York, but everyone pretends it's not irritating as hell because it's not humid. There's not enough water in the whole damn state to fill a thimble. I don't know how anyone can live here."

"Hey."

"Hey, yourself," he said.

"How are the boys?"

"Good. They actually *like* it here. Can't be my genes doing that."

"Tastes differ," I said. I'm nothing if not insightful.

"So I find. Tell me about your case."

"Oh, it's the usual," I told him. "Someone's dead, and I don't know why. Remember, Saturday, we heard it on the news, the man who was killed on West Street by a bicycle? The old guy who owned Harbor View?"

"He's the dead guy?"

"Yeah."

"So it's a rich dead guy?"

"Very rich. I was just reading his obit. It says Harbor View cost him a million six a year to run and that he gave over a million a year to research and other charities."

"Where the hell did all that money come from, and why aren't we doing that?"

"It didn't say. But you always think it's something fabulous, like the guy's great-great-grandfather found the cure for pneumonia, then it turns out he did something you'd never think of, like he invented Tupperware."

"No, that was Earl Tupper."

"How do you *know* that?"

"I know a lot of stuff," he said.

"I wish I did. The woman who hired me, the manager of Harbor View, thinks Harry's death wasn't an accident and that her life is in danger. But she hasn't explained why. Isn't that weird?"

"No more weird than your average dog-training client—hires you to train the family dog, then accidentally on purpose leaves out the most important detail of the dog's history."

"That he's a biter."

"Exactly."

"But that's about money, Chip. They're afraid you'll charge more to work with a dog that could put you out of business for a good long time. Or that you won't come at all—especially now, with all the so-called dog trainers who only handle puppies or refer if the dog shows any signs of aggression."

"Maybe this is about money too. Or about you not taking the case if you heard the whole story up front."

I held the phone to my ear, but I didn't say anything.

"Rach?"

"Maybe both," I said. "Get this—I have to meet her every day at her gym. She only talks to me on the treadmills, the two of us working up a sweat side by side. I'm going to be one skinny detective by the time you get home."

"I love you just the way I saw you last," he whispered into the phone. "Working up a sweat, side by side."

For a moment, neither of us spoke.

"I have to go. I'm taking the kids out to dinner, some fish place they like on the Santa Monica pier. It should be fun. And Betty will get the chance to dip her toes in the Pacific."

"How'd she do on the plane?"

"She lay down at my feet and slept right through takeoff, got up when the food was served, wisely decided it was unworthy of her attention, and didn't get up again until we'd landed. Piece of cake."

"And did they get it this time, that she's a therapy dog flying to a gig, or did they bust your chops?"

"It wasn't as bad as last time. Only two passengers asked if she was a Seeing Eye dog. I was reading both times."

I laughed.

"What did you tell them?"

"After last time, trying to explain. It's too . . ." He sighed. "I told them yes, she was."

"You didn't."

"I did. This one guy, he looks at her, he looks at me, he looks at the book, he says, 'So you're the trainer, and you're transporting her?' I told him, 'Right.' It made it easier all around. Look, Rach, it's the only reason people know that a big dog can be in the cabin. They just want a little reassurance that they understand the world, that it's not chaotic, as they fear, but orderly and safe."

"Good luck on that," I said. "So when's your gig?"

"It starts Monday. I'm doing five sessions. If they need a few more, there'll be time to add a few before I leave."

"What's the deal?"

"Training staff at a residential treatment center for disabled adolescents. They want to get a live-in."

Like Lady, I thought. "There was a resident dog at Harbor View, Chip. She went missing a couple of weeks before Dietrich got killed."

"And they weren't able to find her?"

"No, I'm working on that, too. But she's still missing."

"I miss you," he whispered. "I want to come home."

I held onto the phone for a while after he'd hung up, then looked back at Harry's picture, his weedy eyebrows, potato nose, Dumbo ears, big, fat lips—mean lips, I thought. A prune of a face, not a looker, this Harry Dietrich.

I started reading the obituary again.

"Harry Knowlton Dietrich, 74, died yesterday of head injuries incurred when he was hit by a bicycle on West Street as he was leaving Harbor View, the small, private residential treatment center he cofounded with Eli Kagan, the psychiatrist who had treated Dietrich's younger sister, Betsy. Ms. Dietrich suffered from autism and died in 1957 at the age of twenty-two, two years before Harbor View first opened its doors.

" 'We are deeply shocked over the untimely death of Harry Dietrich, who gave of himself so generously to this population as well as other neglected and needy causes,' " Kagan was quoted as saying. " 'Harbor View will operate as always,' he added, 'continuing to offer care and shelter to people with special needs, the fulfillment of Harry Dietrich's vision and his passion.' "

There would be a private funeral, the article said. It didn't say where or when. It also mentioned that Mr. Dietrich was survived by a sister-in-law, Arlene Poole of Manhattan, a niece, and a nephew.

Dashiell had come up on the couch to sleep, his head leaning against my leg. I leaned down and put my cheek on his back, listening to him sigh in his sleep as I did so. I closed my eyes, thinking about Charlotte in her red gloves and earmuffs, following Dashiell down the stairs. There'd been a dark line on the wall opposite the banister, starting on the top floor and going all the way down to the lobby, about two feet from the ground, a grease mark from a puli's coat, Lady rubbing against the wall, the way so many dogs do, as she ran up and down the stairs, visiting her charges, making sure everyone was taken care of every day.

Harry Dietrich was not the only one who would be missed at Harbor View.

Then all I could think about was Chip, how far away he sounded.

I hadn't asked where he was—maybe at the new house, waiting for the boys to get ready?

I hadn't asked about Ellen either, if she liked it there, that hot, dry place that had no seasons, if she liked it that Chip had come to visit, if she were listening on the other side of the door, if that's why he had sounded so far away, almost like a stranger. Until the end, when he'd whispered.

Then I thought about waking up to the smell of pancakes, neither dog in bed, Chip standing in the doorway with the tray of food, a vase of flowers from the garden on it, how he'd put the tray down on the nightstand, how it sat there untouched while we made love, how after he and Betty had left for the airport I'd taken the cold pancakes out into the garden and put the plate down for Dashiell, watching him wolf them down without chewing, wondering if, given the way he ate, he tasted anything, or if all that begging, all that desire, was just about the pleasure of not being hungry.

7

FAX ME, OKAY?

uesday morning, after reading the paper, I walked across the street to the precinct and took the stairs at the back to the second floor, where the bomb squad was located, a bomb-shaped balloon hanging from the ceiling and pointing to their door. I knocked and went in. My friend Marty Shapiro was just hanging up his phone.

"It's the working girl," he said. "Have a seat, kid. Long time no see."

I sat at the chair on the side of his desk, pushing away the overflowing ashtray.

"Did it skip your notice, smoking's not allowed in the work-place in New York for what, a couple of years now? In fact—" I said, and pointed to the Smoking Prohibited sign.

"Hey, you expect us to go out and risk our lives on a daily basis, and you're not going to let us have a cigarette when we come back, shaking in our boots? What next, no coffee, no doughnuts?"

"You put it that way, I guess it would be too much to ask."

He lit a cigarette, pulled the ashtray back to where it had been.

"What's up, kid? You working again, another citizen thinks we can't do our jobs, thinks the city pays us the big bucks for nothing?" He leaned back, put his hands behind his head. "I'm glad I'm out of that end of it. No problems like that with the bomb squad. None of the good people we protect think they can do *this* better than we can."

"A girl's got to earn a living, Marty. Someone tells me her life is in danger—"

He leaned closer. "Who's in danger?"

"I've been hired by the manager of Harbor View. She thinks—"

"The old guy has an accident, suddenly everyone gets paranoid."

"Not everyone. Just one person."

"So what's the story?"

I shrugged. "That's what I'd like to know. The detectives are thinking it's an accident?"

I waited, but old stone face didn't respond.

"They come up with anyone yet? Guy who allegedly caused said accident?"

"I haven't heard, Rach. You want I should find out for you, is that what this visit is all about, God forbid you should stop by just to say hello?"

At least he didn't have any control issues. Cops.

"The Dietrich case, right?"

"Right."

"What else you want to know?"

"I was wondering—"

The phone rang, and Marty waited, both of us hoping someone else would pick it up.

"About the bicycle," I continued.

He nodded.

"Anyone from Harbor View see it happen, someone else going home, perhaps, or coming on for the evening shift?"

He shook his head.

"Well then, who called it in?"

"Your client, far as I know. Nine eleven has it on tape, of course, but what I recall, it was the woman who runs the place who made the call."

"But she wasn't a witness?"

He shook his head.

"One of the *inmates* went bonkers."

"Residents, Marty. It's not jail."

"You sure? Where are they going, if it isn't jail?"

I shrugged, wondering if someone saw it happen, or saw it after the fact, started moaning or whatever, and got Venus's attention.

"So if no one *saw* it happen, how do they know it was a bicycle?" I asked him, feeling stupid the moment I did. There had to be evidence of the fact. They wouldn't have just made that up.

Marty moved his chair from behind the desk, putting it right in front of mine.

"Skid mark on the sidewalk, for starters."

I nodded.

"Tread mark on the right pant leg. CSU picked up a piece of a bicycle reflector at the scene. There were a couple of slivers imbedded in the fabric of his jacket, too."

"I see," I said, both of us keeping our voices low, our heads down.

"The vic suffered a broken rib where the handlebars hit him, but he was gone before he realized what happened, knocked clear out of his shoes, poor bastard."

I knew it was a dumb question. There was no way to kill someone, by accident or design, without leaving *some* trace of the method of preference.

At least, I hoped that was so. Because the very least you'd want in either case was to find out who, and in the latter case, make sure whoever it was didn't get to enjoy the fruits of his crime. Without evidence, without witnesses, you couldn't do that. You'd be left hanging, never knowing who. Or why.

"Anyone from the outside see this happen?"

"I'd have to look at the five to tell you that," he said, referring to the DD5, the report the detectives had to file after ringing doorbells and taking names, hoping to find a witness in the area of the crime.

I looked at him the way Dashiell looks at me when I'm eating pasta. I swear, that dog prefers spaghetti to steak.

"You wanna know, we got our eye on any suspects yet?"

"Would be helpful."

I picked up a small pad and a ballpoint pen that had seen better days and wrote a number on it.

"Fax me, okay?"

I handed him the number.

"This is your regular phone number," he said.

"Well, I don't get enough faxes to justify the added expense of a dedicated line. Matter of fact, yours stands a good chance of being my first."

"So when did you catch up with current technology? Fax me!"

"My brother-in-law bought me a fax machine, a laptop, and a printer. Until three weeks ago, the only web sites I was acquainted with were between my dog's toes. Now, whew, I surf, I defrag, I download. I'm practically a techie."

"So what was the occasion for all this equipment giving?"

"He thinks I don't like him anymore."

Marty nodded. "Is he right?"

"Nah."

Marty was staring, like I was his crib notes and the test was tomorrow.

"Well, maybe he's right. I don't know."

"You don't know?"

"He's a charming man. It's just that—"

I stopped, wondering why I was making more of this than I should have. Like it was my business in the first place.

"It's just that?"

"I don't trust him."

A banker was missing, it said in the *Times*, a hundred and sixty-seven thousand missing along with him. Some restaurateur from the Bronx was charged with trying to run over his wife. And yet another mother had killed her children. How did anyone trust anyone?

Marty put out his cigarette. "He cheated on your sister?"

"He did."

"And does *she* still like him, Rachel?"

"She does."

"But you can't find it in your heart to—"

I flapped my hand at him. "Don't get me started, okay?"

I headed for the door, my eyes welling up with tears I didn't want Marty to see.

"Hey. Thanks. I'll watch for your fax."

The door closed. I leaned against it, looking up at the fake bomb, someone's idea of a good thing, thinking about my brother-in-law, wondering, the same as Marty—if Lillian could forgive and forget, why couldn't I?

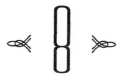

HOW ABOUT A LITTLE TRICK TODAY?

[C]ora was sitting on her bed, her bare feet dangling above the speckled green-and-gold linoleum floor, and for once, Dora wasn't with her.

"Oh, it's my little relative," she said, as soon as she saw me. Then she noticed Dashiell.

"Who woves her mommy?" she asked him. "Lady does."

I gave Dashiell the hand signal for "find." Venus had put a dog biscuit in the pockets of those she wanted me to visit, telling them Lady was coming this afternoon, never mind that *this* time around Lady wouldn't be a little black bitch with dreadlocks, she'd be a big white pit bull with testicles, anatomically, rather than politically, correct.

You stick to the reality they *have* to get, Venus had said—meals are eaten in the dining room; you can't leave the building without an escort; even when you get very angry, you must not hit; that sort of stuff. The rest, poof, you let it go. Because they will anyway.

Dashiell began to nuzzle the pocket with the biscuit. I watched Cora remember the biscuit, the biscuit becoming part of the trail of evidence that would connect her to what she'd been told twenty minutes earlier, help her hold onto the pieces of information she found difficult to grasp. I was interested to see that while she didn't know one dog from another, she remembered the name of the other dog, giving it to this one, generalizing the way young kids do, designating every animal "doggie" until they learn otherwise.

Cora smiled.

"Is the baby hungry?"

She slid the biscuit out of her pocket.

Dashiell looked at it soulfully. Definitely a Patsy-winning performance.

"She is hungry, she is," said Cora, letting him slip the biscuit gently from her bent fingers.

"My other daughter, Eileen," she whispered, "now you don't go telling on me I told you this, she's taken all my things. I tried to get them back, but she has lawyers." Cora's eyes began to tear up.

"Oh, she was the smart one," she said, nodding. "She told me she'd keep everything safe for me. But where? I don't know where anything is. My own daughter. Not a good girl like you. *She* never visits me."

I patted her dry old hand, the skin so thin you could almost see through it.

"I signed documents," she whispered. "I trusted her." Cora folded her arms across her chest. "From that day forward, I never saw another penny, not a bill, not a check, not a bank statement, not my jewelry." She was working herself into a froth, the same story I'd heard a hundred times at the Village Nursing Home. "I don't even have a watch," she whined, tapping her wrist near the

LADY VANISHES | 55

identification band all the residents wore. "I don't know what time it is."

"It's pretty lucky you live at Harbor View, where you get taken care of no matter what time it is, and where Lady comes to visit you. How about a little trick today?" I asked, hoping to distract her from her worries.

"I don't know any tricks," she said indignantly.

"Maybe Lady knows one."

"Lady doesn't do tricks. She's just here to love us."

Dora wheeled herself in from the hallway, her freshly washed hair tight against her head like a cap.

"Oh, goody, Lady's here," she said, "in my—"

"Room," Cora said. "Let's take her—"

"Downstairs. Let's take her out to the garden," Dora said.

"But my daughter's here."

"Where?"

Then they both looked around the room.

"Do you know who *she* is?" Dora was frowning.

"Why, of course."

"Who is she?"

"Don't you know?" Cora said.

They both stared at me.

"Do *you* have children?" Dora finally asked me.

I shook my head.

"They never visit you."

"Tell her to go away," Cora said. She flapped her hands in my direction, shooing me out of her room.

"Would you like to see Lady wave good-bye before I go?"

Cora frowned. "She doesn't—"

"Yes," Dora said, "Oh, goody."

"Goody two-shoes," Cora said.

I signaled Dashiell to wave. Sitting in front of them, he lifted one paw high and patted the air with it. Cora wasn't impressed. She turned her head away, hoping that, one way or the other, I would disappear.

By then, she wasn't the only one who wanted me to move on. Someone's diaper needed changing. *Nu*, my grandmother Sonya would have said, you think you'll smell like Lily of the Valley when *you're* old?

Cora and Dora shared a room on the second floor, facing east, over the garden. Dash and I took the stairs down to the main floor, turning left toward the garden door, straight back from the front entrance. Venus had given me a set of keys so that I could come and go as needed. I unlocked the garden door and stepped outside with Dashiell into the sultry heat of the August afternoon.

The garden was bricked in the center, no grass to mow, with a scattering of weathered teak tables with backless benches and plantings all around the perimeter in raised brick beds, a large tree in the center of it all for shade. I walked out and looked around, checking the gates to the side alleys, finding them high enough to keep both an agile dog and a tall human in, and locked up tight.

Dash began to sniff the places where Lady had left her scent, and I inspected the wall that surrounded the garden. That too was brick and solid; no holes to squeeze through, no way the puli could have gotten out this way.

There was a drawing pad on one of the tables, some colored pencils next to it. I walked over and leafed through the drawings, not knowing which of the residents had made them, since the kind of self-awareness that inspires artists to sign their work was not likely with this population.

Sitting on the bench where the pad had been left, I turned the pages back to the beginning and looked at the drawings, all meticulous renderings of exactly what the artist had seen: that one big tree across from the table. Each drawing was the same, except for one. Apparently a squirrel had scaled the wall a puli could not. But he hadn't remained long enough for his portrait to be completed. The unfinished squirrel, washing his hands at the base of the tree, stood out in contrast to the tree, the trunk neatly colored in four shades of brown, the leaves, pale green where the sun reached them and dark green where they were in shade, each drawn perfectly, the pencils, points up, all neatly replaced in the box.

The glitches were fascinating to me and always had been, one of the many reasons I did pet therapy, for the chance to see what people who worked in homes such as this called tiny miracles, like the time a Down's syndrome boy who was assumed to understand nothing handed Dashiell his plate of cookies when I told another child I had to leave because it was time for Dashiell to eat and he was very hungry, saying good-bye with something he could relate to.

Cora thought I was her daughter, and as she'd wisely told me, she didn't know the time of day, but she'd remembered that Lady didn't do tricks but came to love her.

I flipped back through the drawings once again, stopping at the incomplete squirrel. Only part of the story, like the one Venus was telling me.

I wondered what I'd hear next, the details carefully orchestrated, but for what purpose, I didn't know.

Was she protecting someone?

And if so, who?

I held the door for Dashiell, then tried it to make sure it was locked and followed him down the hall. There were two more residents who had biscuits in their pockets, and though they probably didn't know it, they were waiting for his visit.

HE WANTS TO RUN

I t was one of those triple-H New York summers, day after steamy day so hot, people always say, you could cook an egg on the sidewalk, a suggestion worth ignoring. If the germs didn't get you up front, the cholesterol would surely do it over time.

When we got to the pier, Dashiell lay down, his tongue out. I was thinking that, despite the heat, after his last visit, he'd need to run. But even after finishing most of the water, he refused to move.

I thought about doing a round of t'ai chi, but practicing moves your energy and makes you hotter. So instead, we left the pier and headed south along the path the bicyclers used; no one was dumb enough to be riding while the sun was still up. There was a little shade here, still, the first huge planter we got to—a twelve-by-twelve-foot cement square filled with trees and room for people to sit along the rim—Dash jumped up, walked to the nearest tree, dug away the topsoil until he got to a cooler layer of earth, and lay down.

Jackson, second on my list, hadn't been in his room, but we'd found him downstairs, sitting in the corner of the dining room, dripping paint from his fingers onto one of the pages of a drawing pad.

There were two women I hadn't yet met there, one at either end of one of the rectangular tables. They looked far enough apart in age to be mother and daughter. The older one, wearing a tiara, might have been fifty, the younger one in her late twenties, but when people have no expressions on their faces, age can be difficult to judge.

There was a fat, bald man at one of the round tables, playing with a busy box, his fingers short and wide, the fingertips almost square, his round face flat. Charlotte was there, too, sharpening a stack of colored pencils, watching the curl of wood as it emerged from the sharpener, smelling each new point carefully before she laid the pencil down and picked up the next one. I gave her shoulder a quick squeeze in passing, but she never looked up. Touch is considered pretty much of a no-no with autistics, but I hadn't found that to be the case. If I didn't believe the people I worked with had the same need for contact as everyone else, what on earth was I doing here? Maybe it was because of Dashiell that I could get away with touching. I didn't know. But hadn't Venus done it, too, a quick touch on David's shoulder in passing, over and done with before he even knew it was happening?

When I'd first worked with Emily, a touch would start her trembling, her arms jerking violently up and down, her head shaking from side to side. I'd wait until she stopped, then touch her again, patting her arm and putting a hand on her shoulder for just a second. Each time, her reaction was less violent and shorter-lived until, near the end, before she was to move to a larger institution closer to where her parents lived, she would hug me if I requested it, though never on her own.

By the time we'd gotten to the far corner of the dining room, Jackson had stopped painting. He had wiped his hands carefully on some paper towels and was sitting there, staring straight ahead, a man of about sixty, tall, thin, elegant looking in his collarless shirt, even though he had paint all over his cuffs and on his cheek where he'd forgotten and touched himself before wiping his hands. I took the chair next to his, leaving room for Dashiell to come in between us and place his head on Jackson's leg.

"How are you today?"

I waited for a response, then when none came, I waited for an inspiration.

"I like your painting," I told him, looking at it rather than at him. "What do you call it?"

That went over in a big way. Jackson didn't even blink. I told him my name, then Dashiell's. He never moved.

I waited some more. I didn't mind the waiting. Having done this work for years, I was used to it. Sometimes you could sit with someone for a long time, and nothing discernible would happen. But the dog was there, and somehow, sometimes—no one knew quite how—that helped them forge a path from their shut-off world to the larger world they didn't trust, didn't quite understand. If I was patient, even if I didn't see anything change, sometimes it did. Then next time, or the time after, there might be some communication, or some action. They might pet Dashiell. Or they might just be less tense, less fearful.

This time, with the case on my mind and so little to go on, I was too antsy to sit around as if I, too, were in a semicatatonic state.

"How about if you turn your chair around," I said, figuring, what the hell, it was worth a try, "and I'll show you some neat stuff Dashiell can do. Would you like that, Jackson?"

To my utter surprise, Jackson turned his chair, and keeping my promise, I showed him how Dashiell works on voice commands, hand signals, and whistle signals. I did mostly ordinary stuff—sit, stay, lie down, come, some silent distance work, the seek-back—no big thing for me and Dashiell, but for someone whose life was contained year after year in one building—the world going by without him, hemlines going up and down, sitcoms appearing and getting canceled, books making the list or being remaindered—for this man who lived as if he were being punished for some wrongdoing he could no longer remember, who was virtually in jail, if he were able to concentrate on what was before him, Dashiell's demonstration of basic obedience might have seemed as thrilling as the first time you see fireworks, your father saying, That one's called spaghetti, or Look, goldfish, your mother's favorite, the sky lit up gold and white, your hand in your father's hand, safe and warm.

When I released Dash, he went right back to where he'd been, his chin on Jackson's knee, soulful eyes looking up.

For a moment, Jackson remained as he was. So much for that, I thought, and then, watching him staring at the wall, I found myself wondering why, if so many of these people did that, was the wall blank, just a solid sheet of color, when it could be so much more interesting?

But then it happened, something that made me forget all about a mural for the dining room. Jackson stood. Until then, I hadn't quite realized how tall he was—well over six feet, maybe even six-two or -three. When I looked into his eyes, Jackson was home, looking back at me.

"He wants to run," he said, his voice soft, almost a whisper, but his enunciation clear.

I clipped on Dashiell's leash and held the handle out for Jackson. He took the leash and began to lope around the perimeter of the dining room, his long legs reaching out, covering distance with astonishing leaps. I looked around to see if anyone else was as surprised as I was, but no one was giving the moment a bit of attention, as if it were perfectly ordinary for this quiet, skinny old man to take a big dog twice around the dining room, as if it happened on a daily basis.

When he returned with Dashiell, face flushed, he kept hold of the leash.

"I want to do what you did."

"Go for it," I said, not exactly sure what he meant, but figuring, *something* happening is always better than *nothing* happening, as long as the something was benign and not violent.

Jackson, copying my hand signals perfectly, got Dashiell to sit, lie down, stay, come, and heel. That was when I'd heard it, a choking noise from somewhere behind me. When I turned, it was Venus, standing in the doorway of the dining room, wiping her eyes with the heels of her hands.

At first, I thought something must be wrong. But when I turned back to Jackson, I didn't see what it could be. He was trying the seek-back, taking a clean folded handkerchief from his pocket, dropping it, walking Dashiell away, then sending him back for the handkerchief with one long, low whistle, the way I'd done with my keys, remembering everything I'd done, exactly as I'd done it, except for this one innovation. I hadn't had a handkerchief. And Jackson certainly didn't have a set of keys.

"That was *wonderful*," I said, clapping my hands, meaning it sincerely. "You did a great job."

Jackson handed me the leash and took his seat again. Remembering the biscuit, I put my hand lightly on his arm. "Dashiell must be hungry after all that running. Do you have something for him to eat?"

Expecting Jackson to reach into his pocket and produce the

biscuit Venus said she'd given him, I was surprised when he didn't. I shouldn't have been. The tiny miracles, the little windows of communication, action, or insight, touching moments when a very disabled person seems less disabled, never last. A moment later, or the next visit, it is as if they'd never occurred at all. If I came back tomorrow and tried the same thing with Jackson, he probably would not respond in the same way, which, in part, was why he was here.

For me, the saddest part was that these lucid moments, as Venus called them, were never a sign of a cure, not in this population. Here there were no cures, so these incidents were only what they seemed to be—moments, nothing more.

"Check your pockets," I suggested, but Jackson sat there doing nothing, his eyes looking straight ahead, as mute as he'd been when I'd first sat down.

I told Dashiell to find the biscuit. He began to sniff around, finding it in Jackson's left pocket and carefully slipping it out with the sort of patience you wouldn't imagine a dog could display. Jackson didn't seem to notice, as if he hadn't moved at all, as if he had never spoken to us, as if we weren't there and had never been there.

Venus was still in the doorway, all business now. She tilted her head toward David, who was standing in his usual spot by the sidelight, his head leaning slightly back, the way people do when they want to see something out of the bottom part of their bifocals, his arms stiff, only his fingers moving.

Maybe there hadn't been anything wrong. Maybe her tears were because something was right, because Jackson had had a little miracle.

Or maybe they had to do with something that had happened moments earlier, when she was still in her office.

As Venus had indicated David to me, with a nod of her head,

I did the same with Dashiell. Standing next to her, just outside the dining room, I watched him meander over to David, stand at his side, then slowly sit on the hip closer to David, his legs sprawled straight out in front of him, leaning his weight ever so carefully against David's leg.

David's nervous fingers began to tap at each other more slowly, and in a moment, they were still, the hands relaxed, just swaying at his side, like leaves in a breeze.

"What happened before?" I whispered.

"What do you mean?"

Like Jackson, she had closed the door.

But this time I wasn't having any. I made little lines under my eye with my pointer and shrugged.

"What was it you *did* there?"

"Nothing much," I said. "I admired his work, and Dashiell leaned in for some petting, but he wasn't responding, so I thought I'd show him some of Dashiell's work. It's lively, like his paintings, and it gave me something to do. Then he said *he* wanted to try it. That's all."

Venus turned away for a moment. When she looked back, her eyes were shining.

"Rachel, that man hasn't spoken since he's been here. Not once. I may never let you go."

"It's not *me*. It's Dashiell. He can get to anyone."

"Everyone loved Lady. She was a cheerful, calming presence, rushing about all day on her own, making sure everyone was okay. But nothing like this ever happened. Your boy's good. He gets inside."

"He was born for this."

Venus nodded, her eyes on David. "No heroics. Just hang out. You okay here?"

"I'm fine."

But I wasn't. I didn't feel I'd been told the whole story here either.

"Good. You know where I am if you need me."

She turned and walked back to her office, on the other side of the lobby. I watched her take the keys hanging from her belt and unlock the door. When it closed behind her, I heard the tumbler turn over again—Venus double-locking herself in.

I decided to stay put for a moment and just watch—David standing there, Dashiell leaning on him, no one saying boo. Then, in this place where everything was odd, something unusual happened. David sat. He lowered himself to the floor, stretched his legs out, and sat on his right hip, leaning against Dashiell as Dashiell leaned against him.

After a few minutes I joined them, sitting at Dashiell's side, keeping him between me and David; if a dog could sometimes make a bridge between a visitor and a disabled person, in the middle was exactly where he belonged.

Then I did something else, something that had always worked for me with dogs. When there was a behavior I couldn't interpret, if I could, I'd imitate it. Having already imitated a posture, as David himself had, I now listened as carefully as I could to David's ragged exhalations, then I patterned my breathing after his and stayed that way, on the floor, until I could no longer bear it because if I did it for one more minute, I'd be living here, too.

No wonder Dashiell was exhausted, lying on his side asleep in the dirt under the tree.

I sat looking out over the river, thinking about Lady, the dog I'd never met, the dog I might never get the chance to meet. She was a herding dog, light and quick. She made the kids her flock, the same way she would have were she living with any ordinary family. For her, the job was clear—see where all her little lambs were and keep them safe. Of course, being a dog, she always had a little time in her busy schedule for affection, both the giving and the getting. And maybe sometimes, at night, when everyone was safe in bed, there'd be time for those long snuggles, the sort Dashiell specialized in.

Dashiell was different. You could see the difference in their body types—one built for speed, the other for heavy lifting. No wonder Dashiell was performing miracles here. He started cautiously, waiting for the invitation to press in closer, an invitation that would come in the form of a slower heart rate and deeper respiration, things that told him he was welcome, oh, so welcome, and that he, too, could let go. And when he did, he was just what the doctor ordered—a squeeze machine.

I watched him sleep, his sides moving slowly in and out, his face distorted by his own weight, which seemed to flatten him against the cool earth. I waited until 5:15, then gave him some water, and we headed for the gym and the continuation of Venus's story.

I'D NEVER HEARD HIS VOICE

got to the gym before Venus, tied Dash to the bench, and signed in. Serge put down his newspaper and went for the green water basin.

I took the corner treadmill, putting the power on, starting the belt, and slowly increasing the speed. In front of me, outside the window, which was covered with a taupe shade to keep the sun from blinding anyone working out, the orange-and-white striped barrels that blocked off areas of construction, yellow tape strung between them, kept traffic off the newly paved lane closest to the broken sidewalk. The men in their orange hard hats and vests we had seen on our way to the pier had gone home by now, construction work starting and ending earlier than the average workday. How else could they make all that noise, jackhammers, earthmovers, and cranes clanging away when the rest of the world is still trying to sleep?

I hadn't seen Venus arrive, coming from the north, signing in, and going straight to the ladies' locker room, then appearing on the treadmill to my right. I had questions about the kids—David, Jackson, Charlotte, and the twins—and I wanted to know who had made all those pictures of the tree, the one with the unfinished squirrel. But I didn't know how long she'd have today, and I needed to hear her story, find out why she thought her life was in danger, figure out what to do if it was.

"Did you keep writing him?" I asked, as if she'd told me a minute, not a day, ago that the man she'd met on-line was married.

"I did," she said, fiddling with the buttons on her treadmill.

I looked out the window, the hook hanging from the crane parked across the highway dark and ominous looking against the sky. What was the hook here, I wondered, wasting time caring about a man who was married to someone else?

"She was ill, he said."

Uh-huh, I thought. Companion piece to "My wife doesn't understand me," or, more nineties, "We have an arrangement."

"She had cancer. There had been a remission. But after four and a half years, the disease came back. It had gone from the breast to the bone, and she was dying."

"Oh," I said.

"When she was in the hospital, he was there every day. He went in the morning, early. Then after work, he went back. He spent the evening with her. Sometimes he sat quietly by the bed, holding her hand. Sometimes he'd read to her. He'd tell me what he was reading, and I'd get the book. I'd read it, too."

I turned to look at her, dreadlocks loose today, hanging around her pretty face, her big eyes shining as she told about this man she loved, this married man who was so tender when his wife was dying.

Or so he wrote.

"For months, I read the books he read to his wife, listened to each new symptom, knew the names of the medications she was on, stayed up late, writing him, giving him letters for company when he was lonely."

"Did he talk about an autistic kid?"

She shook her head, the curls swinging one way, then the other.

"Did you talk about your kids?"

She shook her head again.

"It was understood, because of how we met, that autism affected his life and mine. But how, I didn't tell him. He didn't say either. We had the autism chat line for that. This was about our own feelings, not about anyone's kid. This was to feel ordinary, like other human beings."

I nodded, watching the light on the river, the peaks of water silver, the water moving on, toward the Statue of Liberty, south to where the ocean was.

"She died last winter, a week before Christmas."

Venus increased the speed on her treadmill, starting to run.

I took a sip of water, going fast enough walking, my T-shirt soaked even before I got here. I could see Dashiell through the open arch, see his back as he lay on the cool floor, fast asleep, his head pressed against the water basin.

"A few weeks after that, he began to talk about us meeting."

"He was local? Close enough so that you could see each other?"

"He was. That's the strangest thing, isn't it? He could have been anywhere, in Iowa, Alaska, New Zealand, anywhere at all. But he was right here, in Manhattan. Sometimes you think something was meant to be. But then—"

Venus looked at her watch.

"I don't have a lot of time."

"Another meeting?"

She shook her head. She wasn't going to say.

"So did you get together?"

"We negotiated for a month."

When she smiled, I realized I'd only seen her smile once before. Whether she was in danger or not, she surely believed she was, a haunted look on her pretty face.

"Then he picked a spot."

"Where?"

"Provence, in Soho. Do you know it?"

I nodded.

"I wondered at the choice."

"A very romantic place," I said.

Venus nodded.

"A place for lovers," she said. "That's what he said. We've never met, I said. You don't know me. I do, he said. And I know I love you.

"Rachel, this was so extraordinary. We hadn't switched from the internet to the phone. I'd never heard his voice. There was so much I didn't know about him. But I felt it, too. My heart would race before logging on to read his letters every night. I felt exactly the way you do when your lover walks into a room. Only this room, it was a computer screen. It was black words on a white screen. No smell. No catching your breath because you see a wrist sticking out of the white cuff of a shirt and it makes you crazy. Nothing like that, like what you're used to."

I began to laugh. "I know what you mean," I said. "All that longing, it can—"

"But there was none of that."

She hit the cool-down button, going from a run to a walk.

"You must have been scared."

"I was. And I wasn't. Both sides powerfully strong."

Venus shook her head, smiling at the memory.

"And?" I said, afraid she'd cut and run without telling me

what I was dying to hear, so absorbed in her story, as if it were a girlfriend thing, forgetting for the moment why I was here and what this was all about.

"Finally, after so many months, after sharing so much, I was going to meet him. Well, maybe that's the wrong word, Rachel. I'd met him long before. But now, I was going to *see* him, this man who made my heart pound, this man I didn't know any of the normal, ordinary things about, the way you do when it's a more traditional sort of thing.

"I didn't know how I'd feel. Or how he would. Trust me, I was scared. There was so much at stake, Rachel. If it was no good, I'd lose my best friend.

"But I was excited, too. I couldn't wait.

"What never occurred to me at the time was that we might already know each other."

"And did you?"

Venus nodded.

"Can you imagine my surprise when I got there, carrying a red rose, as we'd planned, asked for his table, and saw who it was?"

Venus stopped the belt. She turned to face me.

"Who?" I asked, stepping off on the edges and stopping my belt.

She didn't answer, thinking over if she should tell.

"Who?" Sounding like an owl.

"Why, it was Harry," she said.

As if I should have known.

"Harry *Dietrich?*"

Venus nodded.

"Harry Dietrich," she repeated.

"But he was seventy-four," I blurted out. She couldn't have been more than forty, forty-two at most.

"And *ugly*," Venus said. "Homely as a toad. But I loved him to pieces." Venus swiped at her eyes, then took a deep breath. "And he loved me."

"What did he say when he saw it was you?"

"He stood and took my hand, turning it over and kissing the palm. Then he pulled out a chair for me and said, 'Sit down, darling, we have so much to talk about.' "

"As if he *knew?*"

"As if he'd won the lottery."

"And then?"

She seemed lost in thought.

"Rachel, the funeral is at ten, at the Ethical Culture Society on Central Park West. You'll be there? You won't forget?"

I nodded.

"But—"

"I'm sorry to run like this. I have to see the lawyer. I'll speak to you tomorrow, Rachel. You do understand, I couldn't have just blurted this out to you. What would you have thought?"

"There's more, isn't there?"

"Oh," she said, "count on it."

What was she doing, taking her time to build up some trust in me before she blurted out the rest, not unlike the kids in her actions?

But according to Venus, we didn't have time to build trust. We needed a leap of faith, if we were going to find out what we needed to know by Friday.

"Venus—"

"I'm going to be late."

"Just a quick question," I told her, not taking no for an answer this time. "I was told it was you who called nine-one-one. How did you know something was wrong, that Harry had been hurt?"

"Molly told me. She said Cora was arguing with Dora in the dining room and that when she'd had enough, she'd turned her back to her, which meant she was then facing the window. She began to bang on the glass, Molly said, and when Molly rushed over to tell her to stop, that she might break the window and hurt herself, she said she was trying to wake up Harry, that he'd taken off his shoes and was taking a nap on the sidewalk and that that wasn't right. He ought to be in his bed, she told Molly. That's the rule. Molly looked out, saw Harry out there, and came running to tell me."

"Had Cora seen the accident happen?"

"Not that I could tell. I think she must have looked out minutes afterward. You have to understand, Rachel, with this population, there's no way of knowing things like that. I've got to go now. I really do."

I would talk to Cora myself. But if Venus couldn't find out anything right after the fact, there wasn't much chance I'd get a straight story days later.

I watched her walk toward the locker room. When she was out of sight, no one around except Eloise, the gym cat, sitting on the back of the couch watching Dashiell sleep, I turned my belt back on, stepping on and again slowly increasing the speed, as if staying where I was would help me figure out what to do next.

I have to see the lawyer, she'd said.

What lawyer?

Harry's lawyer, I thought, no doubt about it.

I let that sit, feeling the weight of it.

It was time to find out who might stand to gain from Harry Dietrich's demise, I thought, hoping Venus White would not be on that list, knowing she would be, right at the top, her life in danger because of it.

I WANTED TO SHAKE HER

wanted to shake her, push her back onto a chair, stand over her, one finger poking at her chest, demand that she tell me the rest of it, *now*—this exasperating woman, building me up for each piece of her autobiography so I wouldn't think ill of her. What did that have to do with anything anyway?

What did she think—that if she told me everything at once, I wouldn't understand?

Or was it that I would?

She was going to see Harry's lawyer. Shouldn't I be in the locker room, too, cleaning up, telling her, like it or not, I was going with her, that she wasn't letting me do my job, that, no two ways about it, I had to find out what the lawyer had to say, I had to know once and for all what the rest of the story was, whatever was keeping her up nights, scaring the hell out of her?

But if I did go with her, would the lawyer talk? Who the hell was I that Harry's lawyer should talk to me? And what made me think Venus would let me rush this, find out what I needed to know faster than she was willing to eke it out?

There had to be another way, I thought, going over everything she'd said, starting with her first phone call.

She had whispered the night she'd called me, then she'd talked too loud, purposely feeding information to whoever was there. But when I was outside her office door with Charlotte, I could hear her on the phone, talking about something personal, saying she was scared. Why wasn't she worrying about anyone overhearing her then?

She'd called me around midnight, said she was staying over.

Was it the night man she suspected? He'd been there when the dog disappeared, hadn't he?

And he wasn't there, at least not *inside* the facility, when Harry was killed by a bicycle.

I turned and looked at the big round clock on the wall. He'd be there in a few hours. Lonely work, staying up all night taking care of disabled people, people who get spooked easily, can't tell you what's wrong. Maybe he could use a little company to make the time go by. Before he knew it it would be morning, time to go home, and what? Feed his puli?

And where were all the other players? Where were the sister-in-law and her son and daughter, people who stood to inherit a bundle when the old man died? It wasn't at all like relatives to lie back and wait, act casual when there was a fortune at stake. It was more like a feeding frenzy, the sharks smelling blood and moving in close to make sure they had a shot at the biggest portion.

After my father died, some second cousins we used to see once or twice a year, if that often, came to the house, one saying that since my mother only had girls, my father's watch should go to him, that Abe, he was sure, would have wanted it that way—as if my father, who hadn't known the clock was running down when he was still so young, had nothing better to concern himself with than wondering to whom he should leave his few worldly possessions. And the books, his mother said, a dumpy woman with a doughy face, my cousin Abe would have wanted us to have his books.

My mother, sitting on the couch, a Kleenex crushed in one hand, lifted her face and looked at the cousins, then stood and quietly walked to the door, opening it for them.

"Abe's things are staying right here where they belong, with his family," she said, showing them out. "We're not dead yet," she called after them. "Not by a long shot."

A watch. Some books. What would it have been had there been money, the kind of millions Harry Dietrich had to have had to pour millions into Harbor View over the years?

And what of that? Was money set aside to keep the home going? Eli Kagan must have thought so. He'd told the *Times* that Harbor View would operate as always. With Harry gone, would he be managing those millions? And if not, who would?

Beyond the uptown traffic they were building a median to be filled with plants, trying to make the new road more palatable, prettying it up so the quiet community to the east of the roadway would be less offended by the constant rush of traffic—a neighborhood of townhouses built one hundred and fifty years before, wrought iron boot scrapers still in place at the foot of the stoop that took you up to the grand parlor floors, so that you wouldn't track in mud from the unpaved roads. There were still cobblestone streets in the Village, and carriage houses, now converted into homes, like my own, cottages entered through passageways just wide enough for a horse and wagon to pass.

Venus was leaving the gym, wearing a white linen suit, a

peach-colored shell underneath. As she passed the windows where the treadmills were, I could see that the heart was tucked away again, which made me think of something else; the way she'd put her hand on her chest at the gallery, squeezed her eyes closed, and taken a minute to collect her feelings before continuing. It was the necklace she was touching, feeling it through her shirt, getting comfort from it, the necklace Harry had given her, which she didn't want anyone at work to see.

I looked across at the Jersey skyline. Two towers were going up, the window openings still without glass, like dark open mouths. I thought about how quickly the world was changing now, how slowly things seemed to move when I was a kid, the time between my seventh and eighth birthday taking ten times as long as the time between my thirty-seventh and thirty-eighth.

How had time moved for Venus and Harry that first moment, when they understood who it was they'd each been writing to, someone they each had known for years, but in a very different way?

He was easily old enough to be her father, and as Venus had said, he wasn't an attractive man. He had one of those faces, if it were sculpted out of clay, that looked as if someone had placed a hand on top of the head and leaned a little too hard, scrunching everything into a permanent scowl.

Harry, the money man, watching figures all his life.

But kind to his dying wife.

He'd been kind to Venus, too, paying attention to her concerns, listening to her dreams. He'd shared his thoughts and feelings with her, month after month. He'd been truthful with her, telling her he had a wife.

Maybe not at first, but soon enough.

You could hardly fault the man, wanting someone to talk to when his wife had been so sick.

Could you?

Besides all that, he was rich, richer than anyone else Venus had ever known.

How long after that first glimpse did Venus think about the money?

Looking at the river, the light sparkling on the water the way it did on Venus's diamond necklace, I wondered about that, about their first meeting and what each of them was thinking when they saw the other for the first time, Harry sitting there waiting for her, Venus carrying a single red rose.

I slowed down the belt and stretched out my legs. There was work to do, and for the moment, I was glad that Venus was going elsewhere and that I wasn't going with her. I had the feeling I'd find out much more on my own. I touched the outside of my pocket to check for the keys she'd given me, then headed home with Dashiell to shower and change.

ALL FALL DOWN

I decided to get to Harbor View before the night man, though this was just guesswork. No one had told me exactly when he came on, nor who else might be there in the evening. Since it was likely there'd be more than one person around, on the way over I thought up a variety of excuses for my after-hours presence.

When I unlocked the front door, I heard singing from the dining room. David was in the dining-room doorway, the way he had been when Samuel was doing dance therapy, maybe the closest he got to participating in anything, and little as it was, I was probably not the only one there to think this little bit of contact was a result of good care. There were places I'd been with Dashiell where nothing was too generous a term to describe what some of the residents did.

I let Dashiell go to him first, tying his leash around my waist and waiting in the empty lobby, the floor freshly mopped, the doors to all three offices closed, and my guess, locked. I looked at the keys, still in my hand, five of them, wondering if the offices used the same key or separate ones and planning to find out if any of the keys I'd been given would get me where I needed to go.

Dashiell stood next to David, all but touching him, wagging his tail from side to side in slow motion, waiting for a signal to hype up his schmooze. Apparently it came, because he suddenly leaned in, giving David just enough of his weight that had David moved, Dash would have, too.

But David didn't move. I watched his hands, to see if they'd relax the way they had earlier, but this time I saw something else. Now it appeared that David was moving his fingers in time to the singing.

I felt something like a cool breeze on my skin, a fluttering in my chest. Some things did seem to get inside and touch this inscrutable man. If that were so, wasn't it possible that something could get out, too?

I walked up slowly, and not wanting to startle David, I sighed so that he would know I was behind him. If Eli Kagan wanted workers to knock on doors before entering residents' rooms, this was the equivalent, as best as I could figure out.

I stood, as last time, so that Dashiell was in the middle, never greeting David, nor looking directly at him. For a moment, I watched the singers. Only about half the people gathered were actually singing or humming, the rest sitting, staring at the remains of dessert or at nothing much at all.

Samuel Kagan was leading the group. Dance therapy on Monday, singing on Tuesday, a man of many talents and endless dedication, I thought, watching him work. He appeared to be in his early forties. The zealous look on his face was not unlike the spaced-out look of the Moonies, the incandescent lights from above making his nude bean shine, all the more so since it was slick with sweat. He had a round face, a roundish nose, full lips, and a great broom of a mustache. He bounced on the balls of his feet, singing as loud and as clear as a human being could without shouting, his short-fingered hands chopping the air forcefully as he conducted his little choir with such fervor, you'd think there was going to be a performance tomorrow.

For a while I became so enthralled watching him, his short, chunky body, shirt soaked with sweat despite the air conditioning, energetically tapping his feet and moving around, that I forgot all about David. Then I remembered what had happened earlier; one way or another, I'd passed by him without seeing him. Some people do that, I thought; the opposite of the vibrant, little man leading the singing, energy swirling about him, they pull their energy in, so far that they become almost invisible, like prey animals who change their color to blend in with the environment, their only protection against the predators. I wondered if this was just the way David was, if he had been born like this, or if something had damaged him so severely that he needed to hide this way, thinking of what Venus said, how he tugged at her, how even as closed as he was, he'd taken her heart.

I sat then, cross-legged on the floor. After a moment, David sat, leaving only Dashiell standing, but not for long. This time, based on their earlier communion, Dashiell slipped artfully down David's leg, but not into a sit. Instead, he moved his body forward, so that when he finished sliding, he lay across David's lap, gazing up at him with adoration.

The song ended, and Samuel began to clap, those residents who could joining in. When that was that, he turned, noticed me, and came over.

"Samuel Kagan," he said, bending down to shake my hand, his eyebrows rising, asking my name.

"Rachel Alexander," I said, my eyebrows staying right where

they were, "and Dashiell," since he was too occupied to intro-duce himself.

At the sound of his name, Dashiell lifted his head, sneezed, took a sniff, then sighed and laid his head back on David's lap. Samuel squatted so that we'd be face to face, reaching out for my hand and giving it a squeeze. "I'm so glad you've joined the team," he said, leaving my hand warm and damp.

A thin stream of saliva glistened at the corner of David's mouth, stringing its way down to Dashiell's side. I was finally going to have a use for those paper towels I'd been carrying around—two uses—but for now, I let it be and looked back at Samuel.

"I was so sorry to hear about the accident," I said, "and com-ing so soon after the other loss." I couldn't assume that because David didn't speak, he didn't understand, and I didn't want to remind him of the two tragedies that had happened so recently, changes for the worse in a place where nothing was supposed to change at all. "I'm happy to help out during this difficult time."

"Venus says Dashiell is working out really well with the kids." Samuel looked at Dashiell sprawled across David's lap and nodded his approval. "Really well," he repeated.

"How often do you work with the kids?" I asked.

"Oh, I'm here every day."

"They sing every evening?"

"Most evenings."

"What a lovely way to end their day."

"I also do dance and art with them, speech therapy, and a movement class, more structured than the dance class, very im-portant with this population. They can lose motility if not re-minded to exercise their muscles."

I got up and took a few steps away, Samuel following me.

"What about David? Does he ever do more than watch?"

Samuel sighed.

"He's a difficult man."

I looked back at David, Dashiell lying across his legs.

"That's one of the reasons we were so frantic when Lady disappeared. It's the only contact he's ever accepted, other than medical things, you know, a shot, or a checkup."

"He's okay with that? With the doctor touching him?"

"Yes. It's one of those funny things. I worked with a young man years ago, when I was still studying speech therapy. Back when I still had hair," he said, his lips spreading into a smile, dimples showing on either side of his mustache. "He was incapable of most of the activities we take for granted—getting dressed properly by himself, making a sandwich without destroying the kitchen and everything in it, walking without stumbling—but he could drive a car. Not only that, he was a safe driver. I was asked to see a patient upstate once, and he drove me."

"You don't drive?"

"Well, there's not much need for a car in the city. But he had one, and he wanted to take me, too. I think he wanted me to see that there was something he could do well. He was totally sure of himself, confident, a graceful driver, and obviously, smart enough to know the rules and pass the test. But in the rest of his life he was the consummate klutz, in addition to his crippling stutter. The moral of the story is, you never know. Dad calls the phenomenon holes in the clouds, you know, a spot where the sun can shine through.

"David won't mimic activities either. This is as good as it gets, and it took two years before he'd get this close to any activity. I do better with those in wheelchairs than with David, maintaining enough upper body strength and eye-hand coordination by tossing a big, light ball around. I can even get Eddie to do things, but not David."

"Which one is Eddie?"

"The Down's syndrome man. He's a real sweetheart, and game. He tries everything."

I nodded.

"That class is tomorrow. It's usually after breakfast, but because of the funeral, it'll be after lunch. Come and watch, Rachel. And you should come to our Wednesday-night meeting, too, the staff and Dad, um, Dr. Kagan, talking about progress and problems. He's—Dad is—very receptive to suggestions, and being new, I bet you'll have some. And some questions, too. It's here, in the dining room, eight o'clock."

"Thanks, I'll come."

"See you then," he said, the sweat still running down his full cheeks.

"And in the morning," I said, "I thought I'd go to the service."

"It seems to me you're part of the family already," he said, then he turned back to the kids, walking over to an older woman in a wheelchair, the one who wore the tiara.

There was a heavyset woman at the other end of the dining room, helping people get ready to leave. It was after nine, time for everyone to turn in, time for me to make like I had a reason to be here other than sheer nosiness.

The woman I'd noticed was crossing the dining room now, headed my way. I began to polish up my fish stories, but she only nodded to me. It was David she was after, not me.

"Time for bed, sweet pea," she said, "follow Molly. Here we go," she said, as if she were helping him up. But she wasn't. David had put his hands on the floor to help himself up. "Good boy," Molly said, so Dashiell, who was also up now, wagged his tail. Then Molly turned to me. "I hope you and Dashiell will excuse us, Rachel. It's time for David to clean up for bed."

"Good night, David." I stepped out into the lobby with them.

"Nice to meet you, Molly." She nodded without turning around. A busy woman.

Two more people who were here in the evening.

I watched Molly head for the stairs, David following, thinking at least he did that, he climbed the stairs a few times a day, something to keep a minimum amount of muscle tone. He was thin as a bone, his arms at his side, his fingers tapping again, trailing after Molly, who moved from side to side, carrying her weight slowly up the stairs, her little lamb behind her.

So he understood Molly.

Or did he just know the routine?

I watched until they were out of sight, thinking that, sure, he probably did understand some of the stuff he heard, glad I hadn't talked about Lady within his earshot, but that he never looked from side to side. He never turned around. For whatever reason, he no longer had the curiosity all of us are born with, the desire to know what's going on, the joy that comes with discovery.

Jackson had the desire to paint, and the Weissman twins their passion for argument. Someone else drew pictures, too, the kid who'd rendered the tree a dozen times, once more when the squirrel had come for its brief visit.

I bent over Dashiell and dried him off with the paper towels, dried my hand as well.

When I looked back at the dining room, the last of the kids was leaving, Samuel heading for the elevator with Charlotte at his side.

"Bedtime stories," he said. "Would you and Dashiell like to join us?"

"I'll pass, but thanks," I told him. "You gave me a wonderful idea a moment ago, and I want to work something out with Dashiell, a surprise for tomorrow's movement class."

His eyebrows went north again. "Oh," he said, clasping his hands in front of his chest, "I can't wait to see it."

And liar that I sometimes am—in undercover work, if you don't believe the end justifies the means, you won't get anywhere—this time I'd been telling the truth. I did have an idea for the movement class. I walked Dashiell into the dining room and began to walk around the perimeter of the room. Then when he got used to my pattern, I sent him on ahead.

Forward, good boy, I told him. Now I was following him. Then, Stop. And again, Forward. As we went, I pictured the kids, adding things to the routine I thought some of them might be able to do, even those in wheelchairs, Dashiell loving every change, turning his head and watching me intently to glean clues not only from the words I said but from my body language, trying to predict my direction—succeeding, too. After forty-five minutes, the building quiet and lonely now, having saved the best for last, I gave a command he wouldn't have needed, one for creatures less observant than my dog.

All fall down.

I hit the ground laughing, Dashiell at my side. He rolled over twice, first away from me, then back, a big grin on his face, his tail banging out a tune on the bare floor.

That done, we got up and quickly crossed the lobby, trying the keys Venus had given me on the door to the left, the one farthest from hers. None of them worked. It had been a bit on the optimistic side to figure I'd be handed the keys to the place that held the secrets I was after. When had life ever been that easy?

But that was okay. Because as soon as I had tried all the keys on all three doors and discovered that I was locked out of not one but all three of the private offices, I thought of another way I might be able to get what I was after, a better way. Just the thought of it gave me an adrenaline rush, Dash feeling it and beginning to bounce around me, letting me know, whatever it was I was planning, he wanted in.

◅ 13 ▻

HE DIDN'T ANSWER ME

I could hear Cora and Dora arguing as I passed the stairs. They must have left their door open. I wanted to talk to Cora about what she might have seen the evening Harry was killed, but I knew the morning would be a better time. The later it was in the day, the less lucid she was likely to be.

I headed for the garden door, shutting off the outdoor lights before unlocking it, letting Dashiell out, then closing it without making a sound.

Once outside in the dark yard, I turned right, walking along the wall of the building until I came to the window of the office farthest from Venus's, planning to try the window in the hope it wouldn't be locked. With the high wall around the garden, the alley gate locked, and staff here around the clock, I was hoping that whoever used that office wasn't paranoid about people sneaking in through the window after hours.

The air conditioner, set into the brick wall beneath the window, was off. And sensibly, someone had opened the window so that the room wouldn't get too stuffy overnight.

I slid up the screen and opened the window the rest of the way, climbing into the dark room first, bumping my shin against what my hands told me too late was a chair, then feeling along the wall for the light. Once I had the light on, I told Dashiell, "Over," and he sailed into the room, landing clear of the chair. He immediately began to check out the thick oriental rug for scents of the people who had been here recently, and perhaps even more interesting, of the dog who worked at Harbor View before he did.

I pulled the shade down and closed the curtain, hoping it would block out most of the light, not knowing if the night man, or anyone else, would be stepping out into the garden for a smoke or a breath of tepid air.

Turning around, I looked at the office—Harry's, I was sure, not only because the middle door had been plastered with drawings that gave a user-friendly impression but because this place was clearly an executive's office, a place where someone could shut the door and deal with the business of running an institution, not a place where the kids might come to talk, those who could or would.

I took two cushions off the butter-colored leather couch and laid them against the doorsill. The fact that I didn't have the key to this office didn't mean that no one else did, and I had no desire to attract company with light shining from under the door.

Working quickly and quietly, I pulled out the leather desk chair and sat, hearing only the sound of Dashiell's nose, a flood of air exhaled every few minutes to make way for the new scents he needed to analyze. Then I began to open the drawers. I wasn't checking for random items, anything at all that would tell me something about this man or this place. There was something specific I was after, the thing Venus had gone to the lawyer about this very afternoon—Harry Dietrich's will. I hoped there'd be a copy in the desk or in the files.

I was in the office of a methodical man. In no time I saw the pattern in his files, found out where the personal things were, and had in my hand the copy of Harry's will. Curious as I was, I thought it was risky to stay put to read it. Instead, I took out the staple that held the pages of the copy together and placed them in Harry's fax machine, punching in my number and sending everything home.

I was about to leave, having found what I was after and not wanting to press my luck. After all, other people were in the building, people whose habits I did not know.

But I thought back to Venus's first call, and so I took a chance on staying a few more minutes, enough time to pick up Harry's phone, unscrew the mouthpiece, and find what I hoped I wouldn't, sure now that I'd find the same thing in Venus's phone, perhaps in Dr. Kagan's too.

Venus had tried to protect herself the wrong way. Whispering doesn't keep a conversation from being overheard when the phone you're whispering into has been tapped. Whatever it was she'd wanted to hide was out.

And whoever it was she was hiding it from wasn't being fooled by my cover.

How dangerous this was, I didn't know. But suddenly Venus wasn't the only one playing beat-the-clock. Her deadline was Friday. At least she knew.

Before leaving, I stapled the will back together and returned it to the file. I put the cushions back on the couch, looked around the room one more time, then picked up the picture that sat in a silver frame at the corner of Harry's desk, a young woman in a halter top smiling at the camera.

I shut off the lights, pulled back the curtain, and released the shade, holding on so that it would roll up slowly. Telling Dashiell to wait, I went out first, swinging one leg over the windowsill, poking my head out next, feeling as twisted as a pretzel.

The night air was cool against my skin, a breeze moving my hair across my face so that for the moment I couldn't make out anything in the yard, not even the shadow of the big tree someone had drawn over and over again. I leaned out carefully, holding on to the window with one hand, fishing around for the ground with the leg that was outside before pulling the other one through, still seeing nothing, my eyes not yet adjusted to the moonless night.

My toe was touching the brick flooring and I was ready to swing out when it happened—bony fingers, as strong and cold as steel, grabbing my ankle; the other hand, this one wet and sticky, as if covered in blood, encircling my wrist, then pulling in the direction I'd been going, out into the darkness of the yard. As I spilled out the window, completely off balance, my legs buckling under me, the powerful hands that held me propped me up, not letting me fall.

Not letting go, either.

It took all my willpower not to cry out and bring Molly or Samuel to catch me in the middle of a felony.

Or save my life.

But then, before my eyes became accustomed to the dim light in the garden, before anyone spoke, I heard Dashiell's tail, banging against Harry's desk.

And a moment later I too smelled something that allowed me to exhale.

"Thanks," I said. "I might have fallen if you hadn't caught me."

The fingers holding my leg let go. The other hand released my wrist. When he stood up, he towered over me. Facing him

LADY VANISHES | 91

and smiling, I whistled for Dashiell, heard his nails scrabbling on the wooden sill, heard him land on the bricks with a soft thud, and then felt the comforting heat of his body at my side.

Jackson bent to pick up the leash that had come untied and dropped to the ground when he'd nearly scared the life out of me. For a moment we just stood there, me looking at him, him looking at some point beyond me as the smell of paint dissipated in the cool night air.

"How did you get out?"

He didn't answer me. Instead he walked away, Dashiell following him. Standing in the open space in the center of the garden, he lifted his arms above his head, wiggling his fingers in the breeze.

I wondered if I'd left the door to the garden unlocked when I came out here, but I was pretty sure all the doors locked automatically. After closing Harry's window, not quite all the way, and pulling the screen back down, I walked over to the door and tried to open it, but it didn't budge. So I whispered to Jackson. This time, instead of asking him how he'd come out into the garden alone, I asked him to help us back inside.

Jackson bent and clipped Dashiell's leash onto his collar, walking him to the window on the far side of the door, lifting the window as high as it would go, climbing in, then whistling for Dashiell to follow him, the exact note I'd just used to call him out of Harry's office.

I waited. A hand came out from inside. I took the hand—the sticky one—and let Jackson help me through the window. Then he closed it carefully, turned the lock, and did an even more surprising thing. He turned the garden lights back on, leaving a small dab of yellow paint on the light switch that matched the yellow paint on Dashiell's leash and on my wrist.

When Jackson had handed me the leash and gone in the

direction of the stairs, I wanted nothing more than to head home and read my fax. But there was something more important to do now. I wanted to see who stayed late, who Venus might have been afraid would overhear her call. So instead of heading for the front door, I waited for Jackson to disappear; then, with Dash trailing after me, I began to climb the stairs.

IT WAS JUST AN ACCIDENT

I could hear him from the middle of the first flight of stairs; not Samuel, a different voice, deeper, rougher, the voice of someone without much education.

"I'm goin' get it for you right this minute. You stop cryin' now, wipe them pretty eyes, sure now, that's better. You okay? Homer's goin' come right back with it, you wait and see. Nothing to cry about, Your Highness. Homer'll take care of everything for you, just like always."

And then he was in front of us, coming down the stairs we were heading up.

"You Rachel?" he whispered.

"Yes."

"Can you help me, please? Anastasia's lost her tiara again. I know it's aluminum ferl," he said, "we got plenty in the kitchen, but Sammy always makes 'em for her, and he went home already. He's all the way in Brooklyn. I can't call him back. He'd come, I know, but they have the funeral early in the morning, I hate to do it to him. I never made one, but Anastasia, trust me, we been through this before, she won't go to sleep without her tiara."

"What happened to the one she had?"

"Who knows? It might be in her room, but you know how they gets, it could be anywhere. I don't want to get her crying again, she sees me lookin' and I can't find it."

"No problem," I told him. "Follow us."

He was a little man, I mean really little—five-one, five-two at most. He wore a uniform, a navy jumpsuit, his name embroidered on the chest. H. Wiggens, it said, Harbor View. He had a funny walk, a little stiff in the legs, a little bent forward, his head held up though, his thin gray hair slicked down neat, his black leather oxfords shined so high you could use them as a mirror. A sign of growing up poor, I thought, taking such good care of your shoes.

We got to the top of the stairs, and I looked left, where his voice had come from, seeing the lady I'd seen in the dining room, the crown on her head then.

"Bella Romanov," he whispered. "But she don't answer to nothin' but Anastasia, swears she's royal, she survived the massacre. Dr. K. says to go along with it, makes her feel better."

I nodded.

But I didn't call her anything. Nor did I go into her room. Instead, I motioned for Homer to go, moved my thumb and pointer to tell him to talk to her, then bent down and whispered to Dashiell, "Find" and "Bring." In this case, I didn't expect he'd find anything more dangerous than a stray brassiere or hopefully a lost tiara—no bombs, no guns, nothing that would harm him or anyone else, and I didn't want him alerting me in the usual way, with a bark so loud it could shake the paint off the walls.

Quietly, he followed Homer into the room. Standing out in

the hall, I could hear two comforting things: the sound of Homer's voice telling Bella Romanov just where he was going to look for her crown, and the sound of one dog sniffing, music to my ears.

Dashiell wasn't looking for a tiara, of course. He was looking for anything that was out of place, something that, in his judgment, didn't belong where it was.

In no time, there he was, the largest pair of underpants I'd ever seen hanging from his powerful jaws. I scratched his head and sent him back. The second time he didn't come back.

"Oh, saints preserve us, Your Highness, and here it is without me having to go all the way down to the dining room and look under every table and chair. The new dog found it for you, right here in your very own room.

"I'm going to smooth it out, just like this, and now I can get on with my work and you can get a good night's sleep."

A moment later Homer and Dashiell appeared out in the hallway, Homer giving me a thumbs-up sign, me handing him Anastasia's underwear, which he tossed back into her room. I was thinking fast, figuring this man must have the keys to everything; he could get me into Venus's office. I was determined, even if I had to rappel down from the damn roof, to check her phone before I left Harbor View.

"Oh, no," I said, making it up as I was saying it, what my former mentor, Frank Petrie, said was my greatest talent. "Look at the time. I was so busy working on a routine for Dashiell to do with the kids in Sammy's movement class, I didn't pay one bit of attention to how late it is. I have to call my boyfriend. He must be worried sick. Is there a phone anywhere?"

Homer pulled his key ring out of his pocket. "I'll let you into Miss White's office. You can use her phone," he said.

That's when we heard it, a plaintive cry from Bella's room.

"Help! I've fallen and I can't get up."

I turned and started back up the stairs, but Homer grabbed my arm. When I looked, he was shaking his head.

"But she's fallen."

"Did you hear a thump?"

"No. I didn't."

"She says it every night, ever since she heard it on the TV." He shrugged. "They mimic things. Sometimes they don't even know what the words mean."

I followed him down to the first floor, across the lobby, and to Venus's door. He unlocked the door and held it open. I was just about to ask for a little privacy when he spoke first.

"You don't mind if I leave you a moment, do you? I have to do a bed check, make sure all my little ones are tucked in, doing okay. They get scared sometimes and need a bit of comforting. I got to know everyone's hunky-dory before I start my cleaning. Dr. K., he always tells me, if anyone needs you, Homer, leave the dust. It won't go anywhere, he tells me, it'll wait for another day. But I like to make it nice for them, floors all spotless for when they come down for breakfast, everything just right."

"He sounds like he's good to work for, Dr. Kagan."

"He's a fine man, the doctor is, very good to us what works for him."

"How about Mr. Dietrich? Was he a good boss, too?"

"Oh, absolutely, a saint of a man." Homer crossed himself. "I won't be but a few minutes," he told me, not looking at me, still staring down at those buffed-up shoes of his, the way he had when he'd lied about Harry.

"Take your time," I told him, meaning it sincerely.

"You'll wait right here for me, Rachel, okay?"

"You bet."

"I have a little treat for Dashiell. Least I can do to thank him for finding herself's crown, now isn't it?"

I lifted the phone and dialed my house, listening to Dashiell's barking, my outgoing message. When the sound of Homer's shoes going across the lobby floor had faded, I depressed the button and unscrewed the mouthpiece, finding the bug I would have bet big bucks would be there. As I had before, I left it in place.

It would be too much for anyone to hope that all the kids were sleeping. Luckily for me, that wasn't what I was wishing for. I was counting on the fact that someone needed a bed change, a story, a cup of cocoa. I closed the door almost all the way, so that no one could look in but I would still hear Homer's steps as he approached.

The back of Venus's door was plastered with drawings, the way the front of Harry's door was, his to make his office seem less threatening, Venus's for her, a peek at the hidden inner workings of her kids.

There were two of Jackson's paintings, color dripped in swirls and circles. The other drawings were done in pencil or crayon and looked like the work of little kids, primitive, charming, and mostly indecipherable.

I began to check Venus's files, which were also, as I thought they'd be, meticulous and easy to understand—so easy, in fact, that it only took minutes to find Venus's copy of Harry's will, which made me feel so smug that I almost closed the file drawer without looking at it.

That would have been a huge mistake, because when I changed my mind, I noticed something peculiar. This copy was not the same as the one I'd faxed home. This one was only eleven days old. It had been completed and signed a week and a day before Harry's death.

Venus's fax machine was on the shelf behind her desk. I took out the staple, slipped the pages into place, and dialed my number, sending the newer will home, then watched as the originals emerged from the machine, touched down on the skinny shelf, and slid onto the floor.

Just as the machine beeped its loudest signal, telling me the job had been successfully completed, Homer spoke, jump-starting my adrenal gland and making my heart pound. I hadn't heard him over the gurgling of the machine.

"She get a fax?" he asked. "People have no sense, doing business in the middle of the night. Of course, half the time Dr. Kagan's here, coming in eleven, twelve o'clock at night, working until it's almost light out, then grabbing a couple of hours of sleep on his couch. He says he can think better when things are quiet. Says he gets more done then."

"No fax this time," I said, "that was Dashiell. It was just an accident. You know that old expression, Curiosity killed the cat? Well, dogs, they're, uh, just as bad. He's always poking everything with that big nose of his, so he can get the scent of it. He probably just sniffed the send button on the fax."

Dashiell looked up at me, his brow pleated in concern. To him, my heartbeat must have sounded like hail on a tin roof. Not one to miss a serendipitous opportunity, I tapped the desk with one finger, and Dashiell obeyed, his paws landing with a thunk right where I'd pointed.

"See what I mean?" I told Homer. "He probably thinks Venus has a jar of dog biscuits up here, like I do at home. He's a big boy," I said, "with a big appetite. Always looking to snag a snack."

If I kept running off at the mouth, maybe Homer wouldn't notice the pages of Harry's will lying on the rug behind the desk.

"Well, let's get him what he's after. I can lock up here, and we can go to the kitchen. I'm ready for a cup of tea myself. Can I make you one, Rachel, before you head home?"

"It was busy," I said.

"Say again?"

"The phone."

Dashiell ṿ   syched, listening carefully for the next cue. Thinking he'd heard it, he put his paws back up on the desk, lifted the handset, and when he discovered that he couldn't get anywhere with it, because unlike the one at home, this phone had a cord, he dropped it hard onto the desk, which is how I found out that in my haste I hadn't screwed the mouthpiece back on properly. There it was, lying on the desk, inches away from where it belonged.

"Oh, my god, he broke the phone," I said, grateful the bug hadn't been dislodged and gone skittering across Venus's desk. My luck, it would have landed on the floor, right next to the copy of Harry's will.

Homer took a few steps closer, lifted the handset, studied it for a moment, then screwed the phone back together.

"Must have been loose," he said. "Ready for your cup of tea, Rachel?"

"My boyfriend—his line was busy. He was probably trying to call *me*. Do you mind if I try him again?"

" 'Course not."

He stood there, hands on the desk, watching.

"Maybe you could put the kettle up. I could meet you in the kitchen in a minute."

"Sure, I could," he said, but he gave me a funny look.

Then he got it. Or thought he did.

"Young people," he said, starting to pull the door shut behind him.

"That locks automatically, doesn't it?" I asked. "I don't want to leave Venus's office open."

Homer checked the latch. "Locks when you close it," he said. "You know where the kitchen is?"

"I do. Besides, Dashiell could find it. There's food there, isn't there?"

"Right you are."

This time he left the door open.

"I'm going to close this. It's late, and it makes me feel spooky."

"I can wait right here if you like."

"No, I'm dying for that tea. Besides, Dash will close it. Step outside. I'll show you."

Homer backed out the door. I sent Dashiell to close it and heard the lock click as the door slammed shut.

"Terrific trick," Homer shouted from the other side as I picked up the drawing Dashiell's big feet had pulled off the door. What was it? A man, or a woman wearing pants, drawn from the rear, with what appeared to be spoons stuck into the person's hair.

I wondered if it was supposed to be an alien, if the kids watched *Star Trek* or *The X Files*.

I looked at it again. There was a snaky ground line, someone trying like hell to add a sense of place to his art, someone who might not feel that comfort, that kind of connection in his own life.

I taped it back where it had been, shouting back to Homer, "I'll just give this one more try, then I'll join you in the kitchen."

I listened at the door as his footsteps receded.

Quickly picking up the pages of the will, I stapled them exactly as they'd been before and replaced them in the file at the very back of the bottom drawer. Then, just in case Homer had taken off his shoes, come back in his stocking feet, and was listening outside the door, I dialed my house and, a moment later, hung up and headed for the kitchen to see if I might learn something useful, something I ought to know before things got any worse than they already were.

STAR-CROSSED LOVERS, HE SAID

y first three faxes were lying on the desk. I picked them up, tapped them into a neat pile, and turned them over. The first was from Marty. It was handwritten and very short.

"No news." And he'd signed his name.

Sometimes, like two dogs with one bone, the boys in blue don't like to share.

I sat down on the daybed and read the wills, saving the good stuff, I figured, for last. In the older will, Harry's next-to-last will and testament, written when Harry's wife, Marilyn, was alive, monies were in trust so that she would have no trouble living in the style to which she'd become accustomed, for all I knew, since birth, and substantial sums were allotted for her sister Arlene and Arlene's offspring, Bailey Poole and Janice Poole Richardson. Most of the money—about two-thirds of it, all invested in what I assumed was a well-diversified portfolio—was left in trust for Harbor View, and it seemed to me to be enough that at no time in the foreseeable future would the institution be short of cash. The trust was to be managed by Harry's partner, Eli Kagan, whose sons, Nathan and Samuel, were each left what appeared to be a very modest stock package, something that might have been more a gesture to Eli than actual affection for his sons. No surprises at all in this will, everything *glatt kosher*, as my grandmother Sonya would have said.

On the second will, the signatures would barely have been dry if this had been the original, but of course it wasn't. Harry's lawyer had that. This will was full of surprises, some of which I didn't think would go down well at all with most of the people named as heirs. The will still named Marilyn's relatives, Arlene, Bailey, and Janice, who was now Janice Poole—divorced, I assumed, sometime between the last two wills. But this time they were given small amounts of stock and some tokens of their departed relative's affection for them. Actually, when I looked over the "tokens," it occurred to me that the purpose of those gifts might be to make sure it didn't appear these relatives had been overlooked. In other words, the gifts were so trivial compared to those in the earlier will that their presence there might have been to prevent a lawsuit.

Fat chance, I thought, turning the page.

The Kagan boys fared no better and no worse in this will. They had apparently neither fallen from favor nor gained any ground. The surprise was yet to come.

The bulk of the money was left in trust for Harbor View. So far, so good. But the trustee was no longer Eli Kagan. The trustee and manager, the person now named to take over Harry's role, was none other than Venus White, who had every reason to think that as of Friday, which I was sure was the day the heirs would be made aware of the provisions of the new will, her life would be in danger.

Although, if those bugs were still functional, she might already be in danger.

This was no ordinary will—the sort where the lawyer could simply mail copies to each heir. There would be questions, shouting, tears, accusations. Friday was going to be one hell of a day.

I looked back at the will. Interestingly enough, no stock package, real estate, or real property was left directly to Venus. She would, however, as trustee, be able to take a percentage of the estate she was managing as a yearly stipend. Whether or not she would, only she knew.

I got up and erased the note on my blackboard, feeling a pang of guilt as I did. Despite the reminder, I'd neglected to call my aunt Ceil to wish her a happy birthday.

I made three lists. On the left I wrote the names of people who would profit from Harry's new will. On that list I wrote one name: Venus White.

On the right I listed the people who would have gained more had there not been a later will. On that side I wrote: Eli Kagan, Arlene Poole, Bailey Poole, Janice Poole.

In the middle, under the heading No Change: Samuel Kagan, Nathan Kagan.

Then I wondered what Samuel would think, sweating away seven days a week at Harbor View and getting not much beyond the satisfaction the work itself gave him. It was, it seemed to me, a job with no future. And Harry's will did nothing to change that.

As for Nathan, I wondered if he had any connection to Harbor View at all, or if he'd wisely opted out of Eli and Harry's folie à deux.

I wondered how all of them would feel, and when I thought I knew, I went downstairs to give Dashiell one last outing, opening the door to the garden just as the phone rang.

"Alexander," I said, very much in the work mode, both wills still in one hand.

"Did I wake you?"

"No. I'm up."

I walked outside and sat on the steps.

"I couldn't stop thinking about your case," he said. "So, did she tell you who the guy was, the on-line lover?"

"You bet. It was Harry."

"Dietrich? The old man? No kidding."

"Pinkie swear."

"Incredible, of all the people it could have been. Was that the end of it, when they met, saw who the other was?"

"No," I said, thinking about the new will. "They were really in love. It wasn't over until Harry was killed."

"Star-crossed lovers," he said, my hopeless romantic.

"We're not exactly talking Romeo and Juliet here. These are not teenagers."

"He was only seventy-four," Chip said. "That's the prime of life for a man."

"Oh, please."

"Okay, so he was old enough to retire and move to Miami, but still. That doesn't mean he no longer had feelings, desires."

"You're picturing a little love nest in God's waiting room? Look, he was short and fat, as ugly as a cheap motel room, and old enough to be her father. All that aside, he was married to someone else when they fell in love. Some Romeo and Juliet."

"Meaning the families *wouldn't* have been unhappy at the romance?"

"Oh. *That* Romeo and Juliet."

"Rachel, I would still love you if you were short, fat, and old enough to be my father."

There was a pause. He waited for me to comment. I waited

for him to continue his adolescent fantasy, get it done and out of the way.

"You don't think my heart would have seen beyond a homely-as-a-junkyard-dog visage, that I would have seen and loved the real you underneath?"

I kept that answer to myself. "That's not how it was with Venus and Harry. All those hours on-line, they became soul mates. What they saw when they met in the flesh, that wasn't going to change it. At least, that's what Venus said. And then there's this new will—that sure lets me think Harry thought the world of her, both before he met her and afterward."

"Don't tell me."

"It's not what you think."

"What do I think?"

"That Harry left her a bundle."

"He didn't?"

"Uh-uh. No money. No houses. No cars. Not even a stock portfolio."

"Then what?"

"He left her in control of the trust for Harbor View."

Chip whistled.

"So she was right," I said. "She *is* in hot water. More than she knows, because I'm so mad I could strangle her. Do you *believe* this? She thinks her life's in danger, but she neglects to mention the cause."

I must have been shouting, because Dashiell came over to see what I was so steamed up about.

Chip groaned.

"Sorry," I said. But all I could think about was Venus, the way she eked her story out at the gym, that diamond necklace, the one she kept hidden at work, winking at me as she pulled the wool over my eyes. "Damn."

"You're worried about her?"

"That, too."

Then there was a silence. I thought it might be nice if I acted like a normal human being for the rest of the call.

"What did you do today?" I asked.

"Took the kids horseback riding. I'm a little rusty at it. I need to get into a hot tub. But first, tell me what I'm missing by being here and not in New York."

"Ah, the East Coast news. Well, it's all good for a change."

"Truly?"

"Absolutely. For starters, New York was chosen for chip research."

"No."

"It's true. It was in the *Times*."

"Potato or corn?"

"Semiconductor. I don't know what this is, so I didn't read the rest of the article. But still."

He laughed.

"Next, the Donald was foiled big-time. He tried to get some old lady's house in Atlantic City condemned so that he could add more parking for his casino. Get this. He said her house was ugly, and the parking lot would beautify Atlantic City."

"His greed must be boundless."

"Yeah, and he's no gentleman."

"I'll call you tomorrow. Sleep tight," he whispered.

"You, too."

"And be careful."

"I will," I promised, after he'd hung up.

I put the phone down on the top step and walked out into the garden, looking up at the sky, streaks of gray and inky blue, a cloud cover, no stars visible.

Earlier in the evening, while I was returning Harry's new

will to the back of Venus's file drawer, Homer hadn't been listening outside the office door. He'd been in the kitchen, brewing tea, setting out two place mats on the butcher block counter, filling a bowl with fresh, cool water for Dashiell, from the looks of things, polishing up the teaspoon he then set out on the carefully folded napkin, making sure it had no spots on it. When I'd joined him in the kitchen, Harbor View as quiet as a mausoleum, he'd jumped up and pulled out the stool on my side of the counter and taken the napkin off the plate of homemade cookies, then asked if Dashiell could have a dog biscuit—one of Lady's, he'd said, but he'd checked the expiration date on the box, and they were still fresh. He'd taken his napkin, I thought to put it on his lap, but no, he'd wiped his eyes with it. Looking at him, this little man with his polished shoes, I wondered again if he had stolen Lady from Harbor View, if he had taken away the dog that made everyone, including himself, happier than they were before she'd come.

Or if, one recent night, he had lurked outside on West Street, sitting on the seat of a bicycle, then riding it full tilt into the man who had employed him, the man he'd called a saint, unable to look me in the eye when he did.

Despite his lie, I didn't think so. But that was because some unrealistic and juvenile part of me didn't want to believe—as if I didn't know better, that murderers could seem so nice, that a man who had plotted and killed wouldn't think to offer water to a thirsty dog or worry about a senile old lady's aluminum foil tiara.

Someone else could have been here the night Venus had whispered into her tapped phone, someone who, unlike Homer, had something to gain from Harry's death.

Or at least thought so.

Standing in my garden, no sound to distract me, I thought about the service at the Society for Ethical Culture, where I would more than likely meet the person who had executed Harry Dietrich, a person who had great expectations about the benefits that would fall to them upon Harry's death, a person who, when Friday rolled around, was going to be gravely disappointed.

And *really* annoyed.

Unless whoever it was already knew the awful truth.

DON'T GET ME STARTED, SHE SAID

A heavyset man in a dark suit, not a gray hair out of place, a wine-colored handkerchief in his breast pocket to match his tie, walked somberly to the podium. He looked down, studying his hands, it seemed, which he'd carefully placed there, maybe checking to see if the girl had trimmed his nails evenly before she'd coated them with clear polish. After more time than it took a Chihuahua to make all gone with a bowl of kibble, he began to speak, still not looking at his audience, a large group of mourners mostly in shades of black and gray, filling the seats of the flower-lined conference room.

"Putting the needs of others before his own, using his wealth for the benefit of the community, helping those who could not help themselves"—slowly, dramatically, he lifted his head, looking around at the attentive faces lined up before him—"*this* was Henry Knowlton Dietrich, tender caretaker, devoted husband, loyal brother, philanthropist."

At that point a young man in the front row stood. The

speaker came around to the side of the podium, bent his head to listen, then returned to his place and cleared his throat.

"Harry Knowlton Dietrich," he said, "was, in everyone's estimation, a good man."

There was some throat clearing and a few coughs, people trying hard not to laugh.

Whoever the speaker was, he certainly hadn't known Harry. Still, overcome with grief, he removed the handkerchief from his pocket, took off his aviator bifocals, and dabbed at his eyes.

"A life of giving, not of taking, a life of searching for answers, for others rather than himself, a life of devotion to the memory of his beloved sister, *this* was Harry Knowlton Dietrich."

Feeling secure that I'd absorbed the pattern and the theme of the eulogy, enough so that if any of the relatives gave a pop quiz on the way out, I could pass it with flying colors, I tuned out the booming voice as best I could and began to look around the room. I was sitting in the last row, all the way to the left. From there I could see just about everyone in my half of the assembly.

The woman in the front row wearing designer mourning clothes, a dark gray suit with a pale gray blouse, was also dabbing her eyes with a handkerchief, only hers seemed to have a lace trim on it. She had to be Arlene Poole, Harry's sister-in-law. At her left sat a thirty-something woman in a black cloche hat. I couldn't see much of her face, but I could see the utter perfection of her blond hair and just about a thousand dollars worth of her pearl necklace. To Arlene's right was her son, the young man who had corrected the speaker's error, seated again now. A shock of his blond hair kept falling into his eyes, and he'd periodically swing his head to knock it back into place. He didn't have a handkerchief in his hands, but when he turned toward his mother to catch something she was whispering, I saw that his lips were pursed in annoyance. Hey, he might have given up a tennis date for this, and it wasn't as if Uncle Harry could even appreciate, or reward, his sacrifice.

Or perhaps his lips were pursed for another reason. Perhaps Bailey Poole was impatient to inherit what would have been his had the original will not been superseded by a later version, a substantial amount of money—enough, I'd say, so that he'd never have to miss a tennis date again.

Of course, all was not lost. The new will left Bailey one of Harry's cars, the beautiful racing green Jag that probably spent half its life at the shop getting its timing adjusted, but hey, you got a Jag, that's to be expected. Which may be why Harry had several other cars.

Oddly enough, there had been no chauffeur waiting out front the last day that Harry had headed home, the day he was hit by a bicycle and never got to walk over to Fourteenth Street, hop on the subway, and ride to his apartment on the Upper East Side.

And Janice Poole, I wondered if her lips were pursed too. Instead of inheriting a trust fund that would let her spend her summers in France and might inspire her next husband, should there be one, to retire before he reached his fortieth birthday, Janice was getting some of the lovely antique furniture from Harry's apartment, French pieces that might not even be to her taste. *C'est la vie.*

But I didn't think they knew that yet. Just as I didn't think Eli Kagan knew what was in the new will. I was only sure that one other person here had read the will, the person who had hired me because she thought her life might be in danger. A good guess from where I sat, still angry over her sin of omission.

I looked around for the Kagans, but I couldn't see Samuel, so I assumed they were on the other side of the room. What would they be thinking if they knew what I knew? Even if all three of them turned out to be saints, I didn't think they'd be particularly happy with the new arrangements for Harbor View, those putting Venus White in charge of operations, those requiring Eli Kagan, when he needed something, to have to get approval from a former employee.

The eulogy was coming to a crescendo, the stentorious voice even louder than it had been at the onset, the talk more about the eloquence of the speaker than the accomplishments of the deceased and, as far as I was concerned, much too annoying and much too long.

Everyone was standing, so I stood too, just hanging back as people went to give their condolences to Harry's sister-in-law, his niece and nephew, and to say some kind words to the Kagan family as well. As the group thinned out, I walked up front. Venus was talking to Eli, and he was nodding, his face soft, his hands not around her throat. I was right. He hadn't read the will.

Of course not. They would all read the will on Friday, sitting in Harry's lawyer's office, each, at last, with his or her own copy, discovering what Harry had done just days before he'd died. That was why the clock was ticking so fast: on Friday, they'd all find out. That's what was scaring Venus.

I walked up to join her, and she introduced me to Eli, Samuel, and Nathan.

"We've met," Samuel said, his face glistening with sweat the way it had been when he was trying to get the kids to sing along with him.

"I'm sorry I haven't had the chance to welcome you before," Eli said. "There's so much to take care of now. I've been keeping irregular hours, sometimes not even coming in at all, just making phone calls from home."

"I understand."

"Venus tells me you've had some remarkable experiences with our residents already."

He was short, like his former partner, and no youngster. I thought he was probably a few years older than Harry had been. But unlike his son Samuel, he had a grim face. When I looked at his eyes, I got nothing back but reflected light. And his lips, under a trimmed white brush of a mustache, were drawn. Hey, this was a funeral, what did I expect? But Samuel looked almost cheerful. And Nathan looked as if he were here in body only, his attention very far away. In fact, when I took a better look, his attention wasn't that far away at all. It was only across the room, on the Poole family.

Nathan was taller than his father and his brother, heavier too, a mountain of a man. Perhaps his mother had been a large woman, more statuesque than her husband. And large boned.

He was dark, with even features, a long, straight nose, a lovely mouth. Perhaps his mother had been dark, with a lovely mouth. A cupid's bow.

He began to smile. I thought he was finally going to say something to me, but he didn't. I turned again and saw the Pooles approaching, the mother's face a mask with the startled look and pointy chin that come from one or two too many face-lifts. Bailey was still pouting. Perhaps that was his normal expression. And Janice looked bored, as if there were dozens of places she could name where she'd rather be. As they got closer, something struck me as almost funny. Like her mother, Janice was wearing gray, a smart little suit with a short, short skirt and black braid trimming along the neck and fronts of the collarless jacket. Her shoes were dark too, black kid, new and expensive looking. But her handbag was red, one of those designer things that cost more than the annual salary of people in third world countries. Perhaps it was as new as it looked, and she couldn't bear to leave it home.

"Janice," Nathan said. But she was fiddling with those pearls and didn't seem to hear him.

Arlene was talking to Eli, and Samuel was talking to Bailey. I gave Nathan the old Kaminsky grin, thinking I could start a conversation. But he didn't smile back.

"We have to talk," Arlene was saying to Eli.

Perhaps that was what had snagged Nathan's attention. He took a step closer to his father, both of them standing with their hands clasped in front of them, like ushers with no one to escort down the aisle.

"Of course, of course. Why don't we have lunch?" Eli said.

Now it was Arlene's turn at a *farbisen punim*. She seemed to pull her lips in so that they all but disappeared, but then she nodded. "Let's do," she said. "No sense waiting."

"Mrs. Poole," Samuel said, sweating and smiling, "this is Rachel Alexander. She's doing pet therapy at Harbor View now, and—"

"I'm sure she is, dear," Arlene said, never looking at me.

I looked at Bailey, who was flinging some hair out of his eyes. I wondered if I should tell him the good news, that someone had invented hair gel, but thought that perhaps this wasn't the place for it.

Janice had opened her red purse and was fishing around inside. Perhaps she'd talk to me. After all, she looked to be about my age, give or take any work she might have had done—cheek implants, dermabrasion, whatever. But that didn't happen either. Anyway, Venus was pulling on the back of my jacket, trying in her subtle way to get me out of there.

"Let's go," she whispered to my back.

We said good-bye quickly, and I followed her out.

"They don't seem close," I said in the hallway.

She rolled her eyes. "Don't get me started," she said.

"Get started," I said, as we headed down the stairs. "I have a job to do. I need information."

Venus stopped and looked at me, as if that had never occurred to her.

"They're the kind of rich people that give rich people a bad name, snobs without, in my humble opinion, anything about which to feel superior."

Finished, she headed down the stairs and out to the street.

"Is that it?"

"Harry didn't like them," she said, "but he was always decent to them."

"Well, they are his wife's family."

Suddenly Venus looked grim.

Or was that an angry look? Well, in that case, she had some company.

She walked up to the curb and stuck her arm up. As a cab pulled up, she turned back to me. "They weren't exactly his favorite charity." She opened the door and waited for me to get in first.

I knew that, I thought, sliding over to make room for Venus. In fact, I knew a lot more than that.

If Venus wasn't telling me what she knew, perhaps I should be the one talking. It was high time *someone* gave out with some information. Besides, it was getting more and more difficult for me to contain myself.

Especially since Friday wasn't all that far away.

« 17 »

YOU KNOW HOW FAMILIES ARE

I could barely keep my mouth shut until Venus closed the door and told the driver to head downtown, to Jane and West.

"What in hell's name were you thinking," I said, "hiring me and not giving me the information I need to do my job?"

Venus looked away.

"I have my reasons."

"I *know* your reasons," I told her, so angry I was trembling. "I know why you wanted me to find out who killed Harry by Friday."

She turned and looked at me, then turned away again.

"We've got to talk."

"Okay, Rachel. But we have to go someplace where no one will overhear us."

"And where would that be?"

"Six six six Greenwich Street," she told the driver.

"I don't think so." I shook my head. "Make that Hudson and Tenth," I told him.

"Why?"

"Your phone at work is tapped. Can you assure me that your apartment isn't bugged?"

"But how—"

"Harry's is bugged, too. I couldn't get into Eli's office. Any bets on that one?"

She shook her head.

"How did you—?"

"Harry's, through the window. It wasn't locked."

I thought about Jackson, out in the garden where he wasn't supposed to be, but kept my mouth shut. Maybe the worst thing about being in an institution is that you have no secrets.

But then I thought the opposite was true at Harbor View. For people like Jackson and David, almost everything about them was a secret. Nonetheless, I kept the faith, at least for now.

"And my office? How'd you get in there?"

"Homer."

She shot me a look.

"I said I had to call my boyfriend, and he let me use your phone."

Venus nodded.

"When?" she asked, a moment later.

"Last night. I took Dashiell back to Harbor View a couple of hours after we spoke, worked with him for a while in the dining room, something to try in Samuel's class, and then I decided that, since you weren't telling me what I needed to know, I'd see if I could find out on my own. When you said you were going to see Harry's lawyer, well, it didn't take a genius to figure out where I'd find some of the answers I was looking for. Turns out, I found more than I was banking on."

We passed the Italian specialty shops on Ninth Avenue, then got caught up for a block or two in traffic for the Lincoln

Tunnel and the Port Authority terminal. After that, we sailed downtown, neither of us speaking again until we were out of the cab.

"It's right here," I said, taking out my keys and unlocking the wrought iron gate. "With a little bit of luck, no one bugged my house. At least, not yet."

Dashiell seemed relieved to see me. He sniffed Venus, then squeezed between us to get out into the garden, let the world at large know he was still a player.

We walked inside, and Venus sat on one side of the couch. I got two bottles of spring water from the fridge and joined her.

"Do you have an extra set of keys?" I asked her.

"Why?"

I sighed. "I'm a detective. I need to snoop."

"At my—"

I waited.

Venus fished in her purse for her keys and dropped them into my hand.

"Twelve D," she said.

"I left the bugs in at work. I don't want whoever did this to know we know. I don't want you to act funny in any way. We'll have enough to handle on Friday, when they get to see the will."

"You don't know the half of it."

"Then tell me. Everything, Venus. There's no more time for cat and mouse."

"I wasn't playing cat and mouse with you, Rachel. And it's not what you think."

"Which is?"

"That I don't trust you."

I waited.

Venus waited, too.

"Venus, I don't know what your thinking is—that the relatives will chip in and hire a hit man? What's going to happen is that they're going to contest the new will."

"You are thorough."

"Isn't that what you're paying for?"

She opened the water bottle and took a sip.

"They can't contest it."

"Why not?"

"We were married."

That sat between us for a minute, stopping the conversation dead in its tracks.

"Venus, why didn't you—"

"Tell? Tell Bailey and Janice that I was their auntie now? Tell Eli that for all intents and purposes I was his boss now? Tell you, Rachel, the first day? What would you have thought if I had told you right away that I'd married the rich old toad who'd just been killed, that he'd just made a new will, a week before the accident, that I was now director of operations and finances at the place where I'd been working for a modest salary? You would have figured it for true love, is that what you would have thought, no notions that I duped him somehow, got him to change his will, put me in charge? Tell me about it."

I didn't. I just sat there, waiting. Behind my back, I could hear Dashiell drinking in the kitchen, his tags clanging against the bowl.

"You might have wondered, was he seeing me before Marilyn died, maybe even before she got sick? It wasn't like that, and I wouldn't want anyone thinking that about Harry. Not anyone.

"Or you might have wondered if he was senile, doing something so crazy."

She put the water bottle on my makeshift coffee table and wiped her eyes with the balls of her fingers.

"So you think the family might be upset?"

"It's a possibility."

"Figuring old Harry wouldn't have married a recovering alcoholic black lady for love?"

"How did you—?"

"The first part, that you're a recovering alcoholic? A pretty good guess, apparently. You've obviously got an addictive personality—the gym, the internet, even the way you talk about work and the kids. You said you were lonely. It wasn't too big a leap."

Venus nodded, putting her arms around herself as if she were cold.

"The second part, that you're black? Observation. A result of my extensive professional training."

Venus laughed. I think this was the third time I'd seen her do that, her thousand-watt smile staying in place, too. I smiled back.

I didn't have any problem at all with Harry loving her. But I didn't think my opinion would garner a lot of support, not from Harry's family, not from the Kagans, not from the cops either.

"We're in deep shit, aren't we?"

"Thigh high," I said.

"What's your plan?"

"Other than running for the hills?"

Venus nodded.

"I'm going over to your apartment, check the phones."

"How would someone have gotten in there?"

"Depends how this was done."

"What do you mean?"

"These people who are going to be mad at you—"

"To say the least."

"Some of them have got a lot of money. They could have hired someone. You can always get into someone's apartment, with the gift of gab or a good set of picks."

"But they don't have as much money as you might think. With the Pooles, it's all on their backs. Arlene's a widow. She wasn't left all that much, enough to live on, not enough to live the way she thinks she ought to, the way her sister was able to. She's been supplemented by Harry for a long time."

"Why, if he—"

"His wife. It made her feel guilty that she could go to Palm Beach, and Arlene couldn't."

"What about Bailey and Janice?"

"Snotty little leeches."

"Is that your opinion or Harry's?"

She didn't say.

"Did Harry support them, too?"

"Bailey keeps starting degrees, then dropping out. He'd rather gamble than study. Harry bailed him out of debt lord knows how many times, always at Marilyn's insistence. But he recently told him that the last time was just that, the last time. He said he wasn't going to do it again, that if Bailey got himself into debt, he could just get himself out. He told him to get a job. He even offered him one, busboy at Harbor View."

"Oh, that must have gone over big. So, did he get a job?"

"*Please.*"

"And his sister?"

"Recently divorced. Unemployed. No time to work, what with the time it takes nowadays to accumulate material possessions."

"Credit card debt?"

"Probably. But it's just a guess. We're not exactly bosom buddies."

"All that shopping can be very time-consuming."

"Yeah, it really cuts into your workday. Anyway, she gets alimony. Women like that always do. But not enough. It never is."

"Still, it doesn't cost *that* much to hire someone to do your dirty work. People like that, I wonder if they do anything for themselves."

"But why, Rachel? Why would they bug the phones?"

"That's one of the things I don't know yet. Any ideas?"

"It depends. Was Harry's death a result of eavesdropping? Or did the eavesdropping come afterward?"

"Good question."

"But you don't know the answer yet?"

I shook my head. "No. I don't. Not that I'm complaining," I told her, "but I've been working with a bit of a handicap. My client was keeping me in the dark."

"I'm sorry, Rachel. But—"

"No time for that now. I have to get over to your place, then Dashiell and I have to get to Harbor View for Samuel's class. I know you wanted answers before Friday, Venus, but the most telling thing might be what happens when the heirs read the will. Any way I can be there?"

"I don't know how. I'll call the lawyer. Maybe he can think of something."

"Okay. But don't call from your work phone. And unless I tell you it's okay, don't call from your home phone. In fact, it wouldn't hurt for you to pick up a cell phone today, use that until we have this figured out. That way, if you need to reach me you can. And we'll still meet at five-thirty, on the treadmills."

"Have to. I'm addicted."

She smiled again, but I could see the exhaustion behind it and wished I could tell her everything would be okay, that in no time Janice and Bailey would be calling her Aunt Venus, inviting her for Thanksgiving dinner, feeling blessed to have her in the family.

"Okay, let's get moving," I said instead. "Keep your eyes and ears open, Venus, tell me anything you hear that might relate, no matter how trivial. Oh, and can you get me a key for Eli's office? I couldn't think up a lie that would get me in there last night, and I couldn't go in through the window once Homer had invited me to tea."

"It's on the key ring I gave you. But be careful. Eli's a workaholic, comes in early, stays late, comes back at night sometimes. Three in the morning, he thinks of something he wants to do in the office, he takes the subway back from Brooklyn, gets a jump on the day. It's his life, the only thing he cares about. I've found him there in the morning, sleeping on his couch, too tired to truck back to Brooklyn after working late. With Eli, you can never be sure what his schedule will be."

"I'll be careful. Maybe we can get to the bottom of this *before* Friday."

I walked Venus out so that I could lock the gate behind her. She stopped and looked around the garden.

"This is lovely," she said.

And that's when I began to wonder about something else.

"Venus, how come Harry didn't leave you any money, or his apartment, anything tangible?"

"I wouldn't let him," she said. "Harry was worried sick about Harbor View. Eli and his sons are devoted to it, but none of them has the experience of running it. The unwritten agreement was that if anything happened to Harry, Eli would take over. It makes no sense to assume he could, but that was so long ago, Harry didn't give it that much thought. It was something far away in the future, and in the beginning, he was so ecstatic to get Eli to join him in this, that's all he cared about. When you think about it, it's ridiculous. Eli's talent is with the kids, reaching them, comforting them, finding activities that help them to function better, creating an atmosphere that's safe for them, in which they can flourish. No one would have expected Harry to have been able to take over Eli's role had Eli died first. So why should it be so the other way around?

"The fact is, I've been doing a great deal of this all along. I'm not only familiar with what Harry did, I've always done a lot of it. Harry wasn't always around, and even when he was, he was a busy man, into other things as well, though Harbor View is where his heart was.

"Harry convinced me that I was the one who could best keep Harbor View going in the way he'd been able to. When he was alive, when he was saying it, it seemed so logical. And neither of us thought this would come up so soon. He was seventy-four, but he was a vigorous man. We didn't think this would be an issue for years and years."

"Did Eli know you managed the money?"

Venus looked down. "Not really."

"Not really?"

"I don't believe Harry ever mentioned it."

"Which means what, Venus?"

"That he thought Eli would be insulted that he trusted me and not him. But Eli isn't a money person."

"What about his sons?"

"Samuel is just like his father. He's totally devoted to the kids, and just as naive about business. Nathan probably thinks he could run Harbor View because of his fund-raising experience. And he has raised money for us, mostly finding backers for specific projects. But none of Harry's decisions were made purely on the basis of return on the dollar. The welfare of the kids was always most important to him. He was funny, Rachel. He wouldn't bat an eye about spending thousands on equipment, anything they needed. But if he was around at night, he'd go around shutting off lights to save money. I had to convince him that leaving the garden light on was a safety factor. He used to shut it off after the kids went to bed."

"And Nathan—Harry thought he wouldn't be able to handle the money the way he did, the way you do?"

"Well, no. Despite Harry's stingy quirks, he always put the kids first. He thought Nathan was too bottom-line. That's the phrase he used. Too bottom-line. It's a different generation, he used to say. People of that age tend to be—"

"What?"

"More self-centered. More materialistic."

"Some people. Not everyone. Maybe he was judging too much by his niece and nephew."

"Maybe."

"You're not like that."

"Harry thought I was different," Venus said, her voice almost a whisper, her eyes shining.

"Venus, when Harry left that day, the last day, was he going home?"

"Yes."

"And where was that?"

"My apartment. That was our home. He went back a few times a week to the apartment he had shared with Marilyn to check his mail, his messages, take care of things. Even then, he didn't sleep there. He'd come home late so that he could sleep in his own bed, our bed. He said he never wanted us to spend the night apart."

I nodded.

"So he was facing south because he was heading south, not necessarily because he'd heard the bike coming toward him on the sidewalk?"

She nodded.

"Did Harry want to announce the marriage?"

"He did."

"Then why didn't he?"

"I begged him not to, at least not so soon. I didn't want his family to think ill of him. Marilyn was gone so short a time. But they say that when a marriage has been happy, people want to get married again quickly. He was crazy about her, Rachel. But how would you explain that to her sister, given the circumstances? You know how families are."

"I do," I said.

After she left, I went upstairs to change. Then Dashiell and I headed for the Archives, Venus's keys in my pocket.

MAYBE HARRY OWNED A BOAT

I bought some yellow daisies on the way to the Archives, something to pave the way.

"Venus asked me to take these upstairs, put them in a vase for her, she's coming back with company," I said, showing the concierge the daisies and the keys.

This was a new one. He frowned, trying to decide what to do.

"I work for her," I told him, "at Harbor View. We do pet-facilitated therapy with the residents."

He leaned over the concierge desk, looked at Dashiell. Then he nodded.

I walked back to the bank of elevators, barely feeling the floor in my new sneakers as I followed the wide, deep lobby around to the left.

We rode up alone, walking down the carpeted hallway until we came to Venus's door. Opening it, we faced the river through double-height windows looking west. The afternoon sun filled the living room. I walked down the hallway, where a staircase on the left led upstairs. Dashiell took the stairs. I walked through the living room and looked at the view—the Hudson flowing south, New Jersey beyond, no sound of construction up here.

There was a big, soft couch, pale gray, with lots of loose pillows on it, on the north wall of the apartment. An enormous painting hung over it: a worn wooden walk, flowers all around, bursting with color and energy. The coffee table was glass. There were already flowers there, roses the color of seashells in a crystal vase.

I walked into Venus's kitchen and found another vase. Filling it with water, I arranged the daisies for her. I put these on the dining room table, looking at the fine china in the breakfront, the silver candlesticks, the champagne flutes. Venus had a taste for the things I'd sent to Goodwill for a tax deduction, all the things that reminded me of Jack and a brief marriage that in retrospect didn't seem brief enough.

Or maybe it was Harry who'd liked the table set with bone china—the way Jack had, everything just so, his wife at home tending to his needs, not having any of her own.

But Harry was different. He didn't see Venus as the happy housewife. He believed her capable of managing the finances of Harbor View and, more than that, preserving his original intent. He'd put his money where his mouth was, too.

How had they found each other, people who'd worked together all those years, meeting on-line? It was a curious thing, an annoying coincidence.

I turned on Venus's computer, and while it was booting up, I unscrewed the mouthpiece of the kitchen phone and checked for a listening device, not finding one. Dashiell was coming down. We passed each other on the stairs. There was no bug in the phone next to the bed either.

I opened the closet, which held half Venus's things, half Harry's: suits, sport jackets, slacks, three pairs of loafers, some underwear, I was sure, in Venus's dresser drawers, too, but I didn't check.

The bed was big, queen-size, with white sheets and a white cotton blanket—no dog to shed on it, leave his dirty footprints on the pretty blanket, keep Venus company while she read in bed or slept.

Venus's bedroom was a balcony overlooking the living room, the view of the river even more luscious from up here. There were roses here, too, on one of the nightstands, red ones. A man's watch was on the other one; perhaps Harry had forgotten to put it on that last morning. And now Venus left it there. I sat on her bed, picturing her here, picking up Harry's watch and holding it in her hand. I picked it up, felt its weight, warmed it in my hand. Then I got up, as she might have, went to the closet, and pressed my face into one of Harry's cashmere jackets, for a moment thinking he'd be back, slip it on, take Venus out to Provence for dinner. I could see him then, smiling, his hand dipping into his pocket, the box coming out, that heart inside, lying on velvet.

Back at the computer, I didn't log on; I fished around the files, the things Venus had downloaded and saved. And found what I'd been looking for: conversations with Harry, and more than I'd hoped for, the answer to how they'd found each other.

Harry's on-line name was Skipper.

The dog he had when he was a kid?

Or maybe Harry owned a boat?

It would be pretty funny if Skipper had been Harry's dog, because Venus too had used a dog's name, which explained everything. Venus had signed on as Lady Day.

Lady Day. Of course, not a dog's name to most of the world. A singer's name. It must have made Venus smile, using the dog's name, both of them covered with dreadlocks, the kids' hands always reaching out to see what they felt like, Harry reaching out, too, at first, to a name that meant something to him, Lady Day, making everyone feel better, just the ticket, just what Harry needed, too, his wife dying a little at a time, all that money and nothing he could do to save her.

I looked at Harry's watch, which I'd placed on Venus's desk. It was late. If I didn't hurry, I'd miss the movement class, not get the chance to show off Dashiell's game, help Samuel teach it to the kids. But I wanted to read what Venus had saved, and I didn't know if I'd get the chance to come back.

I looked at the printer. Then I pressed the button. Running back upstairs to put Harry's watch back on the nightstand, Dashiell right behind me, I had another thought. The necklace. That would be around Venus's neck. I wondered if there was anything else.

Maybe I was just being nosy, I thought, not seeing a jewelry box, looking through the dresser drawers, then in the back of the closet shelf. Maybe not. I never knew what would trigger an insight—a smoking gun, a suicide note, a sapphire bracelet.

I was wondering what else Venus hadn't bothered to tell me.

But she'd given me her key, hadn't she?

Still, that was because she was scared. She hadn't stopped to think it through. Like when the doctor says, I see a shadow here; I'd like to schedule a CAT scan. Fear takes over, does the thinking for you.

Maybe Venus was back at Harbor View now, wondering what the hell was keeping me, knowing her printer was pumping out some private documents she wouldn't have wanted me to see, thinking I was looking in her shoe boxes—which I was, about to call it quits when I found what I was looking for, in a silk pouch at the back of a sewing basket.

I could feel the loot before I opened the bag. Sitting on the bed, I turned it over, spilling the contents onto the white blanket. A diamond cocktail ring, a really old one, ornate, the way things were made decades and decades ago. A bow pin, more diamonds. A wedding ring. I picked it up and held it between two fingers. It was simple, a gold band; inside, one word was inscribed. Skipper.

The other things, I had the feeling, had been Marilyn's. Even the diamond heart. He'd probably given that to her first.

The wedding band was new, no patina of scratches on it. Brand-new, because Venus didn't wear it. But he would have given her anything—emeralds, rubies, diamonds. Had Venus insisted on a plain gold band?

The printer stopped. As soon as I started down the stairs, Dashiell passed me, nearly knocking me over in order to arrive a second ahead of me, turn around smiling, because even the most obedient dog likes to show his physical superiority sometimes, remind you once in a while of the facts of life as he sees them.

Witty, I told him. What's next, the Letterman show?

I rolled the papers and put a rubber band around them, shut down the computer and the printer, took one last look around— everything in place. Then I closed my eyes, thinking of Venus here with Harry, of Venus here alone.

We dropped the papers I'd printed off at home, then slowly, because even though it was nearly two, it was too hot to move any faster, we headed for Harbor View, wiser and sadder, to see who could learn to play All Fall Down.

WHAT WOULD YOU HAVE US DO?

I heard it before I saw it; the shrill whooping of the siren coming our way, turning on when the street was blocked and off when the road was unobstructed. At first, my only concern was for Dashiell. I bent over him and cupped his ears with my hands, trying to deaden the painful noise as best I could.

But when the red, white, and blue fire department ambulance passed us, turning onto West Street, I began to run, getting to the corner of Eleventh and West in time to see it stop where I feared it would, in front of Harbor View, two paramedics jumping out, grabbing a collapsible stretcher from the back, snapping down the legs, then running toward the door and disappearing inside. Someone must have been standing there, waiting for them, holding the door open, not a minute to lose.

By the time Dashiell and I got there, there were three more emergency vehicles on the scene, two from the fire department and a police car. I pulled out my keys, wondering what had happened that was more than Harbor View could handle without help—a bad fall, a heart attack, a seizure—thinking how vulnerable the kids were, how easily they got upset, and how dangerous that could be, wondering who it was, my heart pounding.

Keeping Dashiell on leash and right at my side, I unlocked the door. The lobby was empty, and the doors that led to the dining room doors were closed. I opened them just enough to peek inside. Most of the kids were there, sitting around the tables. But no one was painting or singing or eating lunch. They looked almost like mannequins that someone had placed randomly around the tables.

Even Cora and Dora were quiet, sitting side by side in their wheelchairs, for once with nothing to say. Charlotte was sitting alone, her fingers in her mouth. I didn't see David. And he hadn't been in the doorway. I looked back to make sure I hadn't missed him again. Jackson wasn't there either. I wondered if he was in the garden.

Arlene was off in a corner with her issue, the lovely Janice, the sporty-looking Bailey, looking nearly as blank as everyone else. Only Samuel showed expression, and what I saw scared me. Then Molly came out of the kitchen, holding a glass of water. When she saw me in the doorway, she bit her lip and shook her head, making my stomach lurch.

I heard two more sirens whooping, and I could see the flashing lights outside the dining room windows. Still holding the glass of water, Molly went to look.

I looked, too. From where I was standing, I could see through the sidelight next to the door, where David usually stood, that two more police cars had pulled in and stopped in front of Harbor View. They'd come from Jane Street, driving against the traffic on West Street, and now, double-parked on the other side of the ambulance, they were blocking off a lane of traffic headed north, everyone slowing down to see what had caused all the fuss, me still hoping this was just the usual overkill response to a 911 call.

I had turned around, looking for a sign of the paramedics, of Venus, of Eli and Nathan, wondering where they all were, my heart thudding, when Dashiell began to pull on the leash. He headed for Venus's office, his nose going a mile a minute, blowing air out and sucking it in with an urgency that let me know with no uncertainty where the paramedics had gone.

Molly, the glass of water spilling as she went, was rushing toward the front door to let the uniforms in as I ran across the lobby, praying Venus's door wouldn't be locked. But of course, it was.

Molly was filling in two police officers, talking softly, their heads bent to hear her, one writing in his notebook, the other ready to call in on his radio.

The door to Venus's office pulled open then, and Nathan stepped in front of it to hold it ajar.

Standing in the lobby, Dashiell at my side, all I could see was the back of one of the paramedics, kneeling over someone and working on them, though I couldn't see what he was doing right away.

I wondered if it was Eli, succumbing to all the stress, everything going wrong here, one thing after the next after the next. Most people retire by his age, buy a little condo down in North Miami Beach, wait for the sirens each night, find out in the morning who had died. Not Eli. He was working as hard as he ever had, keeping weird hours, not taking care of himself.

But it wasn't Eli.

When one of the paramedics reached for the gauze bandages he'd placed on the desk, I saw who it was. He pulled away the blood-soaked bandage and pressed a clean one to the wound, a cervical collar keeping her head from moving, her dreadlocks hanging over it, matted with blood.

I heard the radio crackle behind me, then the uniform spoke softly into it.

"Ninety-seven H to Vinnie's."

I couldn't make out the response, if there was one; it was as futile as trying to understand the dispatcher's message when you're sitting in the back seat of a taxi.

Eli was there, looking ashen, standing on the other side of Venus's desk.

A cold wind blew through me.

Maybe it was the air-conditioning. With the door open, the cold air was rolling out of Venus's office like a storm blowing in off the ocean. I'd just been out of doors, running as fast as I could in the unrelenting heat, and Venus's air conditioner was cranked up, the compressor going, the room frigid, the way it always is in hospitals, especially in the emergency room, sick people waiting their turn to see the doctor, trembling with cold. I wondered if the paramedics had made it this cold, if it would have any positive effect on Venus, slow down the bleeding or help her breathe.

I watched as the paramedic wrapped gauze around Venus's head, anchoring it under her chin to hold the compress in place, her head all in white, as if she were wearing a wimple.

"Ready?" he asked when he was finished, a middle-aged Hispanic man with a potbelly. No wonder, I thought, always seeing the ambulance parked in front of the pizza place around the corner, at Baskin Robbins, Taylor's—anywhere where there was food, the richer the better.

On a count of three they lifted Venus onto the stretcher, carefully tightening the wide straps around her, then covering her with a blanket. It should have been red, I thought, but it wasn't. It was blue.

"Careful," Nathan said, stepping forward, one hand holding the door, the other outstretched, as if Venus might tumble off the stretcher, but he'd be ready to catch her if she did.

The two men began to wheel Venus out and get her to the hospital as fast as the ambulance could maneuver through the narrow streets of the way West Village. She was gray, her skin dry, her eyes closed, her mouth slightly open. I looked at her chest to see for myself that she was breathing. Like my grandmother Sonya, I was quick to seek something to be grateful for, even in the worst situations.

The younger of the two paramedics, a blond kid with freckles and a cowlick, began running backward, pulling the stretcher toward the door. One of the uniforms held it open. I watched them wheel Venus out, the stretcher leaving parallel red lines in its wake, tracks that got paler and paler as it neared the open door, heading for the ambulance out front.

Careful to step over the trail of blood, I moved into the doorway.

"What happened?"

"A freak accident," Nathan said.

"A freak accident?"

"She must have gotten dizzy and fallen. It looks as if she hit her head on the edge of the desk."

"How awful."

I glanced at the desk.

"Dad has a colleague at St. Vincent's who he's already called. He'll let us know the extent of the injury as soon as he can."

"Was anyone here? Was she alone?" I asked. "Who found her?"

I tried to make myself slow down, but it was impossible. I was on the job. I felt responsible.

Nathan stepped back and made room for Eli to pass him, then stepped out into the lobby and let the door to Venus's office close. He looked after his father, who had walked out front to talk to the uniforms. Four of them were standing in front of Harbor View now, one of them taking notes.

Then Nathan took my elbow and led me into Eli's office, next door to Venus's.

"She fell and hit *the back* of her head?"

Nathan let the door close.

How come the cops were out there, I wondered, not in Venus's office? What the hell was going on?

"We have to wait and see what the doctors say," he said. "She went down hard."

"No one saw what happened?"

"No one."

"Well, then, how did you know she was hurt? Who found her?"

"Sammy went to get her, to ask her to join us in the dining room. He found her lying on the floor, unconscious."

"None of the kids were in there with her?" I asked.

"No, I already told you," he said, "she was alone. Everyone else was in the dining room. In fact, Sammy used his key to get in."

"His key? But why would he do that if she didn't answer his knock, if it appeared she wasn't there?"

"Because she'd stopped in the dining room a minute or two before. We'd asked her to join us for lunch, and she thanked us and declined. She said she had too much work to do. But then something came up in our discussion, and Dad thought that Venus would be the best person to respond to it."

"I see."

But of course, I didn't. I didn't know what he was talking about nor how I'd find out. He was already looking annoyed. And none of those others was going to talk to me, tell me about their private meeting. I also didn't know when I'd be able to get into

Venus's office and see what I could learn on my own, hoping it would be sooner rather than later, hoping it would be before anyone else got in there.

"I think Samuel's going to teach soon, Rachel. I'm sure Dashiell could help calm everyone down."

"First Lady, then Harry, now Venus. If it's not one thing, it's another," I said.

"We *are* having a particularly difficult time now," he said. "But one way or another, it's never easy around here. You must understand that. You and Dash have been in other institutions of this sort."

"So you were all here when this happened? You were all in the dining room?"

"We'd decided to have lunch here. It seemed the appropriate place to be, after the service."

I couldn't picture the Poole clan getting all excited about eating institutional cooking, but I nodded anyway.

"As I already explained, Rachel, these things happen."

"But—"

"The only thing that's important is that Venus gets the care she needs as quickly as possible. Don't you agree?"

I didn't answer him. For what seemed like much too long, we stood there, staring at each other, neither of us speaking. That kind of eye contact, had we been dogs, would have led to some serious fur flying. But we weren't dogs. We were civilized human beings. Nathan broke the silence.

"What would be the point of implicating that poor soul?" he said, his voice thick with emotion.

Time seemed to stop at that moment, and when Nathan continued, it was as if his voice were coming at me through a long tunnel. It sounded hollow and tinny.

"This may be a first for you, but it isn't for us."

"What—?"

"Do you think this never happened before?" he asked me. "It's old hat for us. What do you think happens in institutions such as this? This sort of violence is part of the risk, it comes with the territory. It might not happen again for a year. Or it might happen again tonight. You never know, and if you work here, Rachel, you best be aware of that."

"But the police—?"

I looked at Nathan again, waiting for the answer to my half-phrased question.

"Our function here," he said, "is to protect these people, not to turn them over to the police."

When I opened my mouth, he raised his hand to stop me.

"As I said, what would be the point? None of our residents can be charged with assault, Rachel. Penal law says that in order to charge someone with assault, there has to be intent to cause physical injury. How would you ascertain that in this case, by questioning David?"

"David pushed her?"

"You were told he has a history of violence, weren't you? I believe Venus tells everyone who works here that."

"Then why did you tell me Venus had been alone?"

"Because the fewer people who know, the better. Some people quit after the first incident that occurs after they're hired. Dad and I didn't want to lose you, Rachel. You and Dash are good with the kids. And that's—"

"All you care about."

"That's why we're here. For them."

"Will the Crime Scene Unit be called at all?" I asked, thinking of the number of people that had already trampled the scene.

"I doubt it, Rachel. It would be a shameful waste of taxpayer money and the valuable time of the unit, coming all the way down here from the Bronx for what? In order to press charges, you have to meet the standard of the law, don't you? There has to be intention. And what would they do then, take David away from us? And put him where? It's an aided case, Rachel, call nine-one-one, and you automatically get police along with the fire department ambulance. That's the law. But it's not as if we haven't been through this before."

"Well, you were just through it, weren't you?"

"Indeed we were. And you know what happened then, I take it? Some overenthusiastic officer aggressively questioned David until he ended up breaking the window with his hands. They won't be allowed near him this time. Dad will make sure of that. Not that he didn't try to stop that oaf who questioned him after Harry died."

"Where is David now?"

"Upstairs. Sedated."

"What do you think set him off? I thought he was doing well."

"His medication was cut this morning."

"I see."

"All the kids pick up the stress around them. That's why we do everything possible to shelter them. However, Uncle Harry's death has affected all of us, and there's no way we've been able to shield them from our own feelings. They're too sensitive."

"Litmus paper."

He nodded.

"Perhaps Dad should have waited until after the funeral, but there are unpleasant side effects, and he thought this was the right time. You can't possibly get it right every time. There's just no way."

I heard music coming from across the lobby—Samuel trying for business as usual.

"I shouldn't keep you any longer, Rachel." He opened the door. "We don't want to hold up Samuel's class."

For a moment I stayed where I was, though clearly I'd been dismissed. I was wondering about the crime scene and how far Nathan might go to protect one of his charges.

But was it a crime scene if the person who caused the damage didn't understand the consequences of what he was doing?

And then there was another question. This one came from Nathan. He put a hand on my shoulder and turned me so that I was looking right at him.

"What would you have us do, Rachel?"

This time I knew the answer.

"Whatever's necessary," I said. Then I headed across the lobby with my dog at my side.

THERE WAS NO ONE IN THE LOBBY

After Samuel's class, Charlotte was still looking unusually stressed, so I sat with her and gave her time with Dashiell. When I said good-bye and got up to leave, she got up too, following me out of the dining room, holding my hand as if we were going for a walk with Dashiell, the way we'd done the first day I was here.

I was about to tell her that I couldn't take her for a walk when I decided I couldn't do that. If she wanted one that badly, I'd take her out, maybe just go around the block with her, but I wouldn't say no to her.

Getting with the program, I thought; everything for the kids.

I looked at Charlotte, clinging to my hand, not reaching for Dashiell's leash, not going upstairs for her gloves and earmuffs, but sucking her fingers and not walking toward the front door, but pulling me to the door to Venus's office.

I was sure it hadn't been cleaned up yet, but Charlotte was

twisting the doorknob, then banging on it, starting to moan. Whatever it was she wanted, it was urgent.

There was no one in the lobby. I quickly took out Venus's key ring and unlocked the door to her office, stepping inside with Charlotte and Dashiell and letting the door close and lock. I stood in the way of the blood stain, dry and brown now, so that Charlotte would have to walk to the other side of the desk, the side where Eli had been standing.

In fact, Charlotte never looked at the side of the room where the blood was. Nor did she go to the other side of the desk.

Against the wall were three chairs. On the farthest one there was a pad, just like the one I'd found in the garden. She picked it up, bent down, and looked under the chair. There she retrieved a box of colored pencils, just like the ones I'd seen her sharpening in the dining room.

When she had her things, I expected her to turn around and leave the office.

But she didn't.

She sat on the chair, opened the pad, and began to draw.

That's when I heard Dashiell sneeze. A team player, he had followed Charlotte, had stood next to her, had even put his big head under the chair when she did, helping her look for he didn't know what, his tail wagging. Now he was headed for the other side of the desk, the part of the room I was trying to avoid. When I put my leg out to stop him, he glanced up at me, confused.

I looked back at Charlotte, working on her picture as if the only thing that counted was now, as if nothing at all had happened in this room earlier in the day.

When, I wondered, had she left the pad and pencils here?

But when I looked at the pad, I stopped wondering. She was

drawing what she saw—Dashiell, his strong white body, the patch over his right eye, careful with her lines and colors, the way she'd been when she drew the tree and started to draw the squirrel, the model who got away.

I watched her put down the charcoal gray pencil she'd used to color Dashiell's patch, careful to place it point to the top of the box, like all the others. Then she took another pencil, a red one this time, and began to color the rug behind Dashiell. Only the rug was blue, a pale Wedgwood. Except for the place where Venus had fallen and bled, the place behind where the dog in the picture now stood.

From where Charlotte was sitting, she couldn't see that part of the rug, the part I'd blocked her view of on our way in.

It wasn't only David who had been here. Charlotte had been here, too.

And that squirrel hadn't gotten away before the artist finished his portrait. Clearly Charlotte could draw from memory. So it must have been the artist who was called away, perhaps for lunch, leaving the portrait undone.

Dashiell sneezed again. Frustrated because I wouldn't let him examine what he felt needed his canine attention, he began to search for something else. He turned around and put his paws up on Venus's desk, trolling, his breathing audible now, his head moving from side to side, his nose telling him what he needed to know, then turning to look at me, then back at the desk, whining now to get me to look, see why his nose was twitching the way it was, find out for myself, the way he was telling me to, what was so interesting on Venus's desk.

At first, I didn't see a thing.

And then I did. Green paint on top of Venus's dictionary, the dictionary lying down because the bookend that usually held it up wasn't there.

Was that what he'd wanted me to see, green paint? Jackson's favorite color.

"Good boy," I told him, touching the paint with one finger, finding it dry. It could have been there since early afternoon. Or for years, for all I knew. But if it weren't fresh, why would Dashiell point it out to me? If the paint were old, it would mean nothing to him, no more than the finish on the desk or Venus's blotter.

That's when I thought to check out the side of the desk, the place where Venus hit her head when David pushed her.

No blood there. I even scraped the lip of the desk with a fingernail to make sure.

What was Dashiell smelling up there?

I looked back at Charlotte, coloring in the rest of the rug now, the part without the blood. She had added something while I was checking the desk: a pair of legs from the knee down, a pair of white Keds, speckled with paint. She'd colored the speckles green. There were some green streaks on the pants, too, as if someone with wet paint on his hands had bent over, hands on his knees, to look at something on the floor.

I heard something in the lobby and looked toward the door, hoping no one was coming in here, holding my breath, my eyes on the door, as if by doing that, I could keep it from opening. Waiting, I looked at the drawings and paintings taped to the inside of Venus's door—Jackson's drips, a portrait of Venus done in colored pencil, just the way Charlotte was drawing now, and a bunch of black crayon marks going every which way I felt sure was a portrait of Lady. There was that other strange picture Dashiell had knocked off the other day, the one where someone seemed to have spoons sticking out of his head, a really odd portrait, done from the rear in a shaky hand, the artist using pencil, pressing hard enough to leave a rut in the paper, someone tense doing that picture.

Someone tense, at Harbor View. Brilliant insight, I thought. Maybe I should go get me a Ph.D., publish in the *Autistic Journal*, make a name for myself.

Charlotte was still coloring the rug. Were they all in here when Venus fell, she and David and Jackson?

I thought about Cora, seeing Harry on the sidewalk—Harry, who had been knocked out of his shoes, knocked clear into the next world; Cora, who had nothing to say about what she saw, nothing, at least, that was useful or made sense.

Could any of these three tell me what had happened here this afternoon?

Maybe they could, but not in the usual way. Wasn't that, in fact, what Charlotte was doing, telling me what had happened by drawing it?

Her head was bent low over the pad, as if she were near-sighted, as she made the bloodstain redder, the color rich now, the way it must have looked when it was fresh. She seemed completely absorbed in the drawing, oblivious to me and Dash and even her surroundings.

Watching her, I realized I was wrong. Dashiell had tried to communicate with me. He'd tried to show me what he'd discovered. But Charlotte's drawing didn't have anything to do with me. She was doing it for herself, recording something she had seen, never mind that she appended an image from the present, Dashiell, to one from earlier in the day.

Was that a mistake?

Or was Dashiell there to help her cope, to protect her?

She had seen something confusing, something that frightened her. I watched her drawing, her fingers white against the pencil, getting the scene down on paper to try to make sense out of it.

But whether or not I'd be able to make sense out of it, that was another story.

WE HAVE WITNESSES, I COULD TELL HIM

y the time we left Harbor View and headed over to St. Vincent's, it had cooled off a little, the sun not overhead anymore but tucked behind the buildings west of us. I bought a yogurt at one of the ubiquitous Korean grocery stores, sat on the stoop of a brownstone, and shared it with Dashiell, watching his big tongue cleaning off the little white plastic spoon until long after all traces of food had disappeared.

We worked our way slowly through the revolving door and stopped at the reception desk, where a sand-colored woman with a profusion of bright gold hair and little flowers at the tip of each vermilion nail was talking on the phone. She pulled the receiver away from her hair and raised her eyebrows.

"Venus White."

One long press-on nail slid down the list of names.

"ICU."

A real New York conversation.

She hadn't looked over the counter, and Dash hadn't done

a paws-up, so I saved the story I had worked out on the way over for later. Only no one asked. St. Vincent's had a visiting dog program, and everyone must have assumed Dashiell was part of it.

Until I got to the ICU.

The nurse was the color of a Tootsie Roll and the size of a Mr. Frostee truck. I asked where I might find Venus. But she wasn't answering me. She had something else on her mind. She was scowling, looking down at Dashiell.

"*He* can't be in here," she said. "How'd you get in here with him anyway?"

"He's a—"

Then I surprised both of us. I began to choke up, tears running down my cheeks, no words coming out, though I know I was trying to tell her that Dashiell was a registered therapy dog.

"He's a cool one, isn't he? He won't jump on the bed, will he?"

I shook my head.

"Therapy dog," she read off his tag. She frowned at me. "You won't let him near the IV?"

"Uh-uh."

"Okay. Follow me." She looked at Dashiell again. "You, too. And mind your manners, you hear?"

Venus was in one of those curtained cubicles, barely bigger than the bed and full of machines that looked as if they ought to be on a UFO.

She hasn't awakened, the nurse told me as she slid the curtain back, they couldn't be sure she would, and I had fifteen minutes.

Another New York conversation.

Who was I going to bother, I thought, sitting there and watching a machine breathing for Venus?

She must have thought the same thing when she looked at

the expression on my face. She flapped her big hand at me. "You can sit awhile," she said. But she was frowning again. "But pull yourself together," she said, straightening out the part of the blanket that covered Venus's feet. "Do you know what she's picking up? No, you don't. So wipe your eyes. We don't need that kind of negative energy in this room."

She waited.

"That's better. Don't you be afraid to hold her hand. She won't break. You can touch her." She nodded. "Yes, ma'am. Talking's good, too. Not just any kind, something *interesting*. You can't expect a person to want to listen if you're boring them to death. You need to engage her mind," she told me, pointing to her own temple. "Let me tell you something, honey, there's a shitload we don't know about what's going on with this girl. You get my point?"

She wheeled around, her white shoes squeaking on the freshly mopped floor, parting the curtain and disappearing. I told Dashiell to lie down and reached for Venus's hand.

"You should have seen Samuel's class today," I told her, "you would have loved it. The night I went back late, you know, to snoop, remember, I told you about that? Anyway, when I got to Harbor View, I worked out this game with Dashiell, a sort of ring-around-the-rosy thing. And this afternoon, Sammy and I taught it to the kids.

"Cora and Dora, instead of falling down, because of course they couldn't do that, unless they were willing to risk breaking something, they bent their heads into their laps. Cora covered her eyes, too, as if she were playing peekaboo. Of course, Dora gave her hell for that one. Dora was having herself one fine day. She could have passed for a chick in her early eighties, she was so with it today.

"I got to talk to Cora while I was showing her how to play

and tried to get her to tell me what she saw the day Harry was killed. You were right, Venus. She didn't say anything helpful. All she did was tell me about the naps she had to take with Dora when they were kids, how their mother would fly into a rage if they left their shoes on and dirtied the sheets. She spoke of it as if it were yesterday.

"But I had to give it a try, just in case. Sometimes the smallest clue, just a hint, can set you in the right direction, set you thinking the way you should be in order to get the answers you need. So you try everything. Just the way you do with the kids."

You ring every bell, Marty said once, talking about the cops looking for a witness. If there's the slimmest chance in the world of getting a piece of the puzzle, you go for it. You have to, he said. That's the job.

"The princess kept losing her crown when she leaned forward, then putting it back on by herself. *That* was a sight to see. Molly finally found her a couple of bobby pins. I haven't seen those things in years," I said, remembering that my grandmother Sonya used gray ones, one on each side, and gray hairpins to hold her hair in a bun at the nape of her neck. Grandmothers don't look like that anymore, bunned old ladies in orthopedic shoes and support hose. Now grandmothers go to the gym and pump iron. "I didn't know they still made them, bobby pins," I said, putting my free hand gently on her arm. "Did you?"

I waited for an answer.

"I'm here, honey," I whispered.

There was no window, so for a while I watched the monitor and listened to the clicking of the ventilator.

"Even Charlotte learned the game. Here's what she did— she got in behind Dashiell and aped everything he did. It worked perfectly, until he started licking the floor. I guess Homer missed a spot last night.

"Everyone who came gave it a try.

"Well, almost everyone."

Three of them there, in Venus's office, not just David.

Hey, I could tell Marty, we had a little incident over at Harbor View. Someone tried to kill the manager. And I have good news and bad news.

What's the good news? he'd ask, that cop look on his face, like the shutters were tilted so he could look out, but you couldn't look in.

We have witnesses, I could tell him. Three of them.

And what's the bad news? he'd say.

We have witnesses. Three of them.

I stood up and leaned over the bed, looking to see what had been done with the head wound, but it was covered. I was wondering if they'd stitched it. Maybe I could ask the nurse on the way out.

But what difference would it make for me to know? It was Eli's colleague in charge, wasn't it? Wouldn't he have done whatever was best for Venus?

I tapped my leg for Dashiell to stand, tapped the edge of the bed for him to place his head there, and then gently lifted Venus's hand and laid it on top of Dashiell's big head, maybe because if I were lying on a skinny bed in an intensive care unit, that's what I would want.

I placed my hand on top of hers, watching her face to see if anything changed. Nothing did.

"I'll come as often as I can," I told her, "but I'm still doing what you hired me to do."

I waited again.

"Your home phone's not tapped," I told her. "That's good. At least whoever did this wasn't able to check up on you at home.

"You know, they could be old, those bugs. They might not

even be functional. You never know," I told her, her eyes closed and still, not moving the way they do when you're dreaming.

Dashiell pushed his head up, bouncing Venus's hand, reminding her to pet him.

I began to think about Venus's apartment, the sound of Dashiell's nails on the stairs, the light coming in the window, Harry's watch on the nightstand, part of their internet love affair printed out and waiting for me at home. The wedding band, the one she didn't wear.

Then I remembered the necklace.

I stood, looked toward the end curtain, as if I thought Nurse Frostee might be watching, making sure I didn't knock over the IV stand or accidentally kick out the plug of the ventilator. But no one was there. I could hear her, in fact, talking on the phone, sitting at the desk waiting for someone's alarm to go off so she'd have something to do.

I leaned over Venus and pulled away the neck of her hospital gown. No necklace there, only abrasions on one side of her neck, as if someone had been too impatient to open the latch and had yanked it off, some narcissist who had to have what he or she wanted that very second.

I smoothed her gown, touched her face with my hand, then sat back in the chair, looking at Venus, then looking at the machinery that was keeping her going; one minute you're fine, you're living your life, the next minute you're hanging on the brink because someone tried to take away the only valuable thing you have, the years ahead of you.

And your diamond necklace.

Now what would David want with *that*?

What did the necklace even have to do with this?

Was this done because of the necklace? The damn thing was worth a small fortune.

Or had the necklace been an afterthought?

I needed to clear my head, and I knew just how to do it.

"I'll be back later, Venus," I told her, waiting again to see if there would be a reaction, anything at all, some tiny movement that would let me convince myself she'd heard me, that any minute she would open her eyes and be all right.

What did I think she'd do, wave good-bye? Blow me a kiss?

Is is, Frank Petrie used to say, trying to get me to act more like a detective, accept things the way they were, stop my wishful thinking; Medea changes her mind at the last minute and takes her kids to Disneyland; some clever engineer patches the hole in the *Titanic* and she sails safely to port, no souls lost at sea; Lady Macbeth discovers Purell and gets those pesky spots off her hands without even having to use water.

I opened the curtain for Dashiell, then watched him walk under another part of it. Standing half in and half out of Venus's cubicle, I wondered if maybe, just this once, I might get my way; Venus would wake up, annoyed as hell, tell me who.

Who. That was only part of it. She'd have to tell me *why*, too.

Yeah, right.

I looked back at the bed, nothing moving without the help of a machine.

I let the curtain close behind me, thinking, What if she did wake up, just as I wished, but when she did, she remembered nothing?

Oy, there's the rub.

SEE ANYTHING YOU LIKE? SHE ASKED

ight outside of St. Vincent's, Dashiell stopped to sniff the pants of some very patient man, carrying his groceries home from D'Agostino's.

"He must smell my dog."

"Knows his name, rank, and serial number by now," I told him.

I stopped by the cottage, fed Dashiell, and packed my backpack with a towel, a change of clothes, a small tape recorder, and the pages I'd printed at Venus's apartment. The staff meeting was at eight. I could work out for forty-five minutes, shower, and still get to Harbor View on time.

Walking over to Serge's gym, I tried to piece together what started all this, what happened to Harry.

He'd turned south, planning to go to Venus's apartment.

I wondered if the person on the bicycle had expected otherwise—that Harry would turn north, heading for the subway on Fourteenth Street, that he wouldn't see what was coming, a bicycle headed right for him, maybe someone he knew on that bicycle.

Maybe someone he knew?

Of course it was someone he knew. At least, that was the premise that made sense to me, looking at the world as I did, through a dirty window.

Someone he knew.

Coming down Bank Street, I looked into the Westbeth courtyard, a place I knew well, a place with lots of memories for me.

Across the street was the t'ai chi studio where I had studied late into the night so that I could better insert myself into the life of a young woman who had died there.

The courtyard, too, had been a place of death, and when I came here now, as I had always done, to play ball with Dashiell in the shade of the trees, I tried to erase those memories and replace them with the scenes of Dashiell running, his back legs hitching together like a rabbit's, his ears flopping, his face alive, his mouth open in a grin, the world in his work, nothing more compelling than getting the ball and bringing it back, acting out the law of the jungle and the demands of genetics in the guise of a game. But even watching Dashiell's joy, I'd been unable to forget what had happened here. It was foolish to try. The best I could do was add to the mix.

I detoured into the courtyard. The sun was almost ready to set now, the air still heavy and warm. Even now, so late in the day, delivery men were lying on adjacent walls, one on his back, arms crossed under his head, the other with his knees bent, lying on his side like a baby. Both were fast asleep.

Their bikes, beat-up one-speeds, one with a basket large enough to hold a couple of orders of Chinese takeout, the other with no basket, the handlebars wrapped in silver tape, were leaning against one of the walls, unchained. Was that the way it worked in China, everyone getting around by bike, you could leave one just about anywhere and it wouldn't get stolen?

Not here.

I wondered exactly how easy it would be to steal one.

And then what? After hitting Harry, just ditch the bike a block or two away?

Of course not.

Abandoning the bike in the street would only bring attention to it, the opposite of what the killer would want. A stolen bike, left near a crime scene, that would be a gift for the cops.

He might as well leave a red bow on it.

Or a confession.

No. The bike wouldn't have been *stolen*. It would have been *borrowed*.

And returned. That way it would disappear back into the crowd of indistinct, beat-up delivery bikes as soon as possible. Perfect.

But what kind of a murderer would take the time to return a stolen bicycle?

A smart one.

And what if one of the little men woke up before the bike was returned? What was he supposed to do about it, call the police?

Most of the delivery men spoke just enough English to make change, not a word more. Come from China and call the police? I didn't think so.

The courtyard went all the way through to Bethune Street, one block north, Westbeth filling the entire block from Washington to West, from Bank to Bethune, a Godzilla among buildings. Perhaps after Harry's accident the bike was dropped off on the Bethune Street side, where the courtyard was dark and gray around the clock, no place for a nap in any season.

You wake up. Your bike is gone. You panic. Then what? You figure one of the kids took it to ride around the courtyard. You hope that's what happened, so you look around. And there it is.

But the basket is bent.

Or there's a flat.

Who would the delivery man tell?

Surely not his employer.

I was taking a nap, and someone borrowed my bike. See—the front wheel is bent now, the reflector broken. Kindly get it fixed.

Yeah, right.

The two bikes leaning on the wall were old, with clunky balloon tires, one painted blue, the other a rusty gray. The paint was chipped on both of them. One had a broken reflector. On the other one, only the frame of the front reflector remained, none of the plastic.

Who would even notice another dent or a set of handlebars out of line?

I'd heard years ago that most of the bikes used for delivery by the Chinese restaurants had been stolen, bikes the restaurants bought dirt cheap for cash and quickly repainted—some kid left without transportation, some old guy having to hoof it to the gym instead of pedaling there.

I wondered if the cops had gone around to all the restaurants and checked the bikes for blood stains.

But Harry had died from hitting his head on the sidewalk. The back of his head, like Venus's wound. There wouldn't have been blood on the bike.

What about fibers? Would there have been fibers from Harry's jacket? Wouldn't those come off on the street if the bike had been stolen and returned? Wouldn't that be one of several excellent reasons to return it?

But the detectives would have checked the delivery bikes anyway. Bike rental places, too, leaving no stone unturned, keeping it close to the vest for now.

No news, the fax had said.

Right.

Homicide with a bicycle, I thought, leaving the courtyard. Pretty hokey. Must have been unplanned, something that happened at the last minute, something improvised, born out of incredible rage, something hot, not something cold, plotted, mulled over, rolled around, and examined. Not something played out over and over again before the fact, enjoyed not once but many times. No, this was a compulsive act, a last-minute thing.

So what had happened at Harbor View that afternoon?

Would Venus know? And would she wake up and remember?

There was a side entrance to Serge's gym on Bank Street. I walked past two chunky guys spotting for each other, an old guy with a headband to catch his perspiration reading the *Times* on an ex bike, and a pumped-up Hispanic man with thick, dark hair moving his torso from side to side, counting as he did.

I settled Dash and took the treadmill in the corner, the one I'd always used when I talked to Venus here. Turning on the power, punching the start button, I warmed up slowly, watching the river and letting my mind drift. When I got up to speed, I pulled the folded papers out of my waistband and began to read.

I'd printed the batch of e-mail correspondence without paying any attention to the dates. The stuff I had was written early on, not exactly in the beginning, but soon after Harry had told Venus he was married and that his wife was ill and dying.

" Lady," Harry had written,

I stayed at the hospital all afternoon again, but she woke up only twice, for too brief a spell each time. The first time, she seemed confused and I thought, oh God, she no longer knows me. But the second time, she smiled and took my hand, holding it as long as she could manage to stay awake. I read to her all afternoon, Robert Frost this time, hoping that the sound of my voice would comfort her as the reading and the time I spend with her comfort me.

And all the while, I was thinking about her so long ago, when I first saw her. She had a part-time job in a bookstore near where I lived. She was standing on one of those rolling ladders wearing stockings with seams, and oh, how those seams caught my fancy. When she turned around, her light brown hair loose around her face except for a barrette on one side, I saw her eyes. And lost my heart.

" See anything you like?" she asked, not strident or offended, merely amused. Perhaps she knew from the start that she could have her way with me.

Now, to see my dear girl like this, her face gaunt, her body barely visible beneath the hospital blanket, my voice sounding hollow to me as I read the poems, thinking, how will I live, how will I go on?

" The doctor has finally said that there is no going back from where we are. He suggested hospice care, but I am reluctant to do that as she will know then that there is no hope. And if she felt that, I think she would die sooner and in despair.

Don't think me an utter fool, L. I understand
that she is aware now of how grave the situation
is. But I think a little hope still burns in
her, and I long to keep it that way until the
end, if possible.

S

Venus's answer was short.

Without hope, there is nothing at all.
I'll read Frost tonight and think of you both.

L

L,

My wife's sister came today. She and her offspring are our only family, but I feel far
closer to you, wherever you are. Her sister
comes once a week. She stays a short time. She
is awkward and does not know what to say. She
usually stands. She never touches either me
or her sister. Her children don't come at all,
and I must admit, I like these people less and
less, and trust their fondness for my dear
girl not at all.

I think, like vultures, they see only the
future, the meal they can have if they are
patient. All she means to them is a tidy
distribution, as if she were gone already.
They do not treasure any moment they can spend
with this gentle woman. Perhaps they never
did, who knows?

S

S,

You remind me of a scene in Zorba the Greek

in which the old woman is dying, and the
townspeople come and strip her things away as
she lies in bed watching.
Some people seem to discount the person at the
first bad news.
L

I folded the pages and put them back under my waistband,
looking at the sun setting on the Hudson, the ball dropping behind
the half-built buildings across the way in Jersey City and Hoboken,
the light so fierce at one point that even with the amber shades to
cut down glare, I had to raise one hand to shield my eyes.

It was fascinating to read the letters, this one-sided conversation—he says, she says, but not at the same time. There were
no interruptions, no changes in the direction of the conversation
because of what you perceived in the other person's facial expression or body language. The phone didn't ring; you were using
the phone line, especially since providers started offering a flat
rate and you no longer had to watch the clock.

There was a heightened intensity to the exchanges, everything made more intimate by the speed with which you could
send your thoughts and feelings across space and time and onto
the small screen in someone else's home, where he would read
your words without the interference of normal life. No one ever
interrupting an e-mail "conversation" by saying, "Hey, did you
remember to take out the garbage after dinner?"

They were good friends, listening to each other's concerns,
offering support. The intimacy was strange, disembodied, verbal
intimacy that had nothing to do with age, race, physical charac-
teristics of any kind. Harry, remembering when he was young,
seeming younger than Venus sometimes. On-line, he was unen-
cumbered by a seventy-four-year-old body: no stenosis, no ar-
thritis, no enlarged prostates in cyberspace.

Venus was the supportive one, the nurturer. Venus was sensible and caring.

So what was *she* getting from all this? The chance to do what she did all day at work, only this time there was someone on the receiving end who could express appreciation? I thought about that for a while, wondering if it had been enough for her, wondering how soon after Harry's wife died did things change.

"I'm here for you, S," she wrote, the sexual charge beginning to appear early on. Even without scents and pheromones, you could feel the charge coming off the words.

But was it real? Would it last? Would it stand the test of a virtual meeting?

Often it didn't.

In this case it did.

I had too little here. But I still had Venus's keys, so I punched up the machine, walking as fast as I could without breaking into a trot, hoping the workout would give me more than it took away so that I would be able to get back to Venus's computer and track the meeting of two minds, a love affair that never would have happened the old-fashioned way.

Out the window, there were three lanes of traffic moving north, the newly built median filled with dirt, waiting for the trees and flowers that would partially block the view of three lanes moving south. Everyone moving, I thought, no one content to stay where he was.

A bus was passing, blocking my view of the runners—an odd-looking caravan, painted over, even the windows. It stopped where I could see it, caught by a red light at Eleventh Street. In the shade my hand created, I read the words painted on the side: FORESIGHT IS THE BEST ARMOR AGAINST THE UNKNOWN.

Where was this bus when it was needed? I wondered. Where the hell was it when Venus was here?

When the light changed, the bus disappeared.

Beyond the traffic moving toward the tip of Manhattan, the John Deere equipment sat, parked and still at this hour, the men in their hard hats long gone.

Beyond that was the "park" where I took Dashiell to run off leash, a concrete strip adjacent to the Hudson, a place for walkers, runners, skaters. Bike riders, too.

What if someone skating or walking there *had* seen the accident? So what? It wasn't a car that struck Harry. There was no license plate. From across West Street, or from a moving car heading north, no one would be able to identify the person riding, more than likely hunched forward, as if to make the bike go faster. What good would that sort of witness be?

Or another sort, Cora or any of the other "kids"? The possibility tantalized, but in the end, whatever they were able to offer, in words or pictures, was worse than useless.

I watched the runners, the sun behind them turning them into dark shadows, arms sawing back and forth as they ran, someone going faster, too, disappearing for a moment behind one of the earthmovers, coming out on the other side, lickety-split, the way Dashiell liked to do it.

And someone running with a dog. I couldn't see the dog, but one arm was stretched forward, the leash invisible from this distance, only implied by the position of the runner's arm. I could imagine the dog, his tongue lolling out, his legs moving rhythmically, feeling his canine runner's high, out front and pulling. If they were racing, she was losing. He was first, top dog, loving every minute of it.

Top dog. Was that the issue at Harbor View, too? Hadn't Harry Dietrich, until he was hit by a bicycle, been alpha?

For a moment, walking in place, I wondered about the others, how they felt about Harry's position, and if there was someone, one of them, who might like to apply for that position his or herself, now that it was available.

If so, which one?

Slowing down the belt, for the moment unaware of the panorama before my eyes, seeing another in my imagination, I found myself wondering if this were yet another version of the game I'd been watching all my life.

Only this time it was being played by humans, not by dogs, and involved far more than teeing up or trying to look bigger than the other guy.

This time, it was deadly.

WHAT'S *THIS* SUPPOSED TO BE?

omer, wearing huge yellow rubber gloves that went nearly to his skinny elbows, was mopping the lobby. He indicated the dining room with his head, never stopping the rhythmic motion as he did.

Sorry, I mouthed as Dashiell and I tracked up the wet floor.

But when I was standing right outside the dining room, the doors open just a crack, I heard something that made me pause. I grabbed Dashiell's collar before he used his big head as a wedge to push open the doors.

When I turned around and looked to see if Homer was watching me, I saw that he had stopped too. The mop was still and Homer was staring, waiting to see what I was up to.

I could have checked my pockets, pretending I was looking for something.

Or bent down to tie my shoelace or fuss with Dashiell's collar instead of just holding it.

But I did nothing, nothing but stand there and obviously

eavesdrop, at first, with my back to the door, watching Homer watch me. Then I turned around so that I could hear better.

I heard the mop hitting the pail and the water running off it as Homer picked it up, then squeezed it out.

"You don't mean *here?*"

The speaker petulant.

"Where else?" Eli. Sounding weary.

Silence. Perhaps a shrug.

"You mean you thought you'd do it from home, without any contact with this place at all?"

"You do have a phone, don't you?"

"I think we're jumping to conclusions here." Nathan, trying to calm everyone down.

"What do you mean?" the first speaker said.

"I mean we have to see the provisions in the will, what is called for, what is set forth legally."

"He was my *uncle,*" the petulant speaker said. "Who do you think he'd have control the investments, someone outside the family?"

Silence.

"And what sort of experience do you have that would make you think you could control the finances of a place you never—"

"I thought the purpose of this meeting was to discuss what's best for the kids," Samuel said. "It's not a business meeting."

"It might as well be," Eli said. "It's obvious, one way or another, there are going to be some radical changes here."

"For one thing, there's the nepotism of the staff."

I wondered if Bailey was flipping his hair back as he spoke.

"What are you waiting for, Eli?" Arlene asked. "Harry's dead. He can't take care of income and expenses anymore. I believe that it was his intention that—"

Backing up, working from the front of the lobby to the rear,

Homer was washing the floor behind me, leaving the patch where I stood snooping for later. When I turned to look at him, he looked away.

"We'll work it out. We all have the same goal in mind," Nathan said, "that things run smoothly here, with as little change as possible for the kids."

I turned again, holding up my pointers to make a T before Homer got the chance to look away. He nodded, the mop never stopping.

When I heard some chairs scrape against the floor I backed up fast, taking Dashiell with me, so that it would appear we were just arriving. But we were still too close for comfort. When Arlene pulled open the double doors, she gasped, wrinkling up her expensive face.

"Oh, hi," I said. "I was just coming for the staff meeting. It's not over, is it?" I looked concerned and checked my watch.

Arlene frowned. She looked up from Dashiell. Now she seemed to be staring at my hair. So I studied hers. The humidity hadn't bothered it. Perhaps it had been coated with polyurethane. I had the feeling the color wasn't natural either, but that was just a guess. Only her hairdresser knew for sure.

Everything about her cost money, lots of it—more than she could afford, was my guess. But she didn't look worried. Maybe she was expecting a windfall sometime soon. Then I found myself thinking that her sister must have left her something when she died. But probably not enough. When is it ever enough for people who care about things like that? I wondered if she'd figured out some way to get more. One has to keep up appearances, doesn't one?

Arlene was still frowning. Either trying to place me, or hoping I'd move the fuck out of her way.

"I was hired to do pet-facilitated therapy, after Lady disappeared," I told her, instead of moving away.

"Of course you were."

She smiled a Melba toast smile, guaranteed to break into several pieces if she dropped it.

I ignored the prettied-up surface and tried to see what was underneath. It was an old habit by now, something I'd done for years as a dog trainer, and now for years as a detective.

Janice, coming along behind her mother, just stared, more like a sullen adolescent than a grown woman. Bailey was checking the backs of his hands, which he found infinitely more interesting than me.

I stepped aside, and they walked out, Arlene heading for the front door with Bailey right behind her.

"I left my purse in Uncle Harry's office," Janice said, holding up her hand and snapping her fingers. Bailey reached into his pocket and flipped her a set of keys.

Turning toward the dining room, I heard the keys land on the floor.

"Don't just *stand* there. Get those for her," Arlene said.

I was pretty sure she was talking to Bailey, but I responded anyway. "Keys," I told Dash, and he picked them up, bringing them to Bailey, sitting in front of him and wagging his tail, waiting for an atta-boy. Well, with this motley crew, he could just wait.

"What's *this* supposed to be?" Bailey said, taking a step back. Weren't there any dogs on the Upper East Side?

"Oh, *please*." Janice yanked the keys out of Dashiell's mouth.

I turned to go into the dining room, but the Kagans were coming out.

"Am I too late?" I asked.

"I'm sorry, Rachel," Nathan said. "I left a message on your answering machine. We didn't know where you were. Dad"—he looked at his father—"we're all exhausted. We've decided not to have the staff meeting tonight. We're"—he took a breath—"all on overload. I hope you can forgive—"

"Please, don't give it a thought. As long as I'm here, is it okay for me to take Dashiell around for bedtime visits?"

"I wonder," Eli said. Then he paused. "I hate to impose, but as long as you're going to do that, Rachel, would you take Dashiell to see David? But ask Homer or Molly to go with you, please."

I nodded. "Has there been any word from the hospital?" I asked, looking at Eli, and when he didn't look at me, looking at Nathan, then Samuel.

"No change," Eli finally said. "We'll stop by on our way home."

"Your doctor friend?"

"Yes?"

"Could he, would it be possible for me to go over really late with Dashiell, after I finish here?"

"Rachel, you need your rest, too. Look at you. Your eyes are all red. You look so—"

"I'd really like to go."

"I'll make sure it's okay."

"Why don't you come with us now?" Samuel asked. "That would be okay, wouldn't it, Dad?"

"I want to take Dashiell around first. I think that's important," I said, nodding for emphasis. "But thanks for asking."

It was also a great time to check Eli's office, since he was going over to St. Vincent's and then home.

I turned to head back to the stairs and saw Janice. She'd found her purse. I couldn't miss it against the gray suit.

There was something else I couldn't miss as well. It wasn't Harry's office she was coming out of, brushing her hands against each other; it was Venus's.

Arlene and Bailey were waiting at the front door. As Janice joined them, I saw Arlene's eyebrows go up.

"It wasn't there," Janice said.

I didn't get it. It was right in her hand. But no one elaborated for my benefit. They walked out into the heat, and a split second later, looking through the sidelight where David usually stood, I saw Arlene's arm go up for a taxi, God forbid they should wear out their Gucci shoes walking to the subway.

Eli had gone to get his briefcase. When he returned with it, both sons followed their father out. Watching them leave, I wondered if I'd made a mistake, not going with them. Couldn't one of them kick out the plug of the ventilator or screw up the IV line? But then I remembered Nurse Frostee and all those monitors at her station, and I knew that Venus was safe. At least for now.

Walking up the stairs, figuring I'd start at the top and work my way down, see who was in the mood for a little visit, I began to think about David. Nathan said they had to protect him. And Venus had told me he did get violent sometimes. She'd told me to be careful.

Still, in view of all the other things that had happened here, I wasn't buying the story. It was too convenient, having someone to blame who couldn't defend himself, a scapegoat whose apparent guilt would allow the whole incident to evade police scrutiny.

It was, in fact, if it weren't true, a brilliant ploy. Now all I had to do was determine which one of the players was smart enough, and greedy enough for power, to have figured it out.

And cold enough to have acted upon it.

I BRUSHED AWAY THE DIRT

I started with Charlotte, singing her to sleep with Dashiell occasionally howling along, his subtle way of telling me to keep my day job. The princess was so taken with Dashiell she removed her crown and tried it on him. But I had to call a halt to her fun when she tried to secure it with bobby pins. I passed David's door without knocking. I'd visit him later, with Homer. We visited the guy we'd seen carrying his shoe around. He laughed when Dashiell kissed him. He seemed to be an awfully nice man who'd simply lost his way as he got old.

Some of the old people seemed to get sweeter as they got more senile, going back to childhood and, in doing so, shedding all the burdens that come with being an adult. A few, like Cora and Dora, perhaps because they were a pair, stayed peppery. Still, what you saw in either case was pretty much what you got. Those with autism were infinitely more complex and unpredictable.

We stopped in on a man who appeared to be in his thirties. Or forties. He said his name was Richard. But then he asked if

Dashiell's name was Richard. I thought of telling him it wasn't, but didn't bother. By then, Dashiell had hopped up on the bed, and for a while both Richards, cheek to cheek, communed. When I told him we had to go, he reached for my hand and patted it. I promised I'd come by again as soon as I could.

Dora wanted to see the dog, but Cora didn't.

"I have gas," she told me.

More than I needed to know.

Homer was in Venus's office, the door propped open with a wedge. My guess was, he'd saved the job he dreaded for last, and he didn't want to be in there alone with the door closed. For a moment he didn't hear me over the sound of the vacuum cleaner. When he noticed me, he looked startled, just staring at me, the vacuum still going. Then he reached under the handle and shut it off.

"How'd you get stuck with this job?" I asked him.

He shrugged. "Who else was going to do it? Anyways, couldn't be done before, while Dr. K. was talking to the police. Couldn't be done until they all left."

"Did the stain come out?" I asked. Some kind of white foam was covering where the blood had been.

Homer shook his head. "I doubt it'll ever come all the way clean," he said. "I scrubbed it three times over. I been in here an hour. It's all I've been doing, that and the vacuuming. Got to vacuum up that foam, then we'll see."

He turned the vacuum back on and ran it over the spot where Venus had fallen, shaking his head when he was finished.

"It's still wet, but a rug this light, it's going to show. Dr. K won't want that, won't want the kids to see that. You never know what they understand."

"Will they replace the rug?" I asked him.

"For now, at least, I thought I'd move the desk. If it's just a couple of feet over, it'll cover the spot nicely."

"Good idea," I said. "Let me help you."

"Went straight down, right near it, I guess," he said, looking at the desk.

I looked at the desk, too.

"If she'd been over there when she fainted, she'da been in the clear," he said, looking at the space between the desk and the shelves. Another wishful thinker.

"Have you seen her, Rachel?"

"It's not good," I told him. "She hasn't woken up."

He seemed not to hear me, reaching out and putting his hands under the lip of the desktop.

"We'll walk it back," he said, "until it covers the stain. I want everything just so for when she gets back here. On three," he said. Then he counted.

When the desk was in place, he noticed the books lying down. Now he was looking for the bookend, bending to look under the desk, see if in all the excitement it had gotten knocked onto the floor, shaking his head when he stood up. Then he stepped over to the bookshelves and took a bookend that was there, a brass sailboat. He laid down the last few books there to hold the rest, and carefully propped up Venus's reference books and wedged them in place with the bookend.

"That's better," he said, straightening the blotter, moving the leather cup that held Venus's pens an inch back. "Now what's this?"

We both peered over the desk at the dark spot that had been hidden by the out-of-place blotter. Homer took a cloth from his back pocket and spit on it. When he rubbed the spot, the stain vanished.

"That's better."

I reached for the cloth and turned it over, and we both stared at it, brownish red where it had cleaned the surface of Venus's desk. Homer had a look of panic on his face.

"The paramedic," I said. "He was holding a compress on Venus's head, and when he changed it—"

"We ought to put some flowers here," he said. "She likes that. Likes it cheerful for them. They all come here, you know, just to be near her."

He went back to the shelves, where there was an empty vase, and stood that on the other end of the desk.

I wasn't thinking about flowers. I was wondering where the missing bookend had gone.

"I'll go out into the garden and cut her some greens," he said. "She hangs their pictures up on her door, too, everything to make them feel good. I wouldn't want for her to come back and have the room looking bad."

"Let me, okay?"

I walked around the desk and opened a couple of drawers, looking for a pair of scissors.

"I'll get the polish," he said, looking over at the dull spot where the blood had been. "I'll make her desk shine."

Dashiell followed me to the garden door, and I noticed no one had remembered to turn on the lights. The lights would attract insects, so I left them off, unlocking the door and letting Dashiell out first. There was a moon, and the pearly gray light it cast into the garden was sufficient for us to see.

As soon as he was outside, Dashiell's tail began to beat so hard that every few times it made a complete circle. It wasn't just that he was out, which for a dog, except when it's raining, is always preferable to being in. It was more than that.

He headed right for the back of the garden, to the southwest corner. Not knowing why, I followed him to find out.

It was Jackson, not stretching skyward and being a tree. He was folded into himself, looking more like a stone, looking unbelievably small for such a tall man. Sitting on the ground, knees bent, head bowed so that I couldn't see his face, arms limp at his sides, his hands encrusted with dirt, lying palms-up on the bricks that covered the garden floor, he was immobile, not even looking up when Dashiell wedged his big head next to his face and began to lick his cheek.

I crouched in front of him, putting the scissors down on the brick ledge.

"Jackson?"

There was no reply.

When I reached forward and lifted his chin, I saw that he was crying.

I leaned forward onto my knees and put my arms around him, and Jackson let me hold him, arms still at his side, his head leaning on my shoulder. I rocked him gently for the longest time. When I pulled back to see if he'd lift his head and look at me, I noticed that Dashiell was no longer there.

It was the noise of his tags that made me look. And another sound—his nails scraping against something hard. Dash was at the center of the back wall, in a space between two round pots of flowers, digging at the bricks.

"Leave it," I told him, but he didn't seem to hear me. I let go of Jackson and went over to Dashiell to stop him.

Looking down, I saw that the dirt all around where he was trying unsuccessfully to dig up the bricks was darker and looser than the compact, sandy-looking dirt a foot or so away. I crouched and quite easily lifted up a brick, then a second one, setting them off to the side.

Dashiell pushed his way in now that there was an opening and dug some more, the dirt flying backward as he worked. Two more bricks came loose. With that, he dug at the dirt, and I could see his nostrils moving, taking in the scents coming up from the ground.

"Back," I told him.

This time he paid lip service to my command. He took the smallest possible step back. His forehead squinched with concern, his head hanging over the hole, Dashiell was pressed against my side, his eyes on the ground.

I brushed away the dirt with my hands and felt something hard and smooth in the hole, grasping it with my fingers and pulling it up. It was Venus's missing bookend, and even in the moonlight I could see two things: the brownish red dried blood on its base, and the green paint at the top.

When I turned back to where Jackson had been, he wasn't there. Concerned, I stood, bumping into him. He had been standing right behind me. I hadn't heard him, but there he was, practically on top of me and tall as a tree.

With one hand, he was reaching out for what I was holding.

In the other, he held the scissors.

COME HERE, I SAID

The garden lights came on, and Jackson blinked.

"Are you having trouble deciding?" Homer asked. "Some greens, I thought. And a little touch of color."

He stopped when he noticed Jackson.

"What are you doing out here at this hour?" he said. As if he expected an answer.

I'm not sure why, but I bent and dropped the bookend back into the hole.

"Dashiell began to dig. Damn dog must think he's on the beach or something," I said, pushing the dirt back over the bookend with my hands and quickly replacing the bricks. I stood then and tamped them down with my feet.

Homer was still in the doorway. I took Jackson's hand and led him with me.

"Give those to Homer," I said, pointing to the scissors. "He's going to cut some flowers for Venus's office, make it look real pretty for when she comes back."

Homer reached forward and took the scissors.

"I'll walk Jackson to his room while you do the flowers. You know what she likes better than I do."

Homer smiled. "That I do," he said.

"You know, I bet Jackson could use a cup of tea," I said, as if I were talking to Homer. But I wasn't. "Should I make you a cup, too?" I asked, turning back now.

"I have to do the bed check first, Rachel. Everything's off tonight, everything's late, because of that extra job. If I'd have done the bed check when I always do, I'd have known Jackson here wasn't in his bed."

"He will be very soon. But first, we'll go sit in the kitchen for a bit. I think that would make us both feel better."

"Settle him right down. Does for me."

"It's so peaceful out here," I said.

"That it is." He tilted his head back and looked up at the moon.

"I think if I lived here, I'd come out to the garden every night, just to be by myself for a little while, have some place that was my own."

I felt Jackson's fingers twitch in my hand.

"I wouldn't care what the rules were. What harm could it do to sit out here, look up at the moon and down at the shadows it makes in the yard?"

Homer walked over to the raised beds of plants against the north wall. I headed for the door, Dashiell looking back where the treasure he'd found had been reburied, then running on ahead.

While the kettle heated, I gave Dashiell water and two of Lady's dog biscuits. Then I wet a small, clean dish towel and washed Jackson's face and hands. There was paint everywhere—streaks of green on both sides of his shirt, paint on one cheek, more paint in his hair, his hands so caked with dirt I couldn't see the paint underneath until I started to clean them, which he passively let me do.

I filled a bowl with warm soapy water, and Jackson let me put his hands in it, to loosen the dirt from under his nails and get the layers of paint off his skin. While the tea was steeping, I rinsed and dried his hands.

Sitting across from each other, we drank our tea without saying a word. Dashiell had fallen asleep on the floor near the water bowl. Listening to him breathe, sounding like a kid with a stuffed nose, I wanted to go home, soak in a hot bath, and then crawl into bed and sleep, too.

But there was only one day left before all hell broke loose.

Sitting there with this shell-shocked man and my sleeping pit bull, I thought, no, what was I thinking, there wasn't one day left, all hell had already broken loose, and if I didn't find out why, things were going to get even worse than they were now.

I stood and reached for Jackson's hand. For a moment, only a moment, he seemed to look at me, the way he had done once before. He looked away, reached into his shirt pocket with two long fingers, and pulled out a piece of bread, holding it out to me, then dropping it into my upturned palm. It was as hard and dry as a bone long ago picked clean by a hungry dog, but I had always been told it was the thought that counted, and I believed that. I went around the counter, standing in front of Jackson and looking at him. His eyes flashed again, like heat lightning on a summer night, a quick, bright light, then darkness.

Jackson stood, again looming over me.

"Come here, honey," I said, opening my arms.

This time he stepped toward me, and when I folded my arms around him, he lifted his. I felt the weight of his lanky arms on my shoulders. Then I felt the tears, mine wetting his shirt, his landing on my neck, warm and wet and sad as death.

LADY VANISHES

Jackson took off his paint-splattered Keds and got into bed with his clothes on, too tired to change into his pajamas. Or maybe he would have needed help, but I didn't know the drill, and at this point it didn't seem very important. I pulled a chair close to the bed and sat, Dashiell sprawled on the floor, everyone exhausted by now.

Paint on the bookend. What did that mean? Had it been Jackson who had tried to kill Venus?

But why?

With a population this disabled, was there a *why* I could understand? These were people who could be stressed beyond my comprehension by the ordinary things that made up my world—the touch of a fellow human, the sound of someone's voice, color, light, noise, change of any kind, the barking of a dog.

With some, their brains couldn't discriminate among the sounds that made up speech, so they could neither speak nor understand when someone else spoke. Some were labeled brain-damaged or retarded because of this, the way people deem animals dumb because they try to judge their intelligence without first understanding how they function. Wouldn't we be considered the dumb ones if the test had to do with following a scent trail?

Charlotte got so stressed by normal city noises that she wore earmuffs to block out the sounds of traffic and construction. Some of the kids became mesmerized by things they saw—curls of wood coming out of a pencil sharpener, light flickering on a wall—or by repetitious activities of their own making—sliding a toy back and forth on the floor or table, moving sand from one container to another, rocking or spinning for hours on end— anything that would replace the sights and sounds that were disturbing with something predictable, benign, and most important, comforting.

Why was I even trying to figure out what might have motivated Jackson? It could have been the sudden screaming of a car alarm, or the pain and confusion when a lamp was turned on. Perhaps he was in the dark the night he surprised me in the garden not to be unseen but because the lights hurt his eyes. How could I possibly understand what might have made him freak? It could have been anything.

Jackson's eyes fluttered and closed. I reached out and shut off the lamp. Sitting there in the dark, thinking about the symmetrical smears of paint on Jackson's shirt, I began to concoct another way the green paint might have gotten onto that bookend.

He might have come in and seen it on the floor next to Venus, picked it up, seen the blood, then dropped the bookend and frantically wiped his hands against his shirt.

That would explain it.

No—it wouldn't. Dashiell had tried to alert me to something on the desk. The bloodstain under the blotter.

Had Jackson picked up the bookend and put it down on the desk while he straightened up the books? That would account for the green paint on the dictionary. And the blood on the desk.

What next?

He'd seen the blood on his hands and wiped his hands on his shirt.

But it didn't end there. He'd picked up the bookend again and taken it outside, burying it in the garden.

Why?

And why had he been out there crying after he'd hidden it?

How I wished he could just tell me.

I reached out and touched his arm, watched him sleeping on his back, his mouth slightly open, his breathing audible, but no competition for Dashiell's.

Jackson, clobbering Venus? It didn't make sense.

Had he come in afterward?

Or had he been there all along, someone figuring it didn't make any difference, these three witnesses, considering who they were? All good news, no bad.

But if it wasn't Jackson who struck Venus, who was it? Were we back to David? Ever the skeptic, I didn't believe that one either.

Dashiell was whimpering, running in his sleep. Or was he dreaming he was digging again, using his paws for shovels? They were brown now instead of white, dirt on his face as well. I'd cleaned off Jackson, but not my dog.

What had alerted him—the fresh dirt? Or had he smelled the blood, something out of the ordinary, something to pay attention to, something, if you were Dashiell, that would make you alert your master?

It couldn't have been planned. You don't plan to murder someone with a bookend from their desk.

Or with a bicycle.

Someone was angry, seething.

Someone's rage was spilling.

Someone was coming apart.

Why couldn't I see it, see who it was?

I decided not to wait for Homer. Getting up, I went to David's room, one flight up from Jackson's, knocking softly, then opening the door. The bedside lamp was on, but David seemed to be asleep, lying on his side, his back to the door. I listened to his breathing, slow and even. Only that wasn't the way David normally breathed. It was the sedative, slowing everything down.

Did that mean it was safe to stay?

Carefully, never taking my eyes off David, I walked around the bed and looked at his face, tense even now, despite whatever tranquilizer he'd been given.

His hands were tense, too, one rigid and clawlike, the other in a fist.

With something sticking out.

In the light of the lamp, something sparkled, something metallic, all but a tiny piece of it secreted in David's hand.

Could I see what it was, this amulet he held in his sleep?

Could I do it without waking him?

Maybe I could.

I called Dashiell, softly, with a whistle. As he ambled over, shaking his head, his ears clapping hard, I patted the bed. Dashiell jumped on and without further ado served up the specialty of the house. He lay down alongside David, sighing as he did. Then he let go, leaning all his weight and the heat of his body against David's back.

I waited.

David stirred. His head moved, but his eyes remained closed. I listened to the sound of David's breathing. After a moment, I carefully reached for the treasure in David's hand, grasping the tiny part that was exposed and sliding it toward me until it was free.

When I held it up in the light from the lamp, it came alive, the diamonds winking and sparkling, mesmerizingly beautiful. I let the heart fall into my other palm, feeling the weight of it in my hand, the chain, its clasp broken, hanging down. For all it cost, it wasn't very heavy. But it was heavy enough, I knew, to keep me up all night wondering what this meant, wondering if David had seen the necklace and been attracted to its sparkle, had reached for it and clobbered Venus when she'd pulled away.

Venus had told me to be careful around David. Had she failed to take her own advice?

Sleeping, Jackson appeared normal. David did not. Even now, even with Dashiell tight against his back like a squeeze machine, he was so tense he was spastic, his face in a grimace, his knees pulled up to his chest, the hand I had robbed of its security object twitching.

There was something else sparkly in the room. It was lying on the nightstand: a key chain with a gold-colored ball set with colored stones, faux rubies, emeralds, sapphires, and diamonds, but no keys. Why would this man need a set of keys?

I held it up and watched the light dance off the metal and the stones, then lowered the ball into David's palm and let go as his fingers closed around it, having neatly pulled a Dashiell. Sometimes, when there was something he knew he couldn't have, something he wanted with all his heart, he'd make a trade, leaving one of his toys in the place the object he so coveted had been, as I had swapped the key chain for Venus's necklace.

Holding it in my hand, it was no longer the weight of gold and diamonds. It was the weight of obligation. David and Jackson could sleep, but no way could I, not until I understood what had really happened to Venus. To Harry. And to Lady.

On the way downstairs, seeing the mark along the wall, the mark that Homer must have purposely neglected to clean away, I thought about her, about Lady, the missing dog, sliding along the wall as she traveled up and down to see her charges.

Coincidence, all this happening at once?

Or is that where this all began? Lady vanishes; everything goes downhill from there.

I WALKED BACK TO WHERE HE WAS STANDING

On the way down the stairs, I heard Homer's voice. Someone was frightened. Homer was soothing.

I moved faster, heading for Eli's office, to look for I didn't know what.

I knocked. Because you never know. Then I used Venus's keys, letting myself and Dashiell in, closing the door, then flipping on the light.

I didn't think I had a lot of time, so I went straight for the files, quickly moving through the patient folders, hoping something would jump out at me, something telling.

Dream on.

There were several file drawers full of medical journals and articles on autism, new drugs, vitamin therapies, homeopathy, acupuncture, aromatherapy, you name it, it was there. Though traditionally trained, it seemed Eli was willing to investigate anything that might help.

I was looking for personal things—his will perhaps, or Harbor View finances—but those were all in Harry's office. Venus had a point. Why would someone think these men's skills were interchangeable? The beauty of the relationship was that they were not, that each was an expert in his separate field, and that each was equally devoted to the small, damaged population at Harbor View. It was, it seemed to me, not a career but a calling. Sure, it took money and lots of it to keep this place going, but money wasn't the point of it. And neither man, I thought, took out more than was needed to survive. Well, of course, Harry hadn't taken money out. He'd put it in. Gobs of it.

I flipped through the rest of the files quickly, stopping at David's to read the overview that started each resident's file, then stopping at Jackson's to read his. I took the phone apart and found the bug, then shut off the light and opened the door, my heart pounding because I didn't have a story ready this time.

But the lobby was empty. Homer would be working his way down from the top. I listened for a moment, but I didn't hear a sound. Eli's office wasn't the place to be. I went next door to Harry's office, unlocking the door and letting Dashiell into the dark room first, then stepping inside after him, letting the door close and feeling his tail start to bang against my leg.

What was he so happy about, just because he'd been here before, because it was familiar?

I felt along the wall for the light, pushing up the switch when I found it, then sucking in my breath when I saw we weren't alone.

He lifted his hand to shield his eyes when the overhead light came on. I stood there, mute, Venus's keys in my hand, too surprised to think of how I could explain my presence here. That's when I noticed he had been crying.

"Please don't tell anyone I was here," he said.

Dashiell approached, his tail going in circles now.

"I didn't want any of them to see me crying. They get upset too easily."

I went and sat next to him on Harry's big leather couch.

He had a wad of tissues in one hand and wiped his eyes with it, but the tears kept coming.

"I don't understand what's happening. And I'm afraid. I don't know who's going to be hurt next, but sure as we're sitting here, Rachel, someone is."

"You may be right," I told him, looking at his small, polished shoes, his feet side by side, as if he were sitting in church. Then I looked back at his face. "What can we do about it?" I asked.

"You and me?"

"Exactly."

"What could *we* do?"

"We could pool our information, for one thing."

"I don't—"

"If you don't know what's going on here, Homer, who does?"

"Well, I hear some things, but—"

He sat up, looking at me critically now, probably wondering what I was up to, if he could trust me.

I was already in it up to my chin, but I was wondering the same thing about him.

Sometimes you just have to take a chance.

"You heard some things yourself, didn't you? This afternoon, for instance, outside the dining room. You were listening to them in there, weren't you?"

"I was."

"How come?"

"Because something funny's going on here, don't you think?"

"I think it's not so funny."

"That's what I meant."

"I never said," he told me.

"What didn't you say?"

"That I saw you listening."

"How come?"

Homer turned away from me.

"Why didn't you tell Eli what I did?"

"Venus brought me here twelve years ago. She took a chance on me."

I looked at the little man's face, the flush across his nose and cheeks.

"You met at AA?"

He nodded. "I didn't think I was ready for no responsibility. The cleaning, okay, I needed the money. We both knew that. And that was something I could do. Because, see, I don't clean one night, I won't disappoint anyone so bad I can't hardly stand the sight of myself in the morning.

"But Venus said I was here for the kids first, to help Molly with the bedtime, to do the bed checks, to sit with any of them when they get bad dreams or night sweats.

"I told her, no, I can't do that. I can't be counted on. I never could be. 'You can now,' she told me. 'I would trust you with my life.' I'll never forget her saying that to me because the way she did, I knew I had to make it true. She went to Mr. Dietrich and worked it out. I don't know what she told him, but knowing Venus, I'd say it was the flat-out truth. That's how she is, you know."

I nodded, thinking about how she'd hidden the truth from me. Or rather, eked it out. For Harry's sake, she'd said.

"When I seen you listening in on them, I figured maybe you was doing it for her, to find out what was happening here."

"That's true. I am trying to help Venus. And I think you can help me do that, Homer."

He looked at those polished shoes of his, the laces even, tied just so, as if by paying careful attention to the minutia, that and going to meetings, you could keep your life from falling to pieces.

"I never mean to—"

"But it happens, right? You're cleaning, and you hear someone on the phone, or you hear an argument. The way you saw me snooping today, by happenstance."

He nodded.

"You see, this here building, it was a seaman's hotel originally, before Mr. Dietrich bought it, got it fixed up so it would be right for the kids. It was meant for short-term visits, people staying here by themselves, not a place for lots of families, thick floors and walls you can't hear through. Voices carry here. Mostly, it's a helpful thing. The princess, she cries a lot at night, but she doesn't get up and call me. From anywhere except the kitchen I can hear her, or any of them that needs me. I know to go to her, make things better. That's my job. That's what Venus hired me to do. She said I could understand them, because I'd been down. She said no one would ever wish to be where I spent a major chunk of my life, no one would ever choose to be a drunk and a failure, no one would ever think any good could come of it." Homer's eyes filled again. " 'But in this job,' she said, 'you could consider it an advantage.' "

Dashiell got up and put his head on Homer's knee.

"But sometimes what I hear," he continued, "it's got nothing to do with what I was hired for. You know what I'm saying?"

"I do."

"Sometimes I find out things in other ways," he said.

"A piece of paper in the trash."

Homer nodded a little too enthusiastically.

"Hey, you're human, right? You're curious."

"I never go through the files or nothing. Just sometimes

there's something right on top of the desk when I'm cleaning up. It's hard not to look."

"I figure you know about as much as anyone," I told him.

"Some would think that."

"Before I came today, Homer, did you hear anything yourself? From the big powwow in the dining room?"

"Seemed like the sister wasn't too happy. Those spoiled kids of hers either. Mr. Dietrich wasn't like that. You could see he was rich all right. But he was a regular guy, too. He wasn't a showoff, like them."

"What were they miffed about?"

"That Bailey thinks it's going to be him doing Mr. Dietrich's job, managing investments, and making financial decisions for Harbor View. I always thought Nathan was preparing himself for that, with his MBA degree and all that fund-raising he does. Maybe he thought Mr. Dietrich would move down to Florida, get hisself a boat, take it easy for a change. If anyone could afford to do that, he could. But it's too late for that now."

"What about Samuel? If Nathan thought he'd take over for Mr. Dietrich, did Samuel think he'd take over for his father one day?"

"You can't take care of the kids with singing and dancing, Rachel. These poor souls have serious problems. They need medical care.

"Oh, it's not that Sammy didn't try. There's nothing he would a liked better'n that, as devoted as he is." He leaned closer and lowered his voice. "The story I heard was that he was in medical school, and pffft. Couldn't cut it. Had the brains for it, but not the stomach."

"Who told you that?"

"Molly did. She's known them boys forever. She was their nanny before she came here."

"No kidding."

"Cross my heart," he said. And he did.

"So Samuel. He was in medical school, but he flunked out?"

"Oh, Mr. Samuel is a smart one. Don't kid yourself. He's always reading something, that one, wouldn't step on the subway without a book. And listening to his music, the classics and opera. He didn't flunk out. He passed out. Fainted at his first autopsy, first year in."

"But lots of people do that and get by the squeamishness and go on to be fine—"

Or go on to be psychiatrists, I thought, doctors who can't stand the sight of blood.

"Not this one. He's here late, he wants a snack, Molly leaves the tomato sauce off his pasta, gives him a little oil and garlic instead. Someone gets cut, or falls, it's not Samuel you call. It's Dr. Eli or me or Molly, that tough old bird. He's always been like that, squeamish. Not Molly. You should see what that woman can handle, and the strength of her, at her age. She can lift some of them, grown-ups, nearly her own size, as if they were babes in arms. Gets them to take their pills, go to bed on time, bathe when they don't want to—she can handle anything. A find, that's what she is for a place like this. But so is Samuel, in his own way. Couldn't follow in his father's footsteps, the way he wanted to, but he does a world of good here with his little classes every night, a world of good."

"What about the poster family for overindulgence? Have they ever done anything here? And what about the wives?"

"What wives?"

"Harry's wife, before she got sick? And Eli's?"

"Eli's wife died when the boys were young. That's why they had Molly. She lived with them, in Brooklyn, while the boys were growing up."

"And now?"

"She lives here, Rachel. I thought you knew."

"No, I didn't." But I hadn't seen where anyone could either. I assumed when Venus stayed, she slept on the couch in her office. But where would Molly sleep? I asked Homer.

"Up top. Southeast corner, nice and quiet, overlooking the garden. Small, but she don't seem to mind."

"Do you live here, too?"

"Not me, Rachel. Venus offered. But I've had my place for thirty-three years now, and the rent's cheap. I got my own troubles without being with theirs every hour around the clock. You're here, your work hours get flexible, you see what I'm saying? Molly don't mind that, or so she says. I do. I got to get to my meetings regular and have some peace and quiet, too. And I need a phone, so's I can call my sponsor when I have to. Like tonight." He looked toward the phone on Harry's desk. "We're not supposed to use the phones here, unless it's for them, the kids, an accident or something. Like we ain't got no needs ourselves."

I patted his hand.

"He told me to hold on, my sponsor."

I nodded.

"Well, I told him, I'm *trying*, aren't I? It's why I'm calling, I said." He nodded. I did, too.

"Homer, you never told me about Harry's wife. Marilyn. Did she come here, work with the kids, or help Harry out?"

"Met her twice, is all. This was Harry's work, not hers. The sister's the same way, I can tell you. The one was here today? That Bailey Poole, her son, he was saying he'd be overlooking the finances. That's what I heard him say, overlooking the finances. Never set foot in the place more'n once a year before now. But that sister woman, when they got here after the services, she was looking the place over, as if now that Mr. Dietrich is gone, it's *hers*. Can you just imagine what *that* crew would do to this place if it were theirs? Turn it into a shopping mall, I guess." He looked at his hands, gnarled with work, the fingers stained a yellowish brown. "Never worked a day in their lives, the pack of them. You can see it by their hands, even the boy. Good-for-nothings, I say. Dr. Eli, he was telling them they were jumping the gun. They had to wait and see."

He looked at me, his eyebrows raised.

"Until they got to see the will," I told him, "see what Harry spelled out for Harbor View. I guess everyone is expecting what they want, as if Harry were Santa Claus."

"I'm sure he did what's right for *them*," he said, pointing up.

"You don't think he would have been concerned about his relatives' feelings? After all, Arlene was his wife's sister, and he has no other family that I know of."

"Don't matter," Homer said. "This is what mattered to him. These people here, the twins and Jackson, Willy and Richard and the princess, Charlotte, David, and all of them, this was Harry's family. This is where his heart was. You'll see."

I nodded. "You okay now, Homer?"

"I'm better. It's good to have a friend."

I reached over and patted his hand, dry from cleaning products, rough from hard work.

"I better finish my bed checks. You done in here?" he asked me, the suspicion coming back into his eyes.

"Yeah, I was just looking for you," I told him. "To tell you I couldn't wait for our cup of tea. I want to get over to the hospital, see how Venus is doing."

Homer nodded. "You tell her I said—"

Then he remembered.

"I will, Homer. No point me sitting with her and keeping

my thoughts to myself. I figure, maybe she hears me, so I talk a blue streak. It couldn't hurt."

"You tell her Homer's keeping her seat for her. She'll know."

He got up and went to the door, holding it ajar for me.

"Keep your eyes and ears open. Anything you hear, you let me know."

He nodded.

Dashiell and I headed for the door, then turned back.

"Homer, were you here when Harry got hit by the bicycle?"

"I wasn't. I went to the six o'clock meeting, got here about seven-thirty, couldn't get in right off, because they were looking for clues out front. Never saw so many police in all my days."

"What about the night before? Did you hear anything then, anything unusual?"

"Sorry, Rachel, I didn't. I don't know anything about Mr. Dietrich's accident."

I walked back to where he was standing.

"You might, Homer, but you might not know that what you saw or heard has any significance. So if something comes up, if you remember some little detail, no matter how unimportant it seems, you let me know, okay?"

"Okay, Rachel. I knew I was right about you trying to help Venus."

"You bet I am. And now you are, too. We're a team."

It was a fifteen-minute walk to St. Vincent's, and I was hoping, at least for that short amount of time, I'd be able to let my mind go blank. There wasn't much hope it would get rest in the normal way that night. After checking in on Venus, I was planning to go back to her apartment and spend the rest of the night reading her correspondence with Harry, hoping for something, anything, that would point me in the right direction.

Digging my hands into my pockets, because it was late

enough that I was chilly now, I felt Venus's necklace and wondered if part of seeing what I had to would mean seeing through David's eyes.

Or Jackson's.

And then I wondered if I was up to it.

Sure, sometimes I could see like a dog, I could understand what should be unfathomable. But this was different. David and Jackson were of my own species, yet more baffling than anything I'd run across.

Still, I couldn't help feeling that part of what I was seeking lay hidden there, with David, Jackson, and Charlotte, maybe with Cora, too—people who were unable to see the world as I needed it seen because they were infinitely more lost and confused than I now felt.

I WHISPERED HER NAME

xcept for the sound of machines doing the work some people's bodies had refused to do, and the occasional squeak of rubber-soled shoes on the tile floors, there hadn't been a sound in the ICU since I'd quietly moved a chair closer and sat next to Venus's bed. Even the receptionist downstairs had only nodded when I came in, maybe figuring if I was here so late, there must be a good reason for it. The night nurse, too, had merely looked up as I passed her, as if making rounds with a pit bull was a normal part of hospital procedure.

For a while I sat still, not wanting to disturb the quiet. Then I reached for Venus's hand, sliding mine under it, hers lying limp on mine, palm up. I watched her breathing for a while before I realized she was off the ventilator, doing it on her own. My heart did a little dance in my chest, enough excitement to get Dashiell up from where he'd wedged himself, head and shoulders under the bed, trunk, rump, and tail sticking out, legs straight back in the frog position. First he looked at me, then at Venus. Head up, nose moving, he began to test the air, going closer to the bed until he had no choice, he had to get up there to get what he was after, and with a quick turn behind me to make sure the curtain was closed, I let him, watched him climb up and stand over Venus, his tail moving slowly from side to side, then suddenly dip his big head and begin vigorously to lick her face. I moved my hand to her wrist to protect the place where the IV needle had been inserted to give her fluids and hoped like hell the nurse wouldn't pick this particular time to do a bed check.

I had a powerful faith in the wisdom of a sound dog, having seen and heard enough miracles to know that animals sensed things that were beyond human knowledge. So as odd as this scene would have appeared to most of the rest of the human race and probably all of the hospital personnel, I sat there with a wait-and-see attitude when anyone else would have kicked the dog off the bed in no time flat.

Dashiell kept licking, and the speed of his tail revved up, enough so that I had to move a bit to avoid getting hit in the face.

And then I felt it: Venus's fingers moved, as if she were trying to close her hand.

I felt a flutter in my chest again, but then I thought, who said they didn't move before? Did a twitch mean anything? I didn't know, and I wasn't about to ask the nurse, but now even I thought it was time to get Dashiell off the bed. It's not that he was doing any harm. It's just that I wanted to get a better look at Venus, and he was in the way.

Off, I whispered, not wanting to hear the nurse's shoes squealing as she came running.

Dashiell backed up and got off the bed, standing next to my chair, his tail still going like a runaway metronome.

Now Venus's eyes were moving, the lids still closed, the way Dashiell's do when he's dreaming.

I took her hand. I whispered her name. Venus opened her eyes.

I knew I should have called the nurse right away, but I didn't. I waited to hear what Venus would have to say. She looked at me for what seemed like ages. I thought for a moment she might need time to focus after being out for so long. But her face didn't look confused. It just looked blank. And then her mouth moved, and Venus whispered something, so softly that I couldn't make it out.

"Say it again," I said, getting up and getting closer, bending over her so that I could hear the word Venus had mouthed. And then I did.

"Pain," she said.

And then her eyes fluttered closed, and her head moved slightly away from me.

I sat a moment longer, my heart pounding, then went out to the desk to tell the nurse what had happened.

IS THIS YOURS? SHE ASKED

It was the middle of the night by the time I left St. Vincent's. I had wanted to go to Venus's apartment and read the rest of her letters to and from Harry, but after what had happened, it seemed a ridiculous plan. For one thing, it would take hours and hours to do that. No way could I stay awake that long if I were sitting still and reading. My head ached, my stomach felt hollow, I was punchy with exhaustion. Whatever the nurse had given Venus, injecting something into the IV drip, I should have asked for some myself. But even more pressing than my need for sleep was my need to tell someone about what had happened, someone who knew Venus and would care.

For some reason I can't explain, halfway back to Harbor View, I changed my mind again. I had been hoping to talk to Homer, maybe have that cup of tea with him and tell him that Venus was breathing on her own, that she'd awakened, even if it was only for half a minute, and only to say she was hurting.

But as I passed the little park at Abingdon Square, empty

now, all the old people from the Village Nursing Home snug in their beds, no one else around, not even the pigeons that swoop in and clean the park of dropped food, I decided there was someone else I ought to tell my story to. Even at this late hour, or maybe especially at this late hour, talking about something as emotional as Venus's "accident" and what looked to me like the beginning of her recovery might open up other topics, might just give me the piece of the puzzle that would allow me to understand the now confusing picture. It could make sense of the jumble of seemingly unrelated facts, like when after a long litany of complaints, a dog owner used to tell me the thing I should have heard first. He was taken from his mother at four weeks of age, they'd say, an aside that had no real significance to them but explained all the aberrant behavior that had led to me being hired.

If only.

She opened her door on the third knock, looking puffy-faced and confused when the light from the hallway hit her eyes.

"What's wrong?" she asked, squinting as she pulled her robe closed around her and tied the belt. She had her slippers on, too, I noticed, ready to go forth and do battle if need be.

"I have to talk to you," I told her, watching her expression change. She was looking at me now as if I were crazy. "Can I come in?"

"What time would it be?" she asked.

"Two-something," I told her without looking. "I've just come from seeing Venus."

Molly reached for my hand and pulled me into her dark room, leaving the door open behind us. In the little bit of light that filtered in from the hallway we made our way to her bed and sat, Molly still holding my hand.

"How is she, that poor child?"

"She spoke," I said. "And she's breathing on her own." And

then before I could elaborate, I began to cry. Perhaps it was the exhaustion, making my eyes feel as if they were full of sand, making my shoulders sag and ache, my feet feel too big for my shoes, my mouth feel dry and sour. As if she knew all that, Molly reached for the glass of water on her nightstand and handed it to me. Then she slipped an arm around my shoulder and pulled me close.

"All she said was 'Pain,' " I said, my voice still choked with tears. "But I think that's a good sign, don't you?"

"I do indeed. And breathing without the ventilator?"

I nodded.

"I've been praying for her, asking our dear Lord to bring her back to us."

I nodded again.

"She's the backbone of this place, Rachel. She knows everything, and quietly, never tooting her own horn like some might, she keeps things running smoothly. She's there for us, too, for the staff. But her way with the patients, it's uncanny, always knowing when a person can handle more responsibility. She's always had more faith in them than anyone. I myself tend to baby them. It's not good for them, she'd say to me. Now Molly, you know they need to do every possible thing, every little thing they can for themselves. It's what gives a body self-esteem, she told me many a time. Because I needed to be told it more than once, that's for sure.

"She was hired to take the phone calls, that one, to see who was coming in the front door. No one knew what else she'd be doing for us all."

"Molly, do you think she'll be—"

"Hush, you. Don't you even think anything else. What would happen to the lot of us without her? Of course she'll be all right. She'll be returned to us. And look at you, shaking like a leaf. What are you doing up all night, worrying about everyone else and not taking a lick of care of yourself?"

I couldn't answer. I drank some more water instead.

"He knows what's best," she said. I thought she was talking about God again, our Lord, but when she stopped talking, all there was besides the whir of the air conditioner was the wheezy sound of Dashiell snoring, and I knew that Dashiell was the *he* she'd been referring to because she was laying me down in her bed, still warm from her body, and pulling the blanket over me. I thought I should be asking her where she would sleep, but I don't think I did. All I remember was the sensation of going backward, as if I were falling in my sleep.

When I opened my eyes, I could see the little room, neat as the dollhouse of an obsessive-compulsive child, light coming in from the windows washing over the pale blue cotton blanket that covered me. There was a small bureau covered with framed photographs opposite the bed, a rocking chair with a small table and a lamp in the corner, and not an article of clothing or a scrap of paper anywhere to be seen.

I lay there for a moment, just gathering my thoughts, and when I stretched my arms and legs, I felt something large and warm at the end of the bed. Molly wasn't here with me, but Dashiell was.

I pushed the blanket back, saw my shoes lined up next to the bed, and, ignoring them for the moment, walked over to the bureau in my stocking feet to look at Molly's photo collection, which turned out to be pictures of the boys: Nathan graduating from college, holding his diploma and looking straight at the camera, Nathan the serious; and Samuel, his eyes closed, his brow covered in sweat, leading an orchestra, or more likely, a small band of developmentally disadvantaged singers. Samuel with rabbit ears?

I took the photo with me and turned on the lamp as the door opened and Molly appeared, still in her robe, holding a tray of food.

"I thought you might be hungry," she said.

"Where did you sleep?"

"On the couch in Venus's office. It's very comfortable, and there's a blanket and pillow in the cabinet because sometimes Venus stays over. You're not to worry about putting me out, Rachel. I was fine, and I'm glad you didn't go back out in the night at that hour. It's not safe out there."

It's not safe in here, either, I thought as Molly turned to put the tray down in the middle of the bed.

"Come and sit here with me. We'll have some tea. Do you feel a bit better, child?"

The photo still in my hand, I walked over and sat at the foot of the bed, next to Dashiell, who hadn't gotten up.

"I'm sorry about this. He does it at home, so—"

"You've nothing to apologize for, neither one of you. It's where Lady slept, and no doubt he knew that. She slept right where Dashiell is, keeping my feet warm, the dear thing."

Molly sat at the head of the bed. The tray was between us. I thought she'd pour the tea, but suddenly her face screwed up, and she was reaching under her hip, fishing around, and then pulling something out she'd sat on, holding it up so that the light of the lamp made it glitter and shine.

"What's this?" she asked.

For a moment, I froze.

Clearly, it hadn't been in Molly's bed before I'd spent part of the night there.

But had she ever seen it on Venus?

There was only one way to go with this, I thought, leaving the necklace in Molly's hand instead of reaching for it. Instead,

I looked down at the tray, then poured a cup of tea.

"Is this yours?" she asked.

"No," I told her. There was no cream or sugar on the tray, so I held out the cup of black tea, meeting her eyes now. "It belongs to Venus."

"Is that so?" she asked, taking the heart between two fingers and turning it over. "It's hers, Venus's, you say?"

"That's right."

Molly looked up at me, still holding the diamond heart, the chain dangling down from her hand, the cup of tea between us in my outstretched hand.

"It's very much like one Mrs. Dietrich had."

I put down the cup and glanced at the photo I'd put on the bed next to me, at Samuel, in what I'd thought were rabbit ears, perhaps doing Easter songs with the kids. Then I poured a cup of tea for myself, taking a sip and reaching out for the necklace.

"It is hers, Mrs. Dietrich's," I said. "Rather, it was."

"But how did—"

"Harry gave it to her."

"I don't—"

"They were in love, Molly. They were married." I watched her doughy cheeks flush and tremble, saw the disbelief in her eyes.

"Venus and Mr. Dietrich."

I nodded. If Venus thought it was Molly who might be listening when she was on the phone, well, unless she'd studied at the Actors Studio, I'd say it wasn't.

"But I don't understand."

"There's a lot going on here that's hard to understand, Molly. The fact that two lonely people with the same devotion fell in love is the easiest thing to comprehend. Why he's dead and she's in the hospital, that's another story."

"But—"

"Here's the question that I believe you could answer best, Molly. I found the necklace in David's hand last night. He was holding it in his sleep."

"David?"

I nodded.

I could see Molly struggling with all the new information.

"Nathan says David is the one who hit Venus, that he's been violent before. Venus also told me that he gets violent sometimes. In fact, she said that if he made me uncomfortable, I didn't have to work with him."

"But he's never hurt anyone intentionally. With the exception of himself, that is." Molly picked up her cup and drank some tea. "He's pushed people, who've then fallen. But it was only to defend himself from what he thought was danger. Not too many people can understand how easily he goes on overload, how frightened he is most all of the time. I suppose he *could* have pushed Venus," she said, as much to herself as to me. Then she looked me right in the eye. "No—impossible."

"Why?"

"Because Venus knew him better than anyone. She'd never go that route with him."

"I don't understand."

"She'd never pressure him. It's when he's pressed that he reacts."

"Like when he was questioned by the police?"

"Exactly. And who did he hurt? The officer? No—himself."

"So he's never attacked anyone."

Molly shook her head.

"Then how do you explain the fact that he had this?" I held up the necklace.

"Well, I can tell why he'd want it, but not how he got it."

"Go on."

"It's the sparkle. That's why he stands at the front door all day, looking up. It's the stained glass he loves, the way the light comes through the colored glass. It seems to mesmerize him. Perhaps it gives him a way to block out all the rest, the jumble that makes no sense to him.

"All of them, those with autism, they create rituals, patterns of behavior that give them a little peace. For David, it's watching the light dance. That's what works for him. That, and the dog."

"You mean Lady?"

"Yes. She helped, too. She was the best thing that ever happened in that man's life."

"So you don't think David would have struck Venus? Not even to get the necklace?"

"No, Rachel, I don't."

"Would he have taken it from her after she was hit, when she was lying on the ground?"

"The catch looks broken. Pulled apart."

"Yes, it is."

"Then your answer is no. He wouldn't have pulled it from her neck like that. But if he saw it on the rug, if the light hit it and made it shine, then he would have picked it up and taken it, yes."

"Nathan didn't tell you it was David?"

"No, he didn't. He said she'd fallen. He'd know better than to tell *me* a story like that."

I nodded. The story had been for my benefit. What did that mean? Was it part of the policy of protection? If so, and it wasn't David who'd hit Venus, then who was Nathan protecting?

I reached behind me for the picture of Samuel in his rabbit ears.

"He made those himself," Molly said. "Anything to make the music sound better."

Easter songs, I'd thought. Rabbit ears. So they were headphones with antennae sticking up from each ear. That's what the artist had drawn in that funny-looking picture on the back of Venus's door, the one in which I thought someone had spoons sticking out of his or her head.

I looked at the picture and smiled. It's amazing what you can come up with when you don't know what you're looking at.

"He should have studied music, not medicine," Molly said. "But like most boys, he wanted his father's approval. He wanted to be like him, anything to get closer, to feel accepted."

"And Nathan? What did he do to win his daddy's heart?"

"Nathan? Why, not a thing. It was always his. He was always the favorite. You know how that is."

I put down the photograph and picked up my tea, cold by now, and bitter too. Then I opened my hand and looked at Venus's necklace, seeing something I hadn't seen before. I got up and moved over to the lamp, holding my hand right in the light. Yes, there was a part of the chain that wasn't shiny. It was dark.

"Do you have a tissue, Molly?"

"I do," she said.

She opened the top drawer of her nightstand and took one out. I took it, dipped it in the water glass, and pulled the damp tissue along the dark part of the chain, Molly and I both watching closely as the chain got shiny again and the tissue came away brownish red.

"Molly," I said, "how is it you recognized this necklace?"

"It was her favorite, Rachel, Mrs. Dietrich's. Leastways, she wore it all the time."

"But I thought she hardly ever came here."

"She didn't. But she and Mr. Dietrich used to come to the

house, in Brooklyn, back when I lived there and took care of the boys."

"You mean they socialized with Dr. Kagan?"

"Not often. Just for the holidays, birthday parties, special occasions, like family. The boys called them Uncle Harry and Aunt Marilyn, just as if they were blood relations."

"And recently?"

"Well, I wouldn't know. I've been here since the boys grew up and moved out on their own."

"Where do they live, the boys?"

"Oh, still in Brooklyn," she said, sitting down on the bed. I sat next to her. "It's too pricey around here. Did you see the signs on those new buildings going up? Everything's a luxury building now, and I wonder where they find all those folk with so much money to spend on housing, half a million dollars and more, just for a place to live. Must be all those Wall Streeters, young people that make more money than they know what to do with. No, the boys still live in Brooklyn, just like their father. Why, it's only three-quarters of an hour or so on the subway. Half a million dollars. My word."

"They're sensible."

"Indeed they are."

I slipped the necklace back into my pocket and tossed the wet tissue into Molly's wastebasket.

"Molly, were you here the day Harry got hit by the bicycle?"

"I'm always here, Rachel. Well, most always. But I didn't see the accident, if that's what you're asking."

"I was wondering something else. I was wondering who else might have been around during the day, you know, before the accident."

"The boys were both in. In fact, the others were here, too, come to think of it."

"Which others?"

"Marilyn's sister, Mrs. Poole, and her son and daughter. They'd come to see Mr. Dietrich about something."

"Did you overhear any of what they were talking about?"

"Oh, I don't go around repeating—"

"I wouldn't tell a soul," I whispered.

"I mind my own business," she said, drawing her robe tighter. "I wouldn't know what they were yelling about."

"They were yelling?"

Molly leaned closer and lowered her voice.

"Both times it was coming from Mr. Dietrich's office."

"Go on."

"Well, the first time was after lunch. Charlotte had brought her gloves and earmuffs down with her. She was just dying for a little walk. It cheers her so. So I'd gone to tell Venus that I was taking her out. She asked us to do that, to always let her know when we were leaving the building with one of the kids. But when I knocked, she wasn't there. It was Mrs. Poole's voice I heard that time, from all the way down the other end of the lobby."

"And what did she say?"

"She didn't *say* anything. She was shouting. All I heard was, 'Well, she was *my* sister. I'm sure she meant—' "

She stopped in midsentence.

"That's all?"

"Mr. Dietrich interrupted her."

"How?"

"By bellowing, 'How would *you* know what she intended?' "

"And then?"

"Well, that was all. You certainly don't think I stayed around to hear more?"

I shook my head.

"Of course not. Anyways, nothing else was said for a while."

I looked at her.

"I was merely making sure the child's earmuffs were on properly. If they don't cover her ears, they can't do her a bit of good, can they?"

"And there was another time that day? Was that also Mrs. Poole?"

"I'd gone to fetch David away from the front door. And again there was shouting coming from Mr. Dietrich's office. It's not like I was trying to hear what they were saying. It's just that—"

"What?"

"Well, he was so loud. You couldn't help hearing him. It even made David more tense. It was lucky I'd come to take him upstairs before dinner."

"Who? Who was so loud?

"Mr. Dietrich. And he was normally so soft-spoken, that one. He hardly ever raised his voice."

"What did you hear that time?"

"Well, on the way to get David, I heard him say, 'It's out of the question.' It sounded like something fell when he said it."

"Could he have hit the desk with his fist?" I asked, thinking about the thick carpet in Harry's office, which would deaden the sound of something falling.

"Yes—it could have been that."

"Was that all you heard?"

Molly shook her head. "When I was passing the office with the lad, I heard him shout again. 'Not even when hell freezes over and gets as cold as your calculating little heart,' is what he said that time."

"And who was in there?"

"I don't know, Rachel. I didn't stay around to find out. I wanted to get David away from the shouting as fast as I could. I took the elevator, so I never heard another word. His loss must be even more painful for them."

"For whom?"

"Why, for the two he fought with on the last day of his life. They'll never get the chance to make up."

"Are you sure it was two different people, Molly? Couldn't Mr. Dietrich have been fighting with Mrs. Poole again, or still, the second time?"

"Oh, they'd gone by then, those three."

"You saw them leave?"

"Couldn't help it. When I was coming back in with Charlotte, she nearly knocked the two of us over, rushing out the front door with those two spoiled brats of hers. And not a word of apology from herself, not to me and not to Charlotte neither."

"And you didn't see anyone come out of Harry's office the second time you heard the shouting?"

"No," she said. "I was up with David."

I stood up to go. "Thanks for last night, Molly. You were right. That was no time to be walking around outside."

But Molly wasn't listening to me.

"It could have been anyone," she said. "He might have even been on the phone, for all I know." She reached up and wiped her eyes. "It was the last I heard of him," she said, tears running down her old face. "An hour later, there was that terrible accident, and he was gone and now I canna' take back the awful thing *I* said to him."

"What awful thing?"

She flapped her hand at me.

"You'll feel better if you tell someone."

"It was about the phones, Rachel. He put in some sort of device, he told me, that would track the outgoing calls."

"*Harry* did that? Why?"

"Cheapness," she shouted. "He said I had free room and board and plenty of money besides, and he wasn't going to have me calling my relatives in Ireland on his nickel. He was obsessed about it, the phone and the electric. You could break your neck walking around in the dark so he could save a penny, running around shutting off lights the way he did."

She pulled up a tissue and blew her nose.

"I was furious, Rachel. The only one left in Ireland is my sister Mary. We haven't spoken in thirty-two years. But it was the principle of the thing." She bit her lip. "I called him an old skinflint, I did, and now—"

"But he *was* an old skinflint," I told her, taking her in my arms.

If Harry had put in the bugs, then whoever killed him didn't know about his marriage and the new will, didn't know they'd done it all for nothing. It wouldn't be until they read the will at his lawyer's office that they would understand the changes that would be instituted because of Harry's death.

"There's one more thing," she said.

I stepped back and looked at her.

"What's that?"

"I didn't see Mr. Dietrich get hit. But I may have seen him just before it happened."

"What makes you think so?"

"Cora and Dora wanted to be near the window. Dora got there herself. Cora wanted me to wheel the chair for her. And I did. I know I baby her too much. Venus always tells me that. But I can't seem to stop myself. Well, when I got her there, I looked out. There he was, Mr. Dietrich, just leaving the building, like this—" She put a hand over her eyes, as if she were saluting. "Perhaps he heard it, the bicycle, and turned around."

"He was headed south, Molly. To Venus's apartment."

"Oh," she said.

"After they married, Harry stayed there."

Her lips were drawn up in a tight little pucker.

"They were husband and wife."

"And here I was thinking he'd heard the bike coming, and when he turned, he had to put up his hand to shade his eyes, so he could see better.

"It would have been better if he had been going the other way. At least then, he wouldn't have seen it coming. When my time comes," she said, crossing herself as she spoke, "I don't want to see a thing."

IS THAT LADY? I ASKED HER

On my way out, I peeked into the garden. Jackson and Charlotte were there, sitting at the same table, both working intensely. I held the door open for Dashiell and let him lead the way.

It's awkward figuring out what to say when you don't expect a response. Working with Emily once, I thought I could sing a song, tell her my troubles, or read from the telephone book for all the good any of it would do me.

But every once in a while, she seemed to understand what I was saying. She'd follow some simple instructions or respond appropriately to what I had asked, her actions, not her words, serving as her answer. When I'd asked if she'd hug me good-bye, and to my astonishment, she did, it filled me with the belief that just because I couldn't understand someone, that didn't mean that nothing was going on there.

Just as the nurse had told me about Venus.

And just as I'd always felt about dogs, that there is far more consciousness, interpretation, and decision making going on there than most humans assume.

Jackson was doing what Jackson did, dipping his fingers in the green paint, then moving his hands in slow, graceful, swirly patterns over the paper. As I watched from the doorway, I saw that when he finished with the green, he waited for it to dry. While it did, he dipped his fingers into a cup of water and wiped them carefully on a paper towel, as if he were cleaning his brush between colors.

Charlotte wasn't sharing materials with Jackson. She was using colored pencils, which she kept close to her and absolutely square with the tabletop. Still, I'd never seen either of them sit near each other, or anyone else for that matter. Had experiencing the trauma of seeing Venus get hit made them bond in their own inscrutable way?

I walked closer and took the seat next to Jackson. Neither of them looked up. Jackson's paper had swirls of green on it, the color of the leaves in the garden right after it rained. Now he dipped his fingers in a second color, a bright red, the color of a kid's wagon, or oxygenated blood. The green had dripped freely, running off his fingers in thin streams. He must have watered it down to speed it up. But the red paint was as thick as pudding, dropping rather than dripping off his fingers, forming clumps and thick lines across the page, pooling in one place where he held his hand still instead of moving it.

I looked across at Charlotte's pad, her head bent so low it was inches from the paper, making it difficult for me to see what she was drawing.

I reached my hand across the table, but not so far that I'd be touching hers.

"That looks pretty," I said. "May I see it?"

Charlotte's pencil kept moving in a way that made me think

she was coloring something in, leaving dense color in one small space. And she was. A moment later, she lifted her head, giving all her concentration to resharpening her pencil. It, too, was red. For a few seconds, like Charlotte, I gave all my attention to the curls of wood coming out of the side of the sharpener, light brown with a red rim, one long piece, reminding me of the way my mother peeled an apple. I used to think it was magic, the way the curling skin got longer and longer as the flesh of the apple was revealed, naked and pale, in the palm of her hand. Then she'd quarter it and hand me a piece, but it was that curl I always wanted, the part I didn't understand.

I pulled Charlotte's pad closer and turned it around. When I saw what she had drawn, I felt my breath catch up in my throat. This time it was a picture of a puli standing over an uneven circle of red, colored so densely and for so long that the artist had lost the point on her pencil.

Pretty indeed.

"Is that Lady?" I asked her.

I heard the sound before Charlotte began to move, a deep moan, loud enough to startle me. But it didn't seem to upset Jackson. Jackson, hell, he'd heard it all and worse. He just kept dipping and dripping as Charlotte balled her hands into fists and began to pound her chest, the sound she made, a sound of grief, getting louder all the time.

I looked around for Dashiell, thinking maybe he could help. But he wasn't near the table. Then I saw him. He was at the far end of the yard, where Jackson had buried the bookend. He wasn't digging though. He was standing there wagging his tail in a way that meant he wanted permission to dig, permission he knew would be difficult, if not impossible, to come by.

I whistled him over, moving around the table to where Charlotte sat. Going against what I'd always been told, I put my arms around Charlotte and pulled her close, but this time, it didn't work. She pulled away and, her back to me, kept punching herself in the chest.

When Dashiell came, he laid his head on her lap as if he were dropping a sack of potatoes that had suddenly become too heavy to hold. He sighed, too, the sound of the Hindenburg losing air. This was a dog who did nothing in a small way.

In a moment Charlotte stopped hitting herself. Her arms stayed bent, as if she were about to punch Dashiell, her hands clenched tight. Then the moaning stopped, but she didn't reach out for Dashiell. Nor did she go back to her drawing, even when I put the pad back the right way, just as she had had it.

Sitting quietly next to her, I looked back at her drawing, the black lines going every which way, the puli's cords not orderly like the cords of a show dog but snarled up against each other and sticking out in all directions.

Except one.

One was way too long. It hung down to the ground, then snaked along to the right of the dog.

Of course. It wasn't a cord. It was a leash.

And just like that, I knew what had happened to Lady.

⊰ 31 ⊱

I GOT SOMETHING FOR YOU, KID

s soon as Charlotte had calmed down, I called to Dash and went back inside, heading for Venus's office. I unlocked the door, let him in, then closed the door behind us, merely turning around to see what I was after. But it was gone. Instead, there was a piece of the door exposed where it had been, smack in the middle of all the other art Venus had taped there, the way proud mothers put their kids' pictures up on the refrigerator.

I looked down. It had fallen off before. Nothing.

But I wasn't ready to give up. I looked on Venus's desk. Homer had put fresh flowers there. There was another vase with greens on the top of the storage cabinet beneath the book shelves. But the drawing I was after wasn't there.

Then I saw it. It was on top of one of the file cabinets in a wire basket, lying on top of whatever Venus had put there to deal with later. It had probably fallen off again, and Homer, too harried to tape it back on the door, or planning to do it later, had dropped it there so that it wouldn't get stepped on.

I picked it up and looked at that funny ground line. Only that's not what it was. It was a leash. And had I been able to see all the way to the other end, I would have seen Lady. But, of course, I didn't, because there was another funny-looking line in the picture. This one came down on the right side of the drawing. It was part of the doorway, and Lady was already outside—not in the garden where she usually went, off leash, but out on West Street, headed for God knows where.

At least now I knew who to ask: the man in the portrait, Samuel Kagan, listening to his music as he stole the dog who had stolen the hearts of all the kids and most of the staff.

I checked my watch. He'd be here after lunch. In fact, I was due here then, too, for a second round of ring-around-the-rosy, with me and Dashiell in the lead. I had a couple of hours, and more than enough to do to fill them.

On the way home, we cut across on Greenwich Street to Tenth, stopped at Action Pharmacy for shampoo and toothpaste— if I remembered correctly, I was running low—and crossed Hudson, heading past the Blind Tiger Ale House toward home.

I fed Dashiell, took my purchase upstairs, and while the tub was filling, put Venus's necklace in the top desk drawer for safe-keeping and then checked my answering machine. There were four messages.

The first was from Nathan, telling me that the staff meeting had been canceled.

The second was from Marty Shapiro, telling me to drop in and see him when I had a free minute.

The third was from my sister. It didn't say much of anything. Typical, I thought. She was acting like a smitten teen. I wondered how long that would last.

The last call was from Chip. I erased the first three and saved that one, playing it again as I got dressed just to hear his voice.

I made some phone calls, took some notes, then stopped at the Sixth on my way back to Harbor View. When I opened the door to the bomb squad, Marty got up and joined me in the hall rather than asking me in.

"I got something for you, kid," he said.

"Really? Great. What is it?"

"It's about the bike."

"Yeah?"

"We found it."

"No kidding? How?"

"Perspicacious detective work. You impressed?"

"You bet. Both with the fancy footwork and your astonishing use of the English language."

"I thought you would be."

I was ready to punch him.

"So?"

"Here's the thing. The driver of said vehicle doesn't have an astonishing use of the language. In fact, he probably only has enough use of it to make change."

"No joke."

"Which means—"

I bit my tongue.

"That someone borrowed said murder weapon whilst a hungry family was paying for their egg foo yung."

"Brilliant. But does that mean you can't tie the thief to the bike, because of all the time that elapsed and the number of people using it?"

"The lab is still trying, but the bike was out on the street all this time, including in the rain."

"Still, it's remarkable—"

"Footwork."

"This is true."

"You come up with anything on your end?"

"I might know who took the dog."

"It figures," he said. "So, hey, you'll be sure to keep us posted on that, kid, right? The captain, he's dying to know what happened to the dog. It's way up there on his list of concerns."

"I promise I'll call," I told him. "Or even better, I'll drop in. As soon as it's confirmed."

I still had at least an hour. I didn't want to waste a minute of it. I walked down to Hudson Street and hailed a cab, telling the driver to take us to St. Vincent's and not spare the horses, falling against Dashiell when, a few blocks later, he made a right on Twelfth Street, taking me at my word.

THEY SAY IT'S GOOD LUCK, HE SAID

illy was first behind Dashiell and me, carrying the pillow from his bed. Charlotte was wearing her earmuffs, but not the red gloves. She had a piece of paper that might have been from her drawing pad crunched up in one hand. Cora and Dora were off to the side, sort of clapping to the music. And half a dozen other people were circling around, waiting for Dashiell to drop so that they could fling themselves to the floor, too.

Jackson, in the middle, had his arms stretched high, his red fingers wiggling like leaves of a Japanese maple blowing in the wind. Fortunately, Dashiell didn't see him as a tree. He kept his cool and kept his mind on the game. Mouth open, tongue lolling out, concentrating on the words so that he wouldn't miss his cue, he ambled slowly in a large circle, his tail wagging, his new friends trailing after him, as best they could.

He was a dog. It was all the same to him; cross-eyed, mute, lame, forgetful. He loved them all. When he got the word, he crashed loudly to the floor. Cora dropped her head as if she were praying. Dora covered her eyes. Willy, clever thing, placed his pillow carefully on the floor in front of him and lay down. Charlotte lay on her back. Staring at the ceiling, or at nothing, she smoothed out the drawing and let it rest on her chest as if it were protective armor. Who knows? Maybe it was. Jackson reached for the sky, and I noticed that the paint had dripped down his arms since I'd last looked. My friend Jackson was having a bad day.

After two rounds of Dashiell's new game, he and I sat off to the side, and Cora and Dora joined the group. Samuel pulled the chairs in a circle for everyone else and started tossing a big, light ball from person to person, trying to get them to catch it and toss it back in time to the music he was playing.

Pretty ambitious, I thought, watching the ball hit Willy's shoulder and land on the floor.

Dashiell and I had gotten to the ICU without a glitch. We looked familiar now. No one questioned where we were going. But when we walked in, I saw that the curtain around Venus's bed was open, the bed stripped. Suddenly my mouth tasted sour, and the room seemed to be moving on its own.

"She's awake."

I'd turned to see Nurse Frostee standing right behind me.

"Down this hall, third door on your left. Pinch your cheeks first, woman, you're as white as he is."

She bent and scratched Dashiell's head.

"Therapy dog," she'd said. "There's days I could use some of that myself, that and a good hot soak for my feet."

So I took a few breaths and headed for Venus's room, to see what she could remember.

"Two of them were sitting along the wall opposite the desk," Venus had said, propped up in bed, her hair so black against the smooth white hospital sheets. "I'd just turned around to get Jackson a paper towel. David was standing at the window, looking up at the light coming in through the leaves of the tree out there."

"What about Jackson? Could he have—"

"No."

She stared right at me, defying me to accuse Jackson, to point the finger at any of her kids.

"Not Jackson. And not David either?"

"Rachel, David didn't hit me. I was looking right at him."

"Did you hear the door open?"

"No. I had the radio on for them and the air conditioner going."

"But the door was locked?"

"I'm not sure. Sometimes when the kids are in with me, I unlock it. They have trouble opening it when it's locked. But I can't say for sure."

"When did they move you?" I asked. She had a room to herself now, a window with a view of Eleventh Street.

"This morning."

"That's great," I said. "I'm so happy to see you're doing better."

Dashiell's tail thumped against the floor.

I wanted to say something about Lady, but I didn't. I decided to wait until I knew more—specifically, where she was now.

If she was, now.

"I have your necklace safely at home," I told her, holding her hand, reluctant to leave.

She reached up and touched her neck.

"I guess it got twisted or something when you fell." I didn't think this was the time to tell her how I'd found it. "I have to go. Dashiell's up for a heavy round of ring-around-the-rosy."

She smiled.

"I'll be back later."

I turned to go, then turned around again.

"Venus, did the hospital inform Eli that you're awake now?"

"The doctor said he was going to call right after his rounds, share the good news."

I nodded. And on the way back to Harbor View, I'd called my old boss, Frank Petrie, to send someone over to sit with Venus, just in case whoever hit her was dissatisfied with the outcome of their efforts.

Samuel was still tossing the ball. This time it landed on Cora's lap and, through no effort on her part, stayed there.

"Good job," he told her, waiting in vain for her to toss it back.

Anyone else would have looked over at me and shrugged, giving it the old one-two, but having a little humor about how it wasn't proceeding. Not Samuel. He kept at it, giving it everything he had, as if midway through the class some miracle might occur, and Willy and Charlotte and Jackson would be lobbing the ball back to him like pros, trying out for the Knicks or the Yankees in a week or two.

When the class was over, he carefully put the chairs back, settling Willy in front of a toddler's puzzle, whispering something to Cora, then Dora, watching as Charlotte returned to where she'd been sitting, her pad, colored pencils, and sharpener where she'd left them.

I got up and followed him out into the empty lobby.

"Dashiell's game went well," he said, disappointed that the ball playing had been a bust. "Not everything works out, but I always try. Dad says that in some places people are just warehoused, fed and clothed, but not stimulated at all."

I didn't respond. Something else had gotten my attention. It was Dashiell, vacuuming Samuel's pants, then moving his attention to the shoes, leaving little wet marks where his nose and lips were pressed to the leather, reading the news.

"I guess someone forgot to scoop," I said.

"What?"

I pointed to his shoes.

"Dog poop. You must have stepped in some."

I looked up, and so did he.

"They say it's good luck," he said, smiling his crushed little smile.

"Not in your case it isn't."

"What do you mean?"

"I mean, we're going for a little cab ride, you and me. And Dashiell."

"What are you talking about?"

"We're going to Brooklyn, Samuel, let Dashiell get the smell he discovered on your pants firsthand."

He stepped back and looked around to see if anyone else was there. I reached for his arm and pulled him back to where he was.

"Listen carefully," I told him. "We're leaving here now. We're going to your apartment to get Lady, bring her back where she belongs."

"I don't know what you're—"

He tried to pull off looking indignant, but I wasn't impressed.

"And on the way," I said, "you're going to tell me why you killed your uncle Harry and tried to kill my friend Venus."

DID IT WORK? I ASKED

re you crazy? I didn't kill anyone. I didn't hurt Venus. David did. I'm not going anywhere with you."

"That's fine. You don't have to."

I pulled out my cell phone.

"Who are you calling?"

His shirt was soaked with sweat, a lot more than he'd worked up in class.

"The Sixth Precinct," I said. Dead calm. "Of course, I know you. We have a relationship. I know that whatever you did, you had your reasons. Or maybe something happened and things got out of hand, you couldn't help yourself. I can understand that, Samuel. I care about what you feel. But the cops"— I shrugged my shoulders—"hey, they have different pressures than I do. They just want to find someone to hang this on. They just want to close the case, be done with it. Why? Why doesn't factor into it. Why gets you no sympathy there. Why only counts right here, Samuel, so make up your mind who you want to talk to. And don't take too long, because if the answer is no, you don't want to talk to me, then I have this call to make. And afterward I'm going to walk across the lobby and knock on Daddy's door, have a few words with him, see what he thinks about all this."

"No—don't do that. *Please* don't do that. He'll believe you. He'll think I did it, all of it, everything. And more. Whenever there's a fuckup, he always thinks it's me."

Harry's death, a fuckup?

"You've got to help me, Rachel. You like me, don't you?"

I waited, eyes hard, enough adrenaline pumping to pick him up like the sack of garbage I thought he was and toss him out into oncoming traffic, the asshole.

"I have her," he whispered. "Lady. But I didn't touch Harry or Venus. I swear to you."

He waited.

I let him.

"Can't you say you found her at the shelter? She could have gotten out, got picked up. It's possible. He'd believe *you*. Couldn't you say that?"

"Only if you tell me the truth."

"I *am*. This *is* the truth."

"Excellent. In that case, let's go get Lady."

Slipping the phone back into my pocket, I indicated the front door with a tilt of my head and followed Samuel out.

"You'll see, I took good care of her. I never hurt her. I only wanted—"

"Let's *move*," I told him. "I don't want to hit rush hour, and we have to drop Dashiell off first. We'll never get a cab with a dog this big. Did you take Lady to Brooklyn in a cab, Samuel, the night you walked out with her?"

He wasn't looking at me. He was looking at his shoes, maybe at the spot where Dashiell had pressed his nose, the moisture in his breath condensing, leaving a dull spot when it dried.

"I didn't have enough money with me. I took the subway. Nobody said anything. Anyway, she's a therapy dog, so she's allowed."

"Going to and from a gig, Samuel. Not being stolen. When you steal a dog, you're supposed to use a car. Or at the very least, a taxi."

We headed over to Washington Street, toward the sound of construction, then kept going east, toward Hudson Street.

He could have slipped out after his daytime class, taken the bike, killed Harry, come back for his evening singsong, Mr. Innocence, Mr. Helpful. I wondered if he'd cried when he heard the news.

And wasn't he the one who'd found Venus? *Found* Venus. Right.

Blaming David. Or had that been Nathan's idea? Was it his brother he'd been protecting all along?

"Okay," I said, "I'm ready for the sad story of your life."

He took out a handkerchief that looked as if it had been out too many times already and wiped his dripping face. It was hotter than Hades. Maybe he ought to get used to it, I thought, because as far as I could tell, that was where he was headed.

"Lady," I prompted. "Start with Lady."

"I told you, she's *fine.*"

Petulant. Not looking at me.

"Why did you take her, Samuel?"

"It wasn't fair."

Four years old.

"Tell me about it."

"Everything she did, every stupid little thing, everyone k'velled about it. Dad and Harry and Venus, even Molly, they kept saying she was the best thing that had ever happened at Harbor View. *She* was the best, a life saver. Not a word about me, about everything *I* did there, day after bloody day for coolie wages. I thought that if she weren't there, maybe Dad would see—"

And then he began to cry, great oceans of water running from his eyes and monsoons of mucus leaking from his nose. He drooled a little, too. It wasn't a pretty sight, a grown man bawling like that in the street because he was jealous of a little dog.

I put my arm around his shoulders, feeling how wet and hairy he was underneath his shirt. I could think of about seven thousand things I'd rather be touching. But none of them would pay the rent. Or get Lady back to Harbor View.

"I took good care of her. I meant to bring her back. After. After Dad appreciated *me* for once."

"Did it work?" I asked. Like a courtroom lawyer, I knew the answer before he responded.

"What do you think?"

Sullen now.

"I think it didn't, Samuel. I think your father and Harry and Venus were too wrapped up in what was helping the kids to think about your feelings. But everyone needs a little appreciation. It's only human."

"Do you really think so?" he asked.

Jesus.

"I do," I told him.

"That's all I did," he said, his voice nearly inaudible. Then he looked at me for the first time since we'd left Harbor View. "I'm ashamed of what I did. I truly am. But I didn't hurt her. I took good care of her. And I meant to return her. I really did. I only wanted—"

"Of course you did. Anyone would."

"But I never hurt Uncle Harry. Why would I?"

"Wasn't he the one paying you those coolie wages?"

I watched his face.

"Wasn't that a pretty big slap in the face, working so hard for so little money? It's not like the old bastard didn't have it. He was loaded. What was he planning on doing, taking it with him?"

"No, no, it wasn't like that. I didn't do that. He's always been—"

"What, Samuel? What's he always been? Arrogant? Cheap? Unappreciative? It was always about his sister, never about you. What, he felt guilty he was normal and she wasn't, he had a life and she didn't? It made him hard, didn't it? Hard-hearted toward *you*, not loving, supportive, appreciative. *Uncle* Harry, my ass. Why, the man should have been treating you like family. Instead, he treated you like a servant. How many years were you supposed to take it? Forever? Who *wouldn't* have wanted to kill the cheap son of a bitch?"

"Is that what people will think, just because I took the dog?"

When we got to the corner, I yanked on his arm. "Hurry up. We can make the light."

We stayed on the north side of Tenth Street. He didn't see the precinct until we were almost on top of it.

"You said—"

"I lied," I told him.

The door opened, and a uniform came out. Samuel waited until he'd walked up the block, toward Bleecker Street, so much equipment hanging off his pants it was a wonder they didn't fall down.

"But they'll think I killed Harry. They'll think—"

"They'll think you stole a bike from one of the Chinese delivery men taking a nap in the Westbeth courtyard and rode it full tilt into *Uncle* Harry. Were you trying to kill him, Sammy, or just trying to get his attention?"

Samuel's mouth hung open. Any moment now, and he'd start drooling again.

"What was the fight about that afternoon, you and Harry screaming at each other? Did you ask for a raise, more compensation for your little classes? Is that what it was? Well, you showed *him*, didn't you? Pretty soon, everyone will know what you're made of, what a big man you are. No one's going to ignore you now, will they?"

But he didn't answer me. He just stood there, blinking, as if the sun was more than his eyes could bear.

"And that wasn't enough for you, was it? You had to try to kill Venus, too, clobber her with a bookend, make a hole in her head. Well, she's awake now, Samuel. And she's talking. The charade is over."

"But—"

"Give me your keys," I said, holding out my hand.

"What?"

"Your keys. What do you want me to do, leave Lady at your house without food and water and someone to walk her while you rot in jail?"

"I thought you were going to help me," he said, his face as wet and crushed as a used tissue. It was about as appealing, too.

"I thought you *liked* me," he whined.

"Keys," I said.

He mustered an ounce of backbone. I could see it coming, right between the panic and the rage.

"I don't have to listen to you. Who the hell are you to tell me what to do?"

"You might want to think that over."

"Why? Why should I?"

"Watch him," I said.

Not getting it, he turned around. There was no one behind him, just the closed door to the precinct.

When he turned back toward me, he still didn't get it. I pointed to my dog. He was facing Samuel, looking alert.

Okay, not alert. Menacing.

"Keys," I repeated.

Samuel looked like a balloon with a leak. He reached into his pocket and handed me his keys.

We went inside. After explaining my visit to the desk sergeant, I waited while he called upstairs. In no time at all, two detectives came down, thick-necked guys with *Try me, asshole* expressions.

I walked off to the side with one of them—Matthew Agoudian, young guy with a big nose, dark eyes, good listening skills—told him what I knew, then stood there until they'd walked Samuel to the stairs, listening to him protesting his innocence, first to one detective, then the other. Bet they never heard that before.

Back outside, I ran across the street, got some cash from where it was cleverly secreted in my top desk drawer under my checkbook, then headed toward Bleecker Street to catch a cab.

VENUS TOOK MY HAND

Hispanic woman who looked as if she ate gravel for breakfast was sitting outside the door to Venus's room. She stood when I approached, her arm across the closed door. I showed her my ID.

"Lourdes Rivera," she said. "I heard a lot of good stuff about you from Frank."

"From Frank? Really?"

"I know what you're saying," she told me. "He never told you to your face how good a job you did, am I right? But he tells everyone else, any chance he gets, 'I had this girl Rachel working for me, walked in off the street, took to it like a golden retriever to water, college grad, too, but okay, you know what I mean? I'd be happy if you was half as good an operative as she was.' He's a piece of work, that Frank."

She was short and thick, big shoulders, muscular legs, a gold tooth right in front, shined at you when she smiled, and a shoulder holster with a gun, her jacket open so you could see it, stop any thoughts of messing around before they got started.

"Go on in, Rachel. She'll be happy to see you."

"Thanks. Glad you're here."

"Hey, no problem."

I opened the door, and Venus grinned when she saw me. Then she winced.

"I feel sooo protected," she said.

"Would have been nice *before* you got a hole in your head."

I stood in the doorway, both dogs behind me.

"I'm going to be okay, Rachel. I'm on the mend."

"I know. I stopped at the nurses' station. The head nurse told me. She wasn't going to, but I told her we were sisters."

"We are."

"Don't go all soft and mushy on me, girl. Keep your edge. You're going to need it."

She nodded, then frowned. "That still hurts."

"Nodding?"

"Moving. Blinking. Smiling. Talking. But I am getting better."

"I have a surprise for you. Might speed up the recovery process."

I stepped aside and patted my left thigh. The dogs got up from their sit-stays and lunged forward.

"Whoa," I said, as if they were horses.

Venus squealed, and her hands shot up to her mouth.

"Lady," she whispered, her eyes filling with tears.

I touched the bed, and both dogs landed on it, one on either side of Venus.

"Don't you even want to know how I got *two* dogs up to your room?"

"No. I want to know where you found her."

A nurse who looked like Olive Oyl walked in with some pills—one red, two yellow, party time—in the tiniest cup I'd ever seen.

"Don't tire her out," she told me, bobbing her funny-looking head on her long, skinny neck. Then, "Oh, a matching dog. Is he her father?" she asked, pointing to Dashiell.

I told her yes, watching Venus's smile light up the room.

She filled Venus's plastic glass with water and waited until she had swallowed all the pills, closing the door on her way out.

Venus had one hand on Dashiell's head, the other around Lady, her face buried in the dog's dreadlocks, impossible to see where one ended, the other began. Except for the bandage.

"Where was she?"

"Samuel had her."

"Samuel?"

I nodded.

"He was the one who 'found' you, Venus, after you were hit."

She reached up and touched the bandage.

"Are you saying he killed Harry?"

"It seems so. I dropped him off at the precinct. The detectives are questioning him now."

She pulled Lady a little closer.

"Why?"

"Why is the hardest part of the work I do, Venus, because you and I wouldn't take the road Samuel took, even if we had identical reasons. Someone convinces himself that killing another human being is okay, how can we expect to understand the why?"

"I'd still like to know. Even if I won't understand. The man killed my husband, tried to kill me. I have a right to know what he was thinking, what he was after."

"Yes, you do. He says he took Lady because she was getting all the attention, all the appreciation."

"Oh, good grief."

"He said he was working really hard and that he was devoted to the kids and Harbor View, as devoted as anyone, but no one noticed, no one gave him the atta-boys he needed. He thought if Lady weren't around, maybe he'd be noticed. Maybe Eli would notice him. He said he planned to bring her back. Maybe he thought he'd do that, be a big hero. I don't know. And he claims he took good care of her, which apparently he did. She's fine. But whether or not he would have returned her to Harbor View"—I shrugged—"we'll never know for sure."

"And Harry?"

"He called him *Uncle* Harry. I guess he expected more from him, maybe an unreasonable amount more, affection, praise, money, respect, all the things he craves and doesn't feel he gets."

"So he *killed* him?"

I nodded.

"I told you we can't understand this. It's crazy, doing what he did. Someone else would have gotten a job elsewhere, found a niche of his own. But Samuel has spent his life beating his head against the wall, trying to get love out of a stone."

"I sure wouldn't want Eli for a daddy. All his energy goes into Harbor View. None of it goes into his own kids. Never did, as far as I can tell. Even with the residents, he's thoughtful, intelligent, willing to experiment with new things, but there's no connection."

"What do you mean?"

"He's a suit. He's formal. He's cold. He never touches anyone." She bent her face to Lady again. When she picked it up, there were more tears. "Lots of people have inadequate parents, Rachel. They don't all go out and murder."

"If he focused his childish needs and expectations on Harry—"

"Because he couldn't get what he needed from Eli—"

"Then, in a perverse way, it makes sense. Look, Venus, once someone walks away from what's considered normal, the pattern of their thinking changes. Sometimes they believe they are forced to do the horrible things they do, that the victim asked for it, or left them no choice, or that they had to teach the victim a lesson."

"A lesson!"

"I know it's bizarre." I shook my head. "My sister used to love to scare me when we were little, and one time she read me this story, maybe it was Poe, I'm not sure, about some guy who got walled up by his father, I think. Because the old man wanted to teach him a lesson. I couldn't get that out of my mind, the insanity of it, because as each brick was put in place, he knew, and I knew, he was going to die there. Some lesson."

"He took Lady to get the positive attention he thought he deserved and that she was getting. And when that didn't work, he killed Harry?"

"Maybe it was the lesser of two evils."

"Meaning?"

"That he couldn't kill the person he was really mad at."

"His father. So Harry was—"

"A stand-in. I told you it wouldn't make sense."

"And me? What was I?"

I reached out and put a hand on Dashiell's back. He looked at me and wagged his tail.

"I wonder if he thought that if all the people who were appreciated at Harbor View were gone, his father would have to notice him," I said.

"That's pathetic."

If it were true, wouldn't this still be the beginning? Who would be next? Molly? Me? Even his brother.

"Thank God he's at the precinct."

I wondered how far he would have gone to get the attention he was after.

The door opened, and Olive Oyl popped her round head in.

"Time to go," she said. "Doctor's coming."

"I'll just say good-bye."

Venus took my hand.

"What about Lady? Is there any special way I should introduce her back to the kids?"

She was quiet a moment. "No matter what you do, there's going to be some confusion. It's the nature of the beast, so to speak. If you go without Dashiell, Jackson will be upset. Dashiell is the dog that moved Jackson."

I thought about the bookend, but I couldn't talk to her about it now. Olive would be back in a minute with Doctor. Anyway, given the circumstances, I guess it could wait.

"Some of them will be puzzled, seeing both dogs, but that's okay. That's the way to go.

"You're not thinking this is wrapped up, are you, Rachel? There's still the problem of the will. We're not out of the woods yet. I still need you. And Lourdes."

I leaned over and kissed her on the cheek. "I don't leave until you tell me to leave."

Out in the hall, I thanked Lourdes and asked her to stay at least two more days. The doctor was down the hall, coming this way. The nurse was trailing two steps behind him, carrying a clipboard. I turned the other way and headed for the stairs.

YOU NEED HIS KEYS? I ASKED

On Twelfth Street, outside St. Vincent's, I began meandering west, toward Harbor View, taking my time so that the dogs could read the news of the neighborhood, post their own messages, be themselves before going back to work.

But as I got closer and closer to the way West Village, I found myself going even more slowly, like Dashiell when he wants to stay out and sees I'm heading home.

So I turned south, toward the cottage. I was feeling funny and wanted to be home, even if it was just for an hour. Maybe I was just hungry. I couldn't remember the last time I had a real meal. So I crossed Hudson Street and stopped at Pepe Verde, getting some pasta and chicken to go, a mixed salad, too, and some of their wonderful bread to go with it.

After unlocking the gate and letting the dogs in first, I picked up the mail, several days' worth, stopped in the garden, and sat on one of the benches, watching the dogs flirt and play. Then, without going inside, I opened the bag of food and started eating my salad with the little plastic fork, feeling how empty I was, and how tired.

What was the rush? Surely tomorrow would be a mess, the Pooles and the Kagans finding out about the new arrangements for Harbor View. No more Venus this and Venus that; she'd be pretty much running things as soon as she got out of the hospital. And the shock of it, that she and Harry had fallen in love and gotten married. That ought to take them some time to get used to.

I didn't know about the Pooles. To hell with them. They had nothing to do with this after tomorrow. But Eli would work it out with Venus, for the sake of the kids. They'd be okay, in time.

Time was all any of them needed, time to adjust to the changes and go on. Time was what I needed, too, I thought, starting the pasta, giving each dog a piece of the chicken, saving a little for myself, feeling so tired I wasn't sure I could make it upstairs to bed.

Why rush over there tonight? I thought, wondering if they knew about Samuel yet. He wouldn't show up for his evening sing-along. So what? They'd wonder where he was and put the kids to bed. If I went over, I'd have to tell them the bad news—where he was, and why. A message like that, mightn't they want to kill the messenger? And who was I kidding? I wasn't merely the messenger. I was the one who'd dropped Samuel off at the precinct, who told them what he'd done and why. No, better to stay home, look at the mail, let Lady spend the night and take her back in the morning, let her settle in with the kids while the Kagans sat in the lawyer's office listening to the news, two of them anyway.

I put the remains of dinner into the outside trashcan and secured the lid. Then I unlocked the door, called in the dogs, and filled two bowls with dry dog food, adding some cottage cheese and yogurt, cleaning and refilling the water bowl. I carried the mail upstairs and took it into my office, dropping it on my desk, opening the top drawer and picking up Venus's necklace, letting the heart spin in the light from the desk lamp.

When the phone rang, both dogs barked. The sound seemed out of place in the quiet house.

"Alexander."

"Rach. It's Marty."

"Hey. How's it going? Any luck with that bicycle yet?"

"Not yet. That thing's been out in the weather for two weeks. Whatever wasn't washed off was rubbed off by other people's hands. Doesn't look too promising, but then again, we shouldn't need it now, should we, now that you solved the case for us."

"How's that?"

"Cute, Rach, cute. Like it slipped your mind, the guy you dropped off here."

"Oh. Him. How's that going?"

"He confessed."

"Hey, great. How'd you get it out of him?"

"The usual—hot lights, rubber hoses, beatings, and of course the stun gun. Agoudian's good at what he does."

"Nothing out of the ordinary?"

"Completely routine, but I tell you, this one's an amateur, a real crybaby. Wet his damn pants before five minutes elapsed. Literally. Anyway, we couldn't have gotten where we are without you, kid."

"Well, it wasn't really *me*. Dashiell got real interested in his pants, so I figured he had the dog, and the rest just fell into place. But it was Agoudian who got him to confess. He only owned up to taking the dog when I had him."

"None of that denial here. He opened his mouth, he didn't shut up until it was all on the table, good stuff, rich with detail."

244 | CAROL LEA BENJAMIN

"That's good. A relief."

"You bet. Always nice when you can close a case. It makes the captain happy. So, you recovered the dog at his place?"

"I did."

"Everything okay on that end?"

"Fine. She's okay. I have her here, Marty. I'm bushed. I thought I'd keep her here tonight, take her back to Harbor View in the morning. That okay?"

"Yeah, Rach. We know where she was. And we know where she'll be. Besides, he wrote it all down and signed it. We got him on video, too."

"You need his keys?" I asked. "I have them here. I can drop them off in the morning. In case someone wants to go out to Brooklyn, get him a dry pair of pants."

"There's nothing in the budget for that, Rach. His old man can get him some clean pants. Or he can get them himself, come tomorrow."

"What do you mean?"

"He confessed, all right. We were running out of fucking videotape. He was ready to take responsibility for World War II by the time we finally shut him up."

I didn't say anything. I had a strong feeling he wasn't finished.

"He started out, it looked pretty good. He had a few of the details down pat, stuff he shouldn't have known, about how the bicycle was obtained, for example."

"I may have inadvertently—"

"But the more into it he got—" I could picture him shaking his head. "He was real wound up, Rach, talking a mile a minute, sweating so much his shirt was as wet as his pants. Agoudian, he can be pretty loud when he has to, he's in his face, asking him how he could have hit the old man with the bike, someone he knew since he was a little kid, and you know what he says? He says, I hit him from behind. I did it so I wouldn't have to see his face. Couldn't have done it the other way, he tells Agoudian, like this makes him sensitive, this makes it okay he killed Dietrich, because he hit him in the back, not the front. What this makes him is not guilty, Rachel. What it makes him is nutty as a fruitcake."

I took a deep breath.

"His father's a shrink," I said.

"Yeah, so it figures, right?"

"Seems to go that way."

"Well, he shouldn't be running around loose, in my opinion."

"But he will be? You're letting him loose?"

"One o'clock. Right after lunch. In case you want to meet him, give him back his keys in person. On the other hand, he might not be too happy to see you, considering. Even after cooling off overnight. Maybe you ought to leave them for him at Harbor View. He might be annoyed with you, bringing an innocent man to the precinct, accusing him of some horrific crimes, only one of which he's guilty of."

"Is that why you're keeping him overnight, to 'cool off?' "

He didn't say anything right away.

Neither did I.

"The guys are pissed about what he did, about the nature of the crime, taking the dog away from those poor souls at Harbor View. The dog disappears, wouldn't they figure any one of them might be next? Must have been a tough time there. So we figured a night of our best hospitality, a couple of our gourmet meals under his belt, he might think twice in the future."

I looked up at the bulletin board, the list of people who'd be disappointed once they read the will, thinking, if not Samuel, then who?

"I'm sorry, Marty. I thought—"

"Hey, the dog's okay, right?"

"Right."

"Then something good came out of this, didn't it?"

"Yeah. Thanks for saying that," I said.

"Don't mention it," he told me.

After I hung up, I'm not sure why, I went to the bathroom, got the tweezers, and, sitting at the desk, holding the necklace under the light, I closed the link on Venus's chain, then slipped it around my neck, fastened the latch, and tucked it under my shirt, the heart that Harry had given Marilyn first and Venus second. I went into the bedroom and crawled under the covers, feeling the bed bounce twice as both dogs joined me a moment later.

But I couldn't sleep. At first, I was thinking about Samuel Kagan, who, when he couldn't get positive attention from his father, had tried for some negative attention, confessing to crimes he didn't commit just so his old man would take some notice of him.

And then I stayed up even longer; whoever had killed Harry and tried to kill Venus was still running around loose. Time was running out, and I didn't have a clue as to who that was.

I TOOK OUT MY CELL PHONE

I decided to take Lady back to Harbor View early, while I still could. With Venus in the hospital, I might not be welcome there once Samuel was released. Unless, of course, he decided to keep mum about the whole incident, saving my face along with his own.

I took the dogs across West Street to give them a good walk along the river, picking at all the loose threads of the case as I headed uptown, Venus's necklace hanging around my neck like a stone, reminding me that I didn't know who tore it off her and why. Nor did I know how David got it, how Jackson got the bookend and why he had buried it, nor what those arguments were about on the last day of Harry's life. I was about to make the list of what I didn't know longer than the Saint Patrick's Day parade when I saw something that momentarily stopped my ruminating.

Someone skating toward me was waving. Since I didn't recognize him, I turned around. There behind me was someone saluting. A second later, I began to laugh at the absurdity of what I thought. The person was waving back, his hand passing in and out of the position it would be in were he shading his eyes from the sun. Only he was facing north.

Harry had been facing south. He could have been shading his eyes. He also could have been waving at his killer. Why not? Wasn't it someone he knew? And then, as the bike got closer, with no signs of slowing down, his hand probably froze, so that someone glancing out the window could think he was saluting. Or shading his eyes.

How easy it is to misinterpret what we see.

The skaters met and now both headed north. I followed behind them, stopping to let the dogs sniff and explore or stop and play-bow to each other, untwisting the leashes as the dogs continually changed places, the dog on the left having to see what was on the right side, the dog on the right needing to check out the left.

Instead of crossing the highway at Eleventh Street, the most direct route to Harbor View, I kept going. I wasn't in any rush. Samuel wasn't getting sprung for hours, and everyone else would probably be at the lawyer's office, trying to figure out what might be involved in overturning Harry's will, the lawyer shaking his head, telling them the rest of the bad news, that the will was airtight because Harry could leave whatever he wanted to his wife.

When I got to Twelfth Street, across from Harbor View, everything changed again. Now I had something else to think about, seeing how lonely the old seaman's hotel looked, the only occupied building on the block. In fact, in no time, it would be the only building standing on the block. That very morning, while I was taking a shower and feeding the dogs, a temporary wooden barrier had been set up around the aqua bar, and the wreckers were there, taking it down.

I looked at Lady, who looked back at me, one eye showing, the other hidden by her dreadlocks, her mouth open, her small pink tongue out, her head cocked, as if to ask me what I wanted.

Maybe her disappearance wasn't how it all began.

Since I didn't have a pen and paper with me, I took out my cell phone and called home, waiting for the answering machine to pick up, then reading into the mouthpiece the information from the sign on the wooden barrier, including the phone number. Instead of taking Lady back to Harbor View, I moved as fast as I could, first going back to the hospital to talk to Venus, then heading back to Tenth Street, to my office, to do some very important research, some by phone, some on-line, watching the clock to make sure I didn't miss Samuel coming out of the precinct, taking a deep breath of fresh air, thinking free at last, free at last, then heading over to Harbor View for some much-needed spin control.

37

IT'S ALL A TERRIBLE MISTAKE

t ten to one, despite the heat, I slipped on a jacket, loaded my pockets, leashed the dogs, and walked across the street. When he came out, I was waiting.

"What do *you* want?"

"I came to give you back your keys," I told him. "And to thank you."

"To thank me?"

"For taking such good care of Lady. Just like you said, she's fine."

He reached out a hand.

I didn't reach into my pocket for his keys.

"Here," I said, handing him the loop of Lady's leash. "I was just going to take her back to Harbor View. Maybe you should do that. It would look better."

"You didn't tell them?"

"Uh-uh."

He took the leash, ignoring the dog at the other end.

"Look, I lied to you."

He nodded.

"And you lied to me."

This time he looked past me, down toward Hudson Street, where I hoped we'd be headed soon.

"And you lied to the police."

"How do you—"

"I know what you're after, Samuel."

Two lines appeared between his eyes.

"Why don't we wipe the slate clean and start again? I promise you, you'll get your father's attention this time."

"How?" Sounding like a little kid again.

"By having found Lady. You can tell him what you wanted me to tell him, that you located her at the shelter, that she must have gotten out, but you never gave up, you kept calling and calling, and finally she showed up there and you went to get her. That would explain your absence last night, wouldn't it?"

"It would."

I reached into my pocket for his keys, handing them over to him.

"By the way, what time was the meeting with Harry's lawyer?"

"How do you know about that?"

"Oh, last night, Nathan said they'd all be gone in the morning, something about Harry's will, that the lawyer didn't want to mail copies to the heirs, he wanted to discuss it with them."

Samuel frowned.

"Only he didn't say what time it would be."

"Eleven."

"Good. Then they should be back by now. You can surprise them with Lady. I'd like to go with you, Samuel, to see the expression on your father's face." I smiled and took a step toward

Hudson Street. "Come on. We don't have a moment to lose."

For a moment, I thought Samuel was glued to the spot, a warning to all who pass the precinct about how alleged felons are treated inside by the cops. He looked, and smelled, like hell. But he seemed to have forgotten all of that. He, too, was anxious to see the expression on Eli's face when he showed up with Lady, when his father would see, once and for all, how capable his older son was.

We had nothing to say to each other on the way. He was thinking his thoughts, I my own. When we got to the corner of West and Twelfth, Samuel turned to look at the demolition site, the roof of the bar history by now.

After a moment, he looked back at me. He seemed to be smirking, but then he moved so quickly, I couldn't be sure. He was speed-walking toward Harbor View, tugging hard on Lady's leash when she stopped to sniff the old neighborhood, to reassure herself that she indeed was nearly home.

I could hear them as soon as I unlocked the door, loud voices coming from the dining room. I hoped the kids had finished lunch and were elsewhere. The shouting would surely upset them.

"Why are we sitting here with this god-awful slop congealing in front of us if we're finished here?" I heard Bailey say.

"It can't be legal," his mother told him. Told everyone. "How can it be legal, that woman running this place?"

"She did it for the money," Janice said.

Samuel walked into the lobby first. I let the door close quietly, looking to my right and seeing David in his spot, his fingers tapping rapidly against each other, his jaw clenched.

"I know you're angry and disappointed," Eli told them, "but what you're saying isn't so. Harry didn't leave her any money, not a dime."

I reached for Samuel's arm. When he turned to question me, I put my finger up to my lips. "Wait until they're finished so you and Lady can make a grand entrance," I whispered.

He frowned, but stopped.

Marty was right. He was as nutty as a fruitcake.

"Really. How about half the estate?" Janice said.

"New York State is not a community property state. Dad's right. She doesn't get a dime. The money is all in trust for Harbor View."

"Well, what about my sister's personal things, her jewelry, for example?" Arlene asked, her voice even louder than it had been before. "Why wasn't that mentioned in the will. It was supposed—"

"Right. Where's the diamond necklace, for example?" Janice asked.

"That was all explained to you," Eli said. "All her personal effects had been left to Harry in her will. He was therefore free to leave them, or give them, to whomever—"

"So *she* gets my sister's things?"

There was a silence then.

Samuel turned to look at me again. But before I had the chance to say anything, Nathan spoke up.

"Shouldn't we table this until my brother gets out of jail?"

"Good luck on *that*."

Had there been a smirk minutes ago, it was gone now, replaced by the panic in Samuel's eyes.

No, not panic. Rage.

"You told them," he whispered through his teeth.

I shook my head. "The police must have called."

"Bailey, how could you think that Samuel killed anyone? It's all a terrible mistake. His arrest, it was preposterous."

"Take it easy, Dad."

254 | CAROL LEA BENJAMIN

"I don't care what they said. I cannot believe—"

And then he looked up, because Arlene and Bailey had seen Samuel in the doorway, me standing right next to him, Dashiell behind me, his tail straight out behind him like a rudder, Lady already in the dining room, wiggling and panting because the kids were there, sitting like zombies at their places, the dirty dishes from lunch still in front of them.

Now no one was listening to Eli. They were all staring at Samuel.

And Lady.

The kids noticed her, too, in whatever way they could.

"It's Lady," Cora called out.

"She's—" Dora began.

"Back," Cora finished, clapping her hands.

"But who's—"

"That other dog?"

Jackson stood. He thrummed his arms up and down in front of his stained shirt, as if he were beating an imaginary drum, then walked out of the dining room, ignoring both dogs as he passed.

Charlotte began to moan and hit her chest with her fists.

Willy got up. He was wearing a pair of socks on his hands. He began to walk toward Lady, but when he saw Dashiell, he stopped, looking from one to the other. Then he began to cry, wiping his eyes with the socks, a method to his madness.

I unhooked both leashes, letting the dogs go to them.

Then Eli was standing.

"Samuel," he said, as if he were looking at a ghost. "What's going on? What's happened? How did you get out? Where did Lady come from?"

And as Samuel walked toward his father, Eli got up. "Excuse me," he said to the Pooles, "I have to talk to my son."

Samuel began to cry. Eli handed him a handkerchief and led

the way out, glaring at me as he passed by, heading toward his office.

"We were just going," Arlene called after him, standing and smoothing her skirt, then patting her hair. "I'll call you, Eli."

But Eli ignored her. He was deep in conversation with Samuel. I watched as they went into the office and locked the door behind them.

After Arlene, Janice, and Bailey left, passing me as they did David, as if I weren't there, Nathan got up. He came and put his hand on my arm, leading me back out into the lobby, then toward the garden door.

"I'd prefer it if you didn't interfere again. My father is extremely upset about what you did," he said.

"Is he?"

"He thinks you should have talked to him about your—"

"Theories?"

"Yes, your little theories. He's not thrilled that you carted his son off to the police."

"I bet he isn't."

"You have a real attitude, don't you?" He unlocked the garden door, and we walked out into the heat.

Homer must have been working here recently. There was a bag of fertilizer near the door and a spade propped against the wall, a couple of small bushes waiting to go into the ground. The hose was uncoiled, too. I stepped over it as I walked away from the door.

"You seem to be enjoying all this, as if it's all some sort of joke."

"Not at all, Nathan. I don't consider the death of Harry Dietrich nor the attempt on his wife's life a joke."

"His *wife*."

I was about to give him the cheeky answer I thought he deserved when I noticed something. It was the place where the bookend had been buried, the bookend that might still have a readable print on it, the thumbprint, perhaps, of the person who tried to kill Venus with it, because of the way the thumb might have curled under the lady's chin, but the bricks were out of place and the dirt had been disturbed. Someone had been digging at the hidey-hole, and though I couldn't be sure from where I stood, I was pretty sure the hole would be empty.

"That's correct," I said, slipping a hand into my pocket and taking a step back. "Venus was Harry's wife."

"Be that as it may, it's no longer your concern. My father wishes to terminate your services, as of today. Now that Lady's been recovered, we no longer need you and Dashiell. If you send me a bill, I'll send you a check for what we owe you."

"Your father didn't hire me."

"Oh, I hope you're not counting on Venus to save your job. That's a laugh. Of course, we'll never know what it was that put Harry over the edge, perhaps the grief over Marilyn's death," he said, shaking his head, "or merely his age, but I'm sure that, whatever caused his senility, the courts won't have any problem overturning that will. In a short time, things will be as they should, with Dad running Harbor View."

"For how long?"

"I beg your pardon?"

"How long before you find some way to get *him* out of the picture?"

Nathan snorted like a bull about to charge. "I think we've had quite enough of your paranoid delusions for now. When the police informed us about the charges against Samuel, it didn't take a minute to figure out who had accused him. There's no one else here who would exhibit that kind of disloyalty to Harbor

View. And now you have another scenario, more accusations? *Please*."

"How about your own disloyalty?" I asked him, taking another step back. "I see they're already at work next door, tearing down the bar, getting ready to knock this place down next."

Nathan just glared at me, his cheeks jumping.

"I thought things started when Lady vanished, no one knowing where she had gone, the kids in turmoil over her loss. But your plan to get Harry and your father to agree to sell Harbor View was well underway by then. It started with the fire at the old paper factory next door, didn't it? Then the bar was closed down by the Board of Health. Rats, I believe. Only no one knew then who the real rats were, rats who couldn't wait until two old men lived out their dream and died naturally, rats who wanted to hurry things along, cash in on the hot real estate market by selling Harbor View to the developer who had been after you for the land, who Harry had turned down enough times that they approached you to see if you could persuade your father to swing the decision, not knowing either of them of course, not knowing that, short of dying, these men would never give this place up for money or any other reason.

"But you kept trying. Next there was the electrical fire in the basement, jeopardy a little closer to home. Luckily Lady was still here then. Venus said she was spectacular, a real lifesaver, barking and backing up, leading her right to where the problem was.

"It was right after that that Samuel took Lady away. It's so nice to see brothers getting along so well. Your father will be *so* proud of your teamwork."

"That's quite enough. No one's interested in your—"

"Little theories?"

He reached out for me, but I got out of the way, taking my hand out of my pocket then, pointing my gun at him.

"Ah, so this time you're not taking any chances," he said, a big smile on his hard face.

"There were two arguments in Harry's office that last day. The first was Arlene, trying to find out where Marilyn's jewelry was, assuming it should belong to her now. The second was you, Nathan, trying to convince Harry to sell. You must have been fuming when you came out of there, angrier than you'd ever been in your life, the old guy steadfast about this place, despite your attempts to scare him off, wear him down, wheedle a yes out of him. Am I doing okay so far?"

Nathan nodded, but not to me. It was as if he were signaling someone behind me.

"Good one," I told him, keeping my eyes forward.

That's when I saw him. He got up and walked slowly in our direction, his hands covered with paint and dirt, one of them cradling something against his chest. Even though it was covered by his hands, very little of it showing, and what was exposed was covered with dirt, I knew what it was, the only thing it could be. And as I watched, horrified, Jackson went over to Nathan and handed him what he was holding, the way he'd given me back Dashiell's leash when I'd dropped that.

Nathan took the bookend, and his mouth slid into a sneer.

"So *there* it is," he said. "I wondered where it had gone."

He turned toward Jackson; for some bizarre reason, I thought it was to thank him. Instead, he grabbed him and pulled him in front of him as a shield.

"Watch out," I screamed, too late. "Keep him out of this. This is between us."

"Are you going to shoot me now, Rachel?" he taunted. He had one arm around Jackson's throat. In the other hand he held the bookend. He brought it up, ready to strike. "I didn't realize quite how hard I had to do it last time," he said. "I won't make that same mistake twice. That David. He's really been on a rampage lately, since Dad cut his medication. First Venus, then Jackson. Why don't you put down the gun now?"

But before I could, something dark and unyielding came from behind me and knocked the gun out of my grasp. I heard a cracking sound, something breaking, the garden tilting it seemed, swaying first one way, then another. There was another sound, the gun skittering across the bricks and stopping, but I couldn't look. Something else caught my eye. The dogs. They had both jumped into the garden through the window some careless person had left open, Dashiell first, Lady right behind him.

Samuel was bending, to try to get the gun, and Nathan was telling him to grab me, so that David could strike again—David, who wasn't even there.

My temperature seemed to shoot up, and my right arm felt numb, but my mind was clear.

"Lady, walk-up," I shouted. "Walk-up, *good* girl."

Samuel was reaching for the gun. I kicked as hard as I could, connecting with his face, dead center.

Jackson was still being held as a shield. No matter. I had a plan, too. And mine also included teamwork.

"Dashiell, paws-up," I yelled, pointing at Jackson, and with Lady right behind Nathan, where I'd positioned her, Dashiell flew into Jackson, hitting his chest with the force of a sledgehammer, sending him, and Nathan, backward, falling over Lady and landing on the brick. I heard the satisfying clunk as Nathan's head hit the unforgiving garden floor, and as soon as I saw that Jackson was fine, cushioned by Nathan's enormous bulk, I took my eyes off them, kicked Samuel once more for good measure, and with my left hand retrieved my gun from under the table.

"Watch them," I told Dashiell, seeing his body start to vibrate with the pleasure of being presented with a task he was magnificently up to.

I slipped the gun into my pocket, offered my left hand to Jackson, helping him up and out of harm's way, then pulled out my cell phone, asked Jackson to hold it up for me, and dialed the precinct.

BE SEEING YOU, I TOLD HER

After sitting in the emergency room for two and a half hours waiting for the doctor to look at my arm, then another hour waiting for the X ray to be taken and read, I had the cast put on my arm. It was a soft cast, layers and layers of thick gauze covered with stretchy purple tape and a no-nonsense sling, navy with an ecru trim. When I looked at my reflection in the big window, it resembled a hammock.

The pills they gave me had started to kick in, replacing the pain with a sense of euphoria. A few more minutes, and I could have played baseball, using the arm as a bat.

By the time I was released, it was dark out. I stopped in the gift shop for some candy bars to tide me over and went upstairs to Venus's room.

She was sitting up, looking wildly beautiful, that long dark hair framing her pretty face, a magazine across her lap. When she looked up, her hands flew to her mouth.

"What happened?"

"Samuel hit me with the business end of a shovel. But you ought to see the shovel."

"You promised after we talked you were going to the police."

"I couldn't. Not after last time. Not until I had it all."

"You could have been—"

"But I wasn't," I told her, sitting on the edge of the bed, crossing my legs so that I could lean the arm on my right thigh, give my neck a rest.

"Poor Eli," she said.

"He'll be here tomorrow. He wants to talk. I think things will be okay at Harbor View."

"I'm going to sell, Rachel."

"*What.*"

"I'm not going to close. I'm going to sell. Harry and Eli were foolish not to take advantage of this offer. I can buy something else in the neighborhood and have it renovated exactly the way I want it, the way Eli and I decide would be best," she said. "We've learned so much since this building was purchased and renovated. I've been thinking, since you left, that with the money we can get for this site, we can have something better. The kids don't appreciate the view anyway. That sort of thing means nothing to them. And I wouldn't mind getting them away from the highway, all that noise and exhaust. What I'd like for them is a pool. And if we had a larger facility, Eli could do some training, one or two young doctors at a time. We can pass on what we've learned. We can learn from others, young doctors with fresh ideas. I think it's a fantastic opportunity."

I nodded, my eyelids feeling as if they'd been weighed down with bricks.

"Are you okay?" she asked, her voice coming from far away.

"I'm fine," I lied. I'd been lying all day. What was one more? I reached for the water, and she poured me a glass.

"Did you find out about the necklace?" she asked.

"Janice," I said. "She'd gone to the bathroom. Samuel 'discovered' you on the ground. He called her over, practicing his shocked look, which was no doubt genuine, given how he feels about the sight of blood, then he left her there and went to call the others, including Nathan, who had already washed his murderous hands and gone back to the dining room to be with the others when Samuel broke the news. She saw the necklace. When you were down, it slid up to your neck, out from under your shirt, which reminds me—" I pulled it out from under my shirt and bent my head. Venus unhooked it and put it on.

"So it was Janice who tore it off me?"

"Right."

"How do you know this part?"

"I called her," I said. "Not much else to do, all those hours I was waiting in Emergency."

"Then how did David get it?"

"She tore it off you and found some blood on her hand, freaked out, and dropped it. She ran out to wash her hands. When she went back, it was gone. In fact, she looked again the day of the funeral, thinking it might have gotten kicked under the desk by accident."

"But David had picked it up, because of the sparkle. He loves this necklace."

"He'd seen it before?"

"Yes, I used to take it off and let him play with it when we were alone."

"And the bookend—Jackson picked that up when Nathan dropped it. As you told me, they were all there. Then he buried it. And dug it up later to give it back. Weird."

"Weird is his middle name," she said.

"They've seen a lot," I said, shaking my head. "Too much."

"But you said they're okay. That's what makes me think I can move them. Of course, finding the new place and having it renovated will take time. It'll put off any new construction at our current site for at least a year."

"But KR Properties has been after the site for two years. One more year won't matter."

She nodded. I closed my eyes for what I thought was a couple of seconds.

"Rachel?"

Venus was smiling at me.

"You've been asleep. Go home and do it properly."

I nodded.

"By the way, you know I can't pay you until I get out of here," she said.

"That's what they all say. Hey, I know where to find you." I flashed her the Kaminsky grin, only slightly drugged and lopsided.

"I hope you will," she said. "I hope you will find all of us, any chance you get."

I lifted my broken arm and waved it slightly up and down.

"Be seeing you," I told her.

On the way home, I pictured the new place—a big cheerful dining room, Cora and Dora bickering by the window, Willy holding a coaster or maybe a T-shirt, Jackson painting, Charlotte drawing, all settled in. I pictured the staircase, too, going up to all their bedrooms, and on the side opposite the railing, a brand-new dirt mark on the freshly painted wall, because Lady was back, and wherever they were, she'd be taking care of them, as nobody but a dog can.